FAMILY
LAW

FAMILY
LAW

Gin Phillips

RANDOM HOUSE CANADA

PUBLISHED BY RANDOM HOUSE CANADA

Library and Archives Canada Cataloguing in Publication

Title: Family law / Gin Phillips
Names: Phillips, Gin, author.
Identifiers: Canadiana (print) 20200259768 | Canadiana (ebook) 20200259784
| ISBN 9780735280861 (softcover) | ISBN 9780735280878 (EPUB)
Classification: LCC PS3616.H4556 F36 2021 | DDC 813/.6—dc23

Text design: Lucia Bernard
Cover design: Lynn Buckley
Cover art: magnolia, Sally Crosthwaite /
Bridgeman Images

Printed in the United States of America

2 4 6 8 9 7 5 3 1

Penguin
Random House
RANDOM HOUSE CANADA

For Lisa A. Woodard

Your children are not your children. . . .
You may give them your love but not your thoughts,
For they have their own thoughts.
You may house their bodies but not their souls. . . .
You are the bows from which your children as living arrows are sent forth.

—KAHLIL GIBRAN, *THE PROPHET*

It's wise to know where you come from, who called your name.

—MAYA ANGELOU

❧ **1979** ❧

Lucia

1.

Lucia Gilbert listened as the two men in sherbet-colored suits spun their fairy tale.

"I bathe her," said the father, leaning forward on the witness stand. "Put on diaper cream. Feed her. She loves peaches. Honestly, my daughter is the best part of my day."

"So you're an involved parent?" asked his lawyer, Rob Letson, syrup voiced, as if he didn't know that over the past year the man had repeatedly left his two-year-old daughter home alone.

"I know every hair on her head," the father said.

He was well packaged, Lucia would give him that. He did not fidget. His pale green suit set off his dark eyes, and his pleasant face was still untouched by his nighttime habits. He kept his hands out of sight, though, and Lucia wondered if Letson had finally noticed that his client's fingertips were like open wounds, chewed so ravenously that the nail beds were infected. Lucia spent a decent portion of her days reaching across one desk or another to shake a hand—sun blotched, meaty, limp, veins bulging, nails glossy as buttons—and hands could tell you things.

Netta Peterson nudged Lucia with a sharp elbow. "He's lying."

Lucia patted her client's hand. Netta and her husband were both white haired and crinkle-eyed: their only flaws were Richard's Lucky Strikes and Netta's chattiness.

"She hasn't touched peaches for months," Netta hissed. "When Bethany was alive, the man never did anything. He didn't even mow the yard. Or change a lightbulb."

"I know, Netta," Lucia whispered.

At the front of the courtroom, Rob Letson scuffed one loafer along the wooden floor. "Your late wife's parents are accusing you of negligence. Do you believe they have any motivation other than the welfare of your daughter?"

"We're accusing him of getting so loaded that we can't wake him up," Netta muttered, warm breathed. She smelled of baby powder and, possibly, bacon. "The baby crying in the crib, soaked through."

Lucia patted her hand more firmly.

"I believe," the father said, "that since they lost their daughter—my Bethany—they want to start over with their granddaughter. It's like—this is terrible to say, I know—they think they're owed a replacement."

Netta jerked hard enough that her chair tipped slightly.

Letson walked to his table, lifting a paper in a plastic sleeve. "Did your in-laws ever express that thought in writing?"

Lucia had known he would try this. The nasty letter had no date and no envelope. It likely had been typed by the father himself.

"I object, Your Honor," she said. "That document has not been authenticated."

"Sustained," said Judge Mitchell, a petite man who looked even smaller in his robes.

Rob dropped his arm, the letter slapping his thigh. "Mr. Thompson, have the Petersons ever attempted to keep your daughter from you?"

"They threatened me."

"How did they threaten you?"

"I object," Lucia said. "At the risk of being repetitive, the document Mr. Letson is referencing has not been authenticated."

The pleasant-faced father lifted a hand, brushing at one smooth lapel. She could see his gnawed fingers.

"Sustained," said the judge.

Letson walked over to Lucia's table and bent down, his gold watch catching the overhead lights.

"Gilbert," he said, quietly enough that the judge couldn't hear, "you don't even know what the word 'authentication' means."

She let her eyes drift to his belt buckle.

"Letson," she said, "your fly is unzipped."

His eyes flickered down, assessing. He ran a hand, quickly, from hip bone to hip bone. His zipper was fine.

Lucia smiled.

"Mr. Letson?" said Judge Mitchell. "Ms. Gilbert?"

Rob delayed one more second. He leaned closer to Lucia.

"Fuck you," he said.

Netta Peterson inhaled sharply.

"It's fine," Lucia said to the older woman as Letson turned away. "He just knows he's going to lose."

He'd known it, surely, from the beginning. Why had he even taken this case? Rob Letson was one of the good ones. He enjoyed the back-and-forth of it all, and when she beat him, he would offer to buy her a drink and then harass her for disliking beer.

"He's hateful," Netta whispered, wide-eyed.

Lucia felt a rush of affection for this woman who had lived so long but could still be shocked by a curse word. She had no idea about real hate, something Letson didn't have. The balding man sitting in the row of chairs behind Letson, though—every line of him was rigid. Now, as Letson rested a hand on his table and faced the witness, the balding man lunged forward, clamping a hand on the lawyer's shoulder.

Letson twisted away. The two men exchanged a handful of words.

"Do you know him?" Lucia asked softly.

"An uncle, I think," Netta said.

As Judge Mitchell slapped his palms against solid oak, the man settled back in his chair. Soon the father was giving smooth answers again, and Netta was back to adding her asides: *Does he even know her birthday? Does he know her shoe size? Never even runs a brush through her hair. How's he gonna teach a girl how to be a girl?*

In another hour, they were finished for the day. The Petersons wanted to hash through every exchange, word for word, and Lucia knew it mattered to them, so she didn't rush. When she was finally free, she turned down a hallway and ran into the lawyer for the Cox case, and they circled around each other for a bit. She passed four men who had already heard the zipper story from Rob Letson.

By the time she pushed through the glass doors of the courthouse, the sun was dipping behind First Baptist Church and the Montgomery skyline was turning to shadows. She was later than she'd intended. She pressed her purse to her hip and tightened her grip on her briefcase. She could set a fast pace, even in heels, and the stoplights were in her favor. Soon enough she was turning onto South Perry Street, the steep roof of her office building showing stark against the sky. She cut across the lawn to the parking lot in back, grabbing for her keys.

Her car was the only one left in the lot. A couple of yards away from it, she skidded on a gravelly patch of asphalt, jerking to a stop. The trees overhanging the lot deepened the shadows, but there was no mistaking what she saw.

A smashed windshield, cracks spidering out.

The strong smell of urine, the wet shine of it running down her front tire, pooling underneath.

She spun, certain she heard footsteps, but no one was there.

II.

Lucia was not sure if she liked this woman. Not that it mattered, necessarily.

"He's a manipulator," the woman said, her red-blond hair curling over her forehead in stiff waves. She was built like a dancer. "It might seem like I should have known that from the beginning, but it took me awhile to figure it out. It works like that, doesn't it? You look back and you can see how obvious it was, but it's not that clear in the beginning, is it?"

Lucia lifted her pen a few inches above her notepad. The clock on the wall read 5:10, and the woman's every statement was a question.

"Of course," Lucia said. "How do you think he manipulated you?"

"He never loved me. Not really."

"Margaret," said Lucia. That was the woman's name. Margaret Morris. "Tell me what you're hoping will happen next. What do you want?"

The typed summary on her desk told Lucia that the husband was already out of the house and that the woman hoped for child support for one daughter.

"He told me over breakfast that he thought maybe we shouldn't have gotten married," said Margaret, shifting in her seat. "We were so young when we did it. We'd only known each other three months. He wanted counseling, he said. He wasn't happy, he said. He'd never mentioned any of that. It's crazy, isn't it? To suddenly say something like that? We were happy. There was nothing wrong except in his head."

Lucia nodded. People wanted to talk. They sometimes embellished or omitted or outright lied, but if she sat long enough, they would tell her everything. They would tell even the parts they were sure they had not told her.

"What was your response to him?" she asked.

"I told him to get out of the house. I told him I wanted a divorce."

"So he told you he wanted to go to counseling and you told him you wanted a divorce?"

Margaret slid one hand along the edge of the desk. One pale peach nail tapped the wood.

"No," she said, scuttling away from her own words. "I went along with what he wanted. I didn't make him do anything."

"And you yourself want a divorce?" Lucia asked.

"I should, shouldn't I? After he said those things to me?"

"I can't tell you what you want."

Lucia thought she had kept her tone gentle, but Margaret straightened. She took a couple of silent breaths, and when she spoke again, her voice was smoother. Professional.

"This isn't about me," she said. "Men can afford to think only about themselves, but we women understand, don't we, that it's never that simple. I'm a mother. That's the most important thing, isn't it? I can take care of my daughter with or without him. But what's best for her?"

It was the first mention she'd made of her daughter, and now Lucia recognized her. She eventually recognized every manipulator and martyr, every achiever and survivor and logic-obsessed Vulcan and child who refused to grow up. This woman, with her fresh lipstick and her jittery hands, was a paper doll. If you didn't like the self she'd chosen, she could strip it off and fold on a different one. She'd be whoever you wanted her to be. For a while.

"You're a concerned mother," agreed Lucia. "Do you want a divorce?"

"He asked me to dinner for next week," said Margaret.

She had begun talking about the difficult left turn into the Steak and Ale parking lot when a rap sounded on the office door. Lucia's secretary, Marissa, slipped inside. Short hair, tiny waist, no hips—she was efficiency manifest.

"I'm sorry to interrupt, Lucia, but I was going to head out," Marissa said, gold beads falling over the dents at her clavicles. "Unless—did you want—?"

"Go ahead," Lucia said. "I'll be fine."

"But if—"

Marissa glanced at the potential client, and Lucia did a quick count in her head. Four days. Four days since she had last walked to her car alone. Facing the familiar Chinese-red walls of her office, it felt ridiculous to want a chaperone to walk to her own car. It was no more than fifty yards. She was not a child.

"You go on," she told Marissa.

Lucia ended the meeting politely. She suggested that the next step was for Margaret to decide whether she really wanted to end her marriage. *Every marriage has its ebbs and flows,* she said. *I appreciate you coming in.*

Then Margaret was gone, and Lucia circled back behind her desk. She straightened the bow on her blouse. She signed the last stack of letters Marissa had typed up. She considered the windowsill, where the Flaming Katy was blooming effusively, the petals nearly matching the walls. Her aloe and jade plants were green and healthy, and for succulents, the whole arrangement looked lush.

Urine running through the treads of the tire.

Bits of broken glass glittering on the driver's seat.

She forced herself to stop staring at her plants. She sorted through the green file folders on her desk: *Campbell, Peterson, Cox. Grounds, elements, facts, financials.* She slid the Lawrence deposition and the tax returns for the Shum case into her briefcase, snapping the brass latches. She made herself turn off the lights and shut the door. She pulled her key chain from her purse, and the dangling canister of mace tangled with her keys.

She was halfway down the hall before she saw the girl in the lobby.

It was a small room, so she'd mirrored one wall of it, and that meant she could see two girls, real shoulder against reflected shoulder. Both versions were sitting sideways, gazing at the arrangement of watercolor paintings behind the reception desk. Lucia was proud of those paintings. The men who had rented the offices before her had filled the space with hunting portraits—it had been barely a year ago that she'd stared at that wall full of hounds and setters. The men had asked her if she'd like to keep them.

Hunting dogs. Dead birds in their mouths.

You needed to comfort people in the waiting room. You needed to help them feel like they'd stepped into a friend's home. Nothing too feminine: even a female client did not trust a lawyer prone to doilies. She'd invested in ocher armchairs and porcelain jar lamps, and she'd found a set of watercolors at an Oak Park art festival, impressionistic takes on movie posters, bright and interesting. Gable. Bogart. Katharine Hepburn. Cary Grant.

The girl turned her pale face. She had deep auburn hair nearly to her elbows. Lavender shirt and stonewashed jeans. Nothing shy about her look. Twelve or thirteen years old—an age Lucia felt unsure about.

"I like your paintings," said the girl.

Her legs were folded under her, and she had a book in her lap. The cover showed a long-haired man running through the jungle.

"Thank you," said Lucia. "Did you come with Margaret?"

The girl nodded. "Yes, ma'am."

"You're her daughter?"

The girl nodded again. "She parked a few blocks away because she wasn't sure she'd find any closer spots. She said I could stay here while she got the car. Is that okay?"

Lucia didn't bother answering that. "What's your name?"

"Rachel." Her eyes fell on Lucia's key chain, with its pink plastic flamingo nudging against the mace. "You're going home, aren't you? I can wait outside on the porch."

"Don't be silly," Lucia said. "You're not waiting outside."

She stood there, considering. Children rarely came to her office. Occasionally a client didn't have a babysitter, but the children would linger in the lobby doing dot-to-dots or something, and Marissa would keep an eye on them. Lucia never had conversations with them.

It was absurd that the woman had left her daughter here without even asking permission.

"You don't have any posters of John Wayne," the girl said. "Have you ever seen *Angel and the Badman*?"

Did most twelve-year-old girls discuss Westerns? Lucia considered whether to address the sociopolitical aspects of the Duke and why she did not hang him on her wall.

"Westerns aren't my favorite," she said.

"I love Westerns," Rachel said. "And John Wayne. On Sundays they always show old movies on TBS, you know? If you think he's not a good actor, have you seen him in *True Grit*? Or *Rooster Cogburn* with Katharine Hepburn?"

Lucia smiled. The girl was not like her mother. A negative reaction had not changed her course in the slightest.

"You're right," said Lucia. "He was good in those. Age added some depth."

Rachel looked back at the paintings, and Lucia studied them, too. At some stage she had stopped seeing them as she came in and out of the office.

"*Adam's Rib*," Rachel said, nodding at the sepia-toned versions of Hepburn and Tracy. "It's about lawyers, so that makes sense."

"One of my favorites," Lucia said.

Rachel faced her, eyes dark and fixed. "Do you think he means to hit her? Do you think it's really a slap?"

Lucia dropped into one of the empty chairs. How were you supposed to talk to girls this age? How to discuss power dynamics and spousal abuse as it pertained to screwball comedies?

"Yes," Lucia said. "I do think it's a slap. I think he meant to slap her, but he can't admit it to himself, much less to her."

Rachel unfolded her legs, and her feet hit the floor softly. She reached an arm up, lifted her hair in one twisting motion that reminded Lucia of twirling cotton candy, then dropped the thick mass of it across one shoulder.

"You're wearing a ring," she said. "How long have you been married?"

"Two years."

"Do you have kids?"

"No."

"Do you and your husband have nicknames for each other?"

Lucia couldn't remember the last time she'd been the one answering the questions. It was easier, in some ways. "You mean do we call each other something adorable like Pinkie and Pinky? Like Hepburn and Tracy in the movie?"

The girl nodded. Lucia cast back her thoughts, letting them arc, ribbonlike, and she was peeking through a doorway in her childhood home, staring at the glossy dining-room table. Her mother and father sat at opposite ends, and two couples from church flanked them, and Lucia was supposed to be in the basement, but she'd tiptoed upstairs under the guise of being thirsty. The grown-ups were using the fancy green glasses, and one of the men—he looked like Abraham Lincoln—was saying, "So what was I wearing when he knocked on the door, Mary? What I always wear when I sleep. Not a darn thing." It was a revelation to Lucia. Men slept naked. Married people slept naked. Married people talked about being naked. Over dinner. She'd clutched her plastic cup and realized there might be patterns other than the ones inside her own house. The possibilities had unspooled.

"We don't have pet names," she told the girl. "Although my husband's friends from college call him Bard. He wrote poetry once upon a time. And his middle name is Bartholomew. So—"

"Bard-olomew?" Rachel sounded out.

"I think it sounds better if you've been drinking heavily," Lucia said, then realized it was probably not an appropriate comment.

"What's his first name?" Rachel asked.

"Evan."

"Is he a lawyer?"

"Nope."

Rachel shifted in the chair again, scanning the lobby. There wasn't much to see, and her eyes fell on the paintings again. "Tallulah Bankhead," she said, nodding at *Lifeboat*. "She's from Alabama, right? My aunt lives on Bankhead."

"Your aunt must live pretty close to me. The street's named for Tallulah's family."

Rachel kept her eyes on the painting. "Are you going to be Mom's lawyer?"

"Your mother may not even need a lawyer."

"If she does, will it be you?"

"She and I would have to have another conversation."

"If you had to guess," the girl prodded, undeterred, "do you think you'll be her lawyer?"

Lucia lifted a hair from the edge of her skirt, watching it drift to the carpet. She suspected the girl's mother would never get around to deciding whether she wanted a divorce.

"Probably not," she said.

"Good."

Rachel gave a small smile, eyes veering toward Lucia but missing slightly, settling on the porcelain lamp with its pattern of twining flowers. Her hands flapped once, twice, in her lap before her fingers found one another, interlocking. It was the first trace of uncertainty she'd shown.

A horn honked outside. Lucia suddenly noticed the patter of rain.

"That's Mom," Rachel said. "Thanks for letting me stay."

She was through the front door before Lucia had even finished waving. As the door eased shut, Lucia could see her leaping down the wet stairs two at a time.

She sat in the stillness, listening to the rain. She missed the sound of the girl talking. After a while she pushed herself to her feet, and she made herself loosen her grip on her briefcase. Whoever had vandalized her car—it had to be a man, surely, because what woman would urinate on a tire?—had wanted to scare her. If she dreaded walking out the door—if she panted and worried and flinched—then he had won.

She was not panting.

She was not worried.

She turned off the lamps. She glanced through the window and watched the steady line of traffic, and then she was opening the door and locking it behind her.

The rain picked up, typing a fast rhythm against the leaves. She crossed the Spanish tiles, a remnant of her building's former life as a home for some long-dead lesser Gatsby type. She angled around the side of the building, where the ivy grew thick and the two big oaks turned every hour into twilight. She could not feel a single drop of rain. The air smelled of green and dirt, and here she did grant herself a pause: she had a clear view of the parking lot from this angle. If anyone was waiting, she would see them before they saw her.

The lot was empty. Only her car and the pit-marked asphalt.

Still, she waited. She leaned against the still-dry concrete blocks of the building wall, a sign that Gatsby's vision might have been bigger than his bank account. She ran her hand along one block: the slight curve of it had the same feel as Evan's shinbone under her fingers. Across the parking lot, the rain ran down her car, streaming over the fender. Puddles underneath.

She could still smell the urine.

Cracks spreading across the glass. A rock? A gloved fist? It would take real force to break a windshield so thoroughly.

The sky had still been tinged pink that night, beautiful. Before she'd gone inside to call the police, she'd backed up against her battered car and threaded her keys between her knuckles like her father had taught her.

Are there any other girls? he'd asked her when she came home after her first month of law school.

There's two of us, she'd said.

But don't they think—he'd started, and she'd wanted to ask who "they" were and what they might think, but she hadn't. Instead of finishing his sentence he'd asked for her keys and showed her how to use them as claws.

III.

Rain poured over the eaves of the carport. Lucia turned the key in the kitchen door, and before she'd opened it an inch, it slammed shut. Every single day.

She peered through the window, meeting Moxie's delighted gaze. The Airedale had her massive paws propped against the glass, all fifty-plus pounds of her straining in welcome.

"We've been through this," Lucia said to the dog through the glass. "You have to get off the door before I can come in. Get down. Get down, Moxie. Moxie. Off."

The dog bobbed and panted. She gave a long lick to one of the panes, her tongue sluglike.

"Honestly, you know how this works," Lucia said. "Get off the door. Off."

The dog tossed her head and lashed her tongue through the air and then, more likely from a loss of focus than actual obedience, dropped to her feet. Lucia pushed open the door, the smell of garlic and rosemary washing over her as she slipped inside. She let her briefcase drop, kicked off her heels, and stripped off her hose, all with Moxie jabbing a dirty snout against her thighs.

"All right," Lucia said, hanging her hose on the coatrack next to yesterday's pair. She knelt, scratching behind the dog's sharply folded ears. Moxie thumped in ecstasy.

Lucia swiped at the soil caking the dog's beard.

"The ficus again?" she said.

Moxie darted forward, scoring a solid lick—hints of potting soil—inside Lucia's mouth. She rested the furry cylinder of her head on Lucia's shoulder, her tail vibrating them both. She was without a doubt the most loving dog Lucia had ever owned. And the stupidest. She literally ate dirt.

Giving the dog one more rub, Lucia walked to the kitchen, where she lifted the lid off the crockpot and stirred the pork and white beans. The green chilies eddied, and she was blowing on a spoonful when the phone rang.

Her best guess was Evan—he should have been home by now.

"Hello?" she said, settling the crockpot lid with her free hand.

"How is everything, sweetheart?" asked her mother.

There was a wiliness to the greeting. It implied that her mother knew of some event and was asking about the aftermath. Occasionally, something actually had happened—her car, for instance—and for just long enough to give herself away, Lucia would be fooled into believing that her mother already knew about it.

"Everything's fine, Mother," Lucia said. Moxie rammed her head softly against her thigh.

"No more trouble with your car?"

Lucia liked that phrasing. And, in truth, although she had let slip a mention of her car, she had not been flustered enough to give details. Her mother only knew that her windshield had been cracked.

"No," she said. "Only a fluke, I think."

"Do you think"—her mother lowered her voice—"that someone might have done it on purpose?"

Lucia propped her dripping spoon on the edge of the stove. *Nudge,* went Moxie. *Nudge nudge.*

"Why would anyone do that?" Lucia asked. She was genuinely interested in what her mother's answer might be. Her mother did not like bad things to take form.

"Well, you know, of course," her mother said. "There are all kinds of people out there."

In a skittering of claws and spray of drool, Moxie bolted across the kitchen tile and flung herself against the door. Eventually, Evan forced his way inside, shirt sleeves rolled up.

"Down," he snapped, simultaneously locking the door behind him, rubbing the dog's neck, and shooting Lucia a roll-eyed look that expressed both a hello and an acknowledgment of the difficulties of this particular dog. She watched him register the phone in her hand and the tone of her voice; he realized she was talking to her mother. His face shifted into a question.

She shrugged, letting him know everything was fine.

"I imagine it was teenagers," she told her mother. "I mean, the office is downtown."

This was speaking her mother's language. In Caroline Roberts's world, downtown Montgomery was Saigon. Beirut. Times Square.

Evan looped an arm around her waist, a hand across her belly. She could smell the Juicy Fruit on his breath, and she leaned against him as her mother explained how something had gnawed clean through a package of Ritz Crackers.

"What do you mean 'something'?" Lucia asked. "What could it be other than a mouse?"

"There's no telling," said her mother.

"No telling? Do you think you have a turtle infestation, Mother? Possums, maybe?"

Her mother laughed. She had a saloon girl's laugh, low and never ending. It was almost worth these phone calls. In another few minutes, Lucia was off the phone, just as Evan set a gin and tonic in front of her.

"Moxie's been in the ficus again," she said. "I haven't checked to see if she ate the Saran wrap."

Evan dropped the needle into the groove on Elmore James singing about dusting a broom, then he bent to examine the planter by the sliding-glass doors. The shelves blocked her view.

"I don't think she ate any," he said. "Just tore it off. We could duct tape it."

"Maybe tin foil would work better."

"Chicken wire," he said, just as the slide guitar kicked in.

"How would we attach it?"

He didn't have an answer for that. He crossed the room again, stepping over Moxie, who had sprawled across the kitchen tiles. He leaned into Lucia's space, reaching for her drink. He always tried her drink, even if he'd made it. Even if they had the same thing.

"Nothing happened today?" he asked.

He had been waiting to ask. She had felt him waiting all this time. The music and the drink and the chatter—all diversions.

"Just work," she said.

"Someone walked you to your car?"

He had asked only two things of her: carry the mace he'd given her and don't go to the car alone. Both were reasonable, and she agreed entirely with his logic. She considered lying.

"Don't you think it's silly?" she said. "To still be worried about it?"

"No," Evan said. "I do not. And neither do you."

"I can't have someone walk me to my car forever."

"We're not talking about forever. We're talking about tomorrow. Have Marissa or a client walk with you to the car tomorrow. Then we can have a whole separate argument about the day after tomorrow."

A laugh slipped out of her. Evan stood there, dark hair falling over his forehead. Hazel eyes serious behind his glasses. Waiting.

"I'm leaving the office early tomorrow anyway," she said. "I have the talk at the Prattville Homemakers Association, remember?"

"You think you should do it?"

"I obviously do," she said. "Do you think a Prattville Homemaker is going to attack me with her chicken casserole?"

"Lucia," he said.

"They'll ask me about some friend who wants to leave her husband," she said. "Or if I can fix a traffic ticket. I won't be saying anything that controversial."

He wandered back to the stereo, pulling out an album. *Hoodoo Man Blues.*

"No?" he said, sliding the record back into its slot. "You've said plenty already. Some people take it seriously, Lucia. All the ERA stuff."

Her speeches had slowed to a trickle, and he knew it. That first year out of law school she'd spoken to any group that would listen. Fifty-two speeches in a year. Cardboard boxes full of mimeographed letters asking *Why is the Equal Rights Amendment important?* and dining-room tables packed with women stuffing envelopes and paper cuts striping her knuckles.

Set up the mailing parties inside women's homes, the organizer from the Women's Political Caucus had said. *If they stay home, their husbands won't get their hackles up.* There had been a long history of hackles. When the courts ruled in 1966 that women in Alabama were allowed to serve on juries, Lucia—still in college—had stared at the editorials warning that females were too delicate to handle lurid details, that they shouldn't sleep in accommodations with strange men, and that, after all, wouldn't they be abandoning their children at home with no one to mind them?

Stay home. Stay home. Stay home.

"Hell," Evan was saying. "It hasn't even been a month since they were snapping pictures of you talking about how the Fifth Circuit nominee list was rigged with white men."

"You surely aren't suggesting that the Democratic Party bashed my car."

"I'm suggesting that you've said all sorts of things that bring out windshield bashers and urinators. When you give these speeches, they know where you are."

He pulled out another album and then another, picking up speed, and she thought of those old-timey switchboard operators, jerking plugs in and out of slots, connecting and disconnecting. He had figured out long ago that if he stayed silent, she would talk. She knew that he had figured this out and yet it still worked.

"I am not canceling my speech tomorrow," she said. "But I'll make sure someone walks with me to my car."

He didn't gloat. He only held up a record.

"Pencil Thin Mustache?" she suggested, and he shook the record loose.

IV.

She'd had a string of late nights in the office, and now a dozen minor chores seemed to flash like dashboard lights as Lucia surveyed the house. The dishwasher was full of clean dishes. The doorknob on the closet was another twist or two from falling off. The dog-food bag was nearly empty, and the milk had expired two days ago, technically.

She'd nearly finished unloading the top rack of the dishwasher when someone knocked on the kitchen door. She flinched hard enough that she banged her hand against the edge of the counter.

"Damn it," she hissed, hopping and flapping, and, in general, acting like a loon in the middle of her own kitchen.

Another knock, softer this time.

Evan was having dinner tonight with a new heart specialist at the hospital, but Lucia was not alone: Moxie came galloping down the hallway, taking the corner so fast she spun out and smacked her flank against the sofa. She hurled herself toward the door.

Lucia stared at her hand. She thought it might swell. It had been two weeks since the car incident, and still every little noise. She kept jumping at the sound of a drawer closing. She caught herself looking left, right, and then left again as she stepped into hallways, like some child who'd barely learned to cross the street. At night, she'd jolt awake when the wind shook the windowpanes. She hated the fear, always ready to break the surface. Break the skin. Bleed out of her.

This was not who she was.

She would not feel this.

A third knock at the door, so whoever it was had not been scared away by the dog. Moxie was on her hind legs, slavering, and if you didn't know her, she would seem threatening. From her angle in the kitchen, Lucia could see nothing through the glass. Whoever it was had stepped out of view. It was still light outside.

Lucia glanced at the knife block. She pressed her face to one of the windowpanes in the door and glanced into the carport.

She caught a swathe of red hair and a bare arm with multicolored bracelets. Shoving Moxie back with one knee, she unlocked the door, and the moment she pushed it open the girl came forward, beaming at her.

"Rachel?" Lucia said.

"Hi," said the girl, with a wave of her fingers. "I didn't mean to bother you. I wasn't positive it was you, and I just thought I'd see. But if it's a bad time . . ."

"How in the world—?"

A satisfied look. A swish of ponytail.

"You said you lived near Bankhead," the girl said. "So I was at my aunt's after school, and I looked you up in the phone book. It turned out there aren't too many Gilberts. There was no Bartholomew and no Evan, but then I saw the E. B., and I figured that must be him. So I walked."

"You walked here? Did you tell someone you were coming?"

"Nah," Rachel said. "Aunt Molly's gone to Hancock's for thread. We won't eat supper until later. I had some time."

Lucia realized she was staring over the girl's shoulder, past the flat stretch of lawn, half expecting a car to come screeching into the driveway. Surely a girl this young could not just wander off without someone coming to look for her?

"You're at a stranger's house," she said. "Won't your mother or your aunt be worried that—?"

"You're not a stranger," said Rachel.

Lucia could not think of how to approach the potential impropriety of this. It seemed possible that the girl's paper-doll mother—who had never followed up on their office meeting—might think that Lucia had invited Rachel, and that would seem extremely unprofessional. She should have thought about this possibility before she hinted at her address.

No—she should not have thought of it. There had been no reason to believe this girl would show up on her doorstep. And yet here Rachel was, one foot propped on the literal doorstep. Her hair was sweaty at her temples, and the damp patches made Lucia remember slicking back her own ponytail, the tree bark hot against her fingers as she climbed.

The girl rocked from one foot to another.

"Would you like to come in?" Lucia asked at last.

Rachel grinned. "Thank you," she said, stepping carefully—almost daintily—inside as Lucia took a step backward.

"Have a seat," Lucia said, motioning toward the sofa, which was half covered by the newspaper and her suit jacket. "Would you like something to drink?"

"Yes, ma'am."

Lucia paused. What was there to drink?

"I have Tab," she said. "And ginger ale and sweet tea."

"I've never had a ginger ale. Can I try that?"

Lucia stepped to the refrigerator, and when she turned back with the soft drink, Rachel was still standing, one hand hovering over the piece of driftwood that ran the length of the bookshelf. She reached for the milk-glass chicken, tweaking its red comb, then yanking her hand away when the glass jangled.

"You're fine," Lucia said, holding out the ginger ale. "My mother carried that across the country during World War Two. It's not that delicate."

Rachel moved to the watercolor of the lighthouse, the great pale tower of it against a blue-black sky, and Lucia could still see Evan standing in the art gallery in Nantucket, saying, *Do you ever fantasize about living in a lighthouse?*

Rachel finally reached for the glass. Lucia waved a hand toward the sofa again. The girl sat—again, carefully—against the sofa arm, leaving the wide expanse of two other sofa cushions completely untouched. It was almost mathematical, the way she kept her leg from straying over the edge of her own cushion. Her feet were flat on the floor, knees properly together.

"This is really good," Rachel said, sipping. "Thank you."

Lucia sat down, occupying two couch cushions. She tucked her bare feet under her. "Do you go to your aunt's every afternoon?"

"Most of them. She picks me up from school."

"Your mom's sister?"

"Yeah. This afternoon she was working on Easter stuff. She sews these little felt eggs, and she puts a quarter inside each one. She brings them to the church egg hunt. They're cute."

Rachel glanced at the end table and then rested the glass of ginger ale on her thigh.

"There are coasters," Lucia said. "On the other side of the lamp."

"Oh," said Rachel. She lifted the glass, leaving a wet circle on her bare legs. She found the coasters. "I like your hair like that."

"Thank you."

"What do you call it?"

"A twist, I suppose," Lucia said, rejecting the word "chignon," which sounded pretentious in the best of circumstances.

"I might get mine done next week," Rachel said. "For the prom."

"How old are you?"

"I turn fourteen in May."

"Junior high has a prom?"

"Ours does."

"You have a boyfriend?"

"No. Just a guy, Reggie, who thinks—" She waved off Reggie, whatever he thought. "But Mom said that maybe the lady who does her hair could fix mine, but we're not sure how expensive it would be, and maybe she has too many clients already, Mom says, or no room in her schedule. So Mom's friend Helen can also braid, and I could just have Helen do a French braid. But I'd like it to be up, you know? Something more unusual than a braid."

"The prom is next week?"

"Friday."

"Where does your mother get her hair done?"

"Gayfers," said Rachel. "Why?"

"What's her hairdresser's name?"

"Mildred?"

"Why don't we check?"

Lucia got up and dug the phone book out of the kitchen drawer. Gayfers department store was easy enough to find: she ran a finger down the list of departments until she hit "salon," and she called the number and asked the relevant questions.

"She'll do any kind of updo," Lucia said, hanging up. "Whatever you like. It's twenty dollars. They said usually late afternoons aren't too busy."

The girl was staring. Lucia wondered if she'd crossed some line.

"Thank you," Rachel said, unmoving.

"I could make you an appointment," Lucia said slowly, "but I imagine you'll need to schedule it for when your mother is free to drive you."

Rachel picked up her ginger ale. The coaster stuck to the bottom of the glass before it clattered to the table. She slapped her hand over it, quieting it. "On Aunt Molly's last birthday, Mom bought her coasters with monkeys on them. And a monkey-shaped candle and a monkey apron. And monkey socks."

Lucia sat down again. She detested monkeys viscerally. She had never been able to make it through *Planet of the Apes*.

"So your aunt likes monkeys?" she asked.

"No. But Mom decided that Aunt Molly needed a hobby. She thought, like, hey, collecting monkeys would be good. So she bought up all the monkey stuff she could find, which is more than you'd think."

"Does your mother collect things?"

"She likes knickknacks. Dad calls them that. Like Fenton glass and china figurines. Hummel, maybe? Little, pretty, breakable things. She likes finding them. It's more like hunting than collecting."

Lucia laughed. She was funny, this girl, now that she'd gotten comfortable. Although was it comfort? There was a certain stagecraft to her patter, not that Lucia begrudged a little acting. It was the next best thing to confidence. Practically the same thing.

"Is your father still—?" she started.

"He has an apartment right now," Rachel said. "I go over there on weekends. Sometimes he gets me for supper on a school night. So where does your husband work?"

Lucia mentioned Baptist Hospital, and as she started explaining the role of the marketing department, it occurred to her that she should omit the specifics. If she dropped enough clues, Rachel might show up at Evan's door. It would involve crossing the Southern Bypass, granted, but Lucia wasn't sure the girl would be deterred by six lanes of traffic.

V.

Two weeks later, Lucia came home and found a blue-and-green egg made of felt on her doorstep. It had a quarter inside.

Two weeks after that, she found a flamingo pen—the bird bobbing on a spring—propped against the door. It matched her key chain. It was three months, though, before Rachel arrived again in person. When Lucia opened the door, her hand tight around Moxie's collar, the girl held out a set of bacon-shaped stickers that said *I bring home the bacon.*

Lucia laughed. "You don't need to bring me anything. I appreciated the flamingo, too, but you don't have to get me gifts."

"It's just something silly," Rachel said.

She wasn't looking at Lucia, though—she was staring over Lucia's left shoulder, and Lucia didn't have to look behind her to know why.

"Come in," she said. "You can meet my husband. Evan, this is Rachel."

There was a moment when they stood there looking at each other—Evan by the countertop with a pair of scissors in one hand and a package of 9-volt batteries in the other, Rachel in the shadows of the carport. Lucia watched Rachel watching Evan. She assumed her husband would see the girl much as she did—pretty in the way of teenage girls, slightly unwieldy, shorts too short—but she wondered how Rachel saw her husband. How did he rank by thirteen-year-old—by now, probably fourteen-year-old—standards? Was he what the girl had expected? Would the glasses count against him?

"I've heard all about you, Rachel," Evan said.

He set down the scissors and held out a hand. Rachel nearly lunged for it across the doorstep. "I've been wanting to meet you," she said, giving a solid shake. "May I call you Bard?"

He smiled. "You may. Are you coming inside?"

Of course she was. She cheerfully accepted the offer of a ginger ale, and she once again took the circuitous route to the sofa. She stopped at the driftwood, then peered around the edge of the bookshelves.

"It's a mandolin," Evan said, nodding at the instrument that hung on the wall. He eased into his armchair, still struggling to open the batteries.

"The guitar?" said Rachel.

"It's not a guitar," he said. "It's a mandolin."

"I gave it to him for his birthday a few years ago," said Lucia, handing over a cold can of ginger ale.

Rachel laughed and asked Evan, "Do you play the mandolin?"

"No," he said. "I don't."

"You could," said Lucia.

"I never gave you any reason to believe that I would like to play the mandolin."

"I don't know why you wouldn't," she said to him, aware that they were hamming it up a bit. She sat down, her armchair facing Evan's, the sofa to her right.

"A *mandolin*," he said.

"So," said Rachel, dropping onto the sofa. Her head turned back and forth between them. "Was that the weirdest gift that Lucia ever gave you?"

She was clearly chumming the water.

"She gave me a mushroom garden," Evan said. "You were supposed to plant them all in a box and harvest them under the moon."

Rachel laughed again. Or maybe she had never quite stopped laughing. Her fingertips dented the metal of her soda can. An off-key percussion.

"It was whimsical," said Lucia.

"I don't care for mushrooms," said Evan.

"You didn't have to eat them."

"I don't like to envision them."

"Envision," echoed Rachel softly. "I got a car hammer last Christmas."

"Is there such a thing?" Lucia wondered.

Rachel nodded. She glanced at Moxie, who was licking her butt next to Evan's chair. "Aunt Molly gave one to me and one to my mom. It's a little hammer that fits in your glove compartment so if your car goes off a bridge, you can break the windows."

"Why do you need your own hammer?" Evan asked. "You can't drive."

"So Mom and me can break the windows at the same time," Rachel said. "Once you break the glass, the water would flood in right away, so you'd need to get out fast."

"Jesus," Evan said.

"She also gave me this necklace that has, like, a vial hanging on it, and she thought I could fill it up with Campho-Phenique in case of an accident. I think she got nervous after I went to the lake with Tina—she's my best friend—and some guy let me drive his four-wheeler, only I'd never driven one before and I fell off and banged my head and talked crazy for a few hours, and Mom was furious and said if I had permanent damage she would sue that guy."

Lucia did not want to interrupt by pointing out that a vial full of antiseptic would not help a concussion. Or that unless a child's father was dead, imprisoned, or shut away in an insane asylum, a mother in Alabama had no legal right to sue over her child's injuries.

"I could put perfume in the vial, too," Rachel added. "Aunt Molly said that would be smart since I'm at the age when body odor starts. So that's good to know."

Lucia glanced at Evan, who had let his head fall into his hands. His shoulders shook. Outside, the wind chimes played their tune.

When Rachel left, the two of them stood under the carport and watched her cross the street, hopping over the curb with more clearance than necessary.

"I see what you mean," Evan said.

"I knew you would."

"Does she make you a little more ready to have kids?" he asked.

Lucia leaned against him, her fingers finding the rough edges of his unbuttoned sleeve. She liked this shirt, with its stripes the color of coffee and toast. She thought of childhood declarations of "best friends." It was the same thing that drove marriage, she supposed. The beauty of pairs. Of fitting flush together, gapless.

"Maybe," she said.

VI.

It was still a shock how early night fell in November. Winding through the familiar streets, Lucia passed the elementary school playground, where two boys were scaling the bars of a metal dome. She felt a flash of disapproval that they were wandering around alone after dark, but then she saw a woman—their mother, she assumed—standing by the fence, and she remembered that it was barely after 5:00 p.m.

She glanced back at the boys in the rearview mirror as one of them made it to the top of the dome, lifting his arms like Rocky.

Evan had liked the idea of living so close to a school.

As she turned onto her street, she recognized the light blue Chevy parked by the curb in front of her house. Rachel's mother had started chauffeuring her daughter once she'd realized she was sneaking over. The woman's friendliness had surprised Lucia. Months after her original appointment, Margaret had called the office to say she would like to start the divorce process. She'd asked for a meeting and Lucia had agreed to it, and then Margaret had called back within a week, wavering, and asked to cancel. When she called again weeks later, Lucia told her gently that she deserved a lawyer more suited to her particular preferences. She'd found one easily enough, Rachel had reported.

Now as Lucia pulled into the driveway, Rachel opened the passenger door, waving, her hand a fan-shaped blur in the streetlamp glow. Lucia waved back, more enthusiastically than she might have expected from herself. She would not have minded a half hour to watch the news or nap on the couch.

And yet. To get that smile, merely for pulling into her own driveway.

By the time Lucia got out of the car, Margaret was standing, one elbow on her car door. She'd not only lacked resentment, she'd been effusive. Every time they met, the woman acted as if they were the sort of friends forged by slumber parties and mai tais. Her smile was as wide as her daughter's.

It was baffling.

"She begged me to stop and see if you were home," Margaret said, her voice low and conspiring. "We were headed to Molly's, but I could drop her off for a little while. As rude as it is for her to impose on you like this."

"Mom," hissed Rachel, empty-handed for once.

Lucia took a few steps closer, tightening the belt on her leather coat. The almost-dead grass bristled under her feet.

"It's always a pleasure to see her," she said. "Although Evan and I have dinner plans tonight. Come in for twenty minutes, Rachel, and then we'll drop you back at your aunt's."

"I can walk," Rachel said.

"We'll drop you," Lucia said. "You don't have a coat?"

"I can't ever get her to wear one," said Margaret. "Where are you going for dinner?"

"The Bamboo Garden."

"Oh, I've heard of it," Margaret said, coming out from behind the car door. "I went to the Lampliter the other night—they're putting on *Guys and Dolls*. The musical? You know it? They did this chicken pasta for dinner, and it was too spicy, really. But, still, it's the theater you go for, isn't it?"

Rachel slammed the passenger door. Her hair whipped around her head, revealing sequined turkey earrings that dangled nearly to her shoulders. She angled through the yard, her daisy-print blouse loose and blowing.

"Bye, Mom," she called over her shoulder.

"Oh, she's always so—" started Margaret, voice low again. "You know how she is. And did you see those ridiculous earrings?"

"I'll have her back soon," said Lucia. "In plenty of time for dinner."

Margaret lifted her hand to smooth her hair, her keys and her bracelets jingling. "You've been in this house for how long?" she asked.

Rachel was waiting with her hand on the doorknob.

"Four years," Lucia said.

"And you still feel good about the neighborhood?"

"Margaret," said Lucia. "*Your* earrings. They're so pretty."

"These? I got them at Parisian on sale."

"Really beautiful," Lucia said, as she started up the drive. A couple of steps, then a look over her shoulder. "So nice to see you."

She had learned this method of escape from her mother, who always needed to get home to start dinner after church on Sundays but inevitably got trapped in the pew by Mrs. Norris, who talked about her granddaughter's ballet recitals, or Mrs. Rigby, who talked about her back pain, or Louis Herbert, who stared at any woman's chest the whole time he talked to her. *Louis,* her mother had said once, *what smooth sleeves you have. Not a wrinkle in them.* She had been building momentum as she spoke, and as he thanked her, she had darted past him toward the fellowship hall, dragging Lucia along by the hand.

"Thanks again," Lucia called.

"Sure," Margaret replied, turning, finally, toward her car. "Sure."

Inside the house, Lucia shed her coat and grabbed a Tab for herself and a ginger ale for Rachel. Evan had obviously put the dog in the backyard because there had been no mass of fur hurtling toward them, only Evan, who kissed Lucia and asked her if jeans were all right for dinner—which was likely a way of making sure she remembered their plans. He exchanged a few words with Rachel and disappeared toward the bedroom.

Rachel took her usual spot on the couch. "I'm nearly done with *The Autobiography of Miss Jane Pittman.* Thanks again for it. It's horrible. Amazing, I mean, but horrible."

"You haven't read anything like it in school?" Lucia asked, although she knew the answer.

"No," said Rachel, frowning. Considering.

If she had to make a bet, Lucia would guess the girl had never heard of the bus boycott. She could imagine the school-board men dickering among themselves in rooms filled with pipe smoke, deciding that it was best to keep teachers from stirring up the past. Not that it was the past. Those black boys on the igloo wouldn't have been allowed on that particular playground a few years ago. *Brown v. Board* hadn't done anything here—it took *Carr v. Board of Education* in 1964, and then redistricting in 1969, and then another round of redistricting in 1974, and the upshot of it was that Montgomery had managed to avoid integration for two decades, and maybe a silver lining was that it let tempers cool. No one got mobbed. No one got beaten.

The consequences were more subtle.

"I heard they used to assign reading with Black History Month," Rachel said. "Before they canceled it. It was, like, really disruptive. Mom read in the paper that the black kids at Lee wanted to skip classes on the anniversary of Martin Luther King's death, and the principal said no, and they did it anyway. He suspended, like, two hundred of them. Mom said they were out of control, acting wild and making trouble."

Lucia considered that Jane Pittman might have a limited effect. *Wild. Out of control.* She knew that Rachel could not feel the age-old currents underneath those words.

"I was in algebra class when Kennedy was assassinated," Lucia said. "The principal made an announcement over the intercom. Kids cheered. You could hear the yelling and clapping all through the school. Those white kids were fairly disruptive."

"They cheered?"

"They did."

Rachel pulled at the metal tab on the ginger ale. It snapped off in her fingers. "Is that when you decided you wanted to be a lawyer? Because of, you know, how unfair everything was back then?"

Lucia told herself she should have expected the question. The girl was especially interested in character. Motivation. She believed an action must have a reason.

"No," Lucia said. "I didn't know law was a possibility when I was in high school. I was in college before I thought about being a lawyer."

"And you love it?"

Lucia tugged at her pantyhose, which had twisted at the knee. She suspected she was incapable of an unedited answer at this stage of her life, particularly with Rachel.

"I feel like I make a difference," she said.

She had clearly chosen the right answer. Rachel smiled and dug her feet into the couch cushions. Her turkey earrings swayed, transcendently tacky. In October, she'd worn silver skeletons and rats that hung from their tails.

"I got grounded," she said.

Lucia looked away from the turkeys. She'd never known the girl to get in trouble. "For what?"

"I roller-skated."

Lucia laughed. She had come to believe that these stories were like the silly presents, a currency offered in exchange for a visit. She increasingly felt the clever engineering of them. The stories were constructions—good ones—but she wondered what was underneath their gloss.

"I couldn't sleep last week," Rachel said. "It was about midnight, and I thought exercise would be good. So I went skating, maybe for half an hour. But Mom woke up and found me gone, and when I came back she was standing at the door, like, 'Where have you been, Rachel?'"

She had a talent for mimicking Margaret's Southern-lady accent.

"I told her—I mean, it was pretty obvious with the skates—that I'd been skating. She said, 'With who?' like I'd had some sort of drug deal or sex date on—"

"Sex date?" said Lucia.

"On roller skates. I told her I'd just been skating by myself, and she said anything could have happened, that there was no telling who was out at that time of night, that I could have been kidnapped or crammed in a van—which are basically the same thing—and she would never have known what happened. She went on like that for a while until she told me I couldn't go anywhere but school and church for the next two weeks. I can't believe she let me come here."

"Two weeks?"

"It's a waste, isn't it? I might as well have had a sex date."

Blues guitar played in the background, and Lucia didn't recognize the song. Evan had a better ear than she did.

"You know I have to kick you out in a minute, right?" said Lucia.

"Yeah," said Rachel, content.

❋ **1981** ❋

Rachel

1.

I closed the back door and dropped my damp purse next to the buffet, careful not to jar the porcelain kittens. My sandal snagged on the turned-up edge of the GOD WELCOMES US ALL mat. An obstacle course of small rugs—Oriental, floral, braided—covered the den carpet. *They add depth,* Mom always said.

I smelled tacos. No surprise. When we weren't eating at Aunt Molly's, Mom did either tacos or fettuccini or Rotel dip. Occasionally stroganoff.

Mom was stretched out on the sofa, mostly hidden behind a newspaper. I could see her bare legs, her fingertips, and the curls sproinging from her bun. She wore it like that to work. I didn't like not being able to see her face.

"Oh!" she said, letting the paper drop. "I was getting worried. Were the roads bad?"

The look on her face was a relief. Not angry. Not sad. Those were the big two.

"They were fine," I said, as if I'd ever admit that they weren't. "Just wet." She stood up, circling around the coffee table.

"That leak is starting again in the guest bathroom," she said.

"It's dripping?" I asked.

"No. But I feel like the ceiling might be discoloring. You want to look?"

I checked the couch for a plate, but she wasn't eating. She hardly ever ate. Since I could smell the tacos, though, I figured they were ready. Sometimes Mom finished cooking and then drifted away and let the food either get cold or turn black, depending on the burner situation.

"I should probably put a bucket under there," she said, "just in case."

Apparently, we were going to keep talking about a leak that was not leaking.

"I'll look in a minute," I said. "But all you can do is put the bucket there, right? And then call someone tomorrow if it does start to drip."

I angled around her, focused on my feet. Heel, toe, heel, toe across the rugs. But Mom didn't head for the bathroom like I expected. Instead she reached for the *Journal.*

"Lucia Gilbert is in here," she said. She was using that tone she had when something mattered to her but she was trying to pretend it didn't.

I kept my voice and face blank. "Oh."

She shook the newspaper at me. "She volunteered at some crisis center for women."

She watched me.

"It says here," she said, "that the Bar Association arranged for real attorneys to man the phones at the Crisis Center for Law Day—have you ever heard of that? Law Day? Battered women could call in and ask for legal advice. They have a picture of Lucia. They interviewed her."

Mom lowered her head to the paper and read, her voice singsong. "'A woman can seek counseling if she doesn't want to take legal action,' said Ms. Gilbert, a self-described feminist. 'But most counselors won't see a wife about abuse unless the husband is willing to go as well. And there are limits to counseling. Sometimes a woman must recognize that she needs to end a relationship.'"

She folded the paper, dropping it onto the coffee table. I didn't look at it.

Mom wasn't impressed by Lucia, not since that first meeting, or, more likely, she was too impressed. It added up to the same thing.

I made things worse, of course.

"That's interesting," I said, not sounding interested. "Can I get some tacos?"

Mom couldn't see me anymore once I stepped into the kitchen. The shells were lined up on a baking sheet, so she had remembered to toast them this time, and that was nice. The meat was still simmering, orangish, in the skillet. I turned off the burner and scooped filling into a couple of shells; I decided I didn't feel like shredding cheese. I just squeezed taco sauce out of the packet.

By the time I'd fixed my plate, Mom had disappeared. She'd gone to stare at the nonleaking ceiling, most likely. I ate a few bites, standing by the kitchen table and staring at the lemon wallpaper until I made the pattern of lemons and leaves blur into fat honeybees with green wings. When the hallway to the back of the house stayed empty and silent, I hurried back into the den and grabbed the newspaper. I spread it across the kitchen table and read the article for myself. It was only a couple of short columns. Mom had covered most of the part about Lucia, but not the ending.

The pretty little blonde has a history of firsts, it said. *Before moving into private practice, she was the first woman to be appointed a deputy district attorney in the state of Alabama.*

First woman to substitute on the bench of the Montgomery County Criminal Court, it said.

One of only two women in her class at Cumberland Law School, it said.

I studied the black-and-white photo. Lucia was talking into a phone, her hair hanging across her face. When I saw her in the afternoons, her makeup had usually worn off, her freckles showing, but in the photo she was a Hollywood version of herself.

"She's not that little," said Mom from behind me, and when I turned she was in a towel, showered and barefoot. One downside of all the carpets: you could never hear her coming.

I bit into my taco. Mom pinched a bite of meat from the skillet, flinching at the heat of it. She'd likely snitch another bite and consider it supper.

The phone on the wall rang, making the receiver jump. Almost surely Will Pearson. He always called between 8:00 and 8:30, which meant that on Tuesdays he interrupted *Hart to Hart*. Honestly, it would have been hard enough to make conversation if he called once a week—why would a boy call if he was just going to sit there and breathe?—but he called every night, which Mom said was a sign of a good boyfriend, but he wasn't my boyfriend, so he wasn't being good at anything except breathing. I'd pace between the kitchen table and the stove, and a silence would seep through the twisted-up phone cord, and eventually I would fill it. I'd talk and talk and he'd laugh at my jokes, and I couldn't stand it, but on a Tuesday? Even worse.

The phone kept ringing.

"Aren't you going to answer it?" Mom said. Her face was slicked with Pond's, which she always said would soak in, but it never did.

"The show's about to start," I said.

Fourth ring. He'd hang up after the sixth.

"It's rude not to answer, Rachel. If a boy cares enough to call, you can care enough to answer."

A piece of shell caught my gums like a shard of glass. I thought about reminding her of John Martin, that nice turtle of a man, no neck but so kind, and Mom made me answer the phone four nights in a row and tell him she was in the shower, until he said, *She takes a lot of showers, doesn't she?*, and finally he stopped calling.

There came a time with every man where she enjoyed ignoring the phone more than she'd ever enjoyed it ringing.

"I don't want him to call, Mom," I said.

"It could be your father," she said.

She knew I would pick up the phone if I thought it was Dad, but if I admitted it, her face would shut down and in whatever invisible point system we had, she would score. Once upon a time Dad used to call most nights, but that had stopped because who could come up with that much conversation? (I'm talking to you, Will Pearson.) Then for a while he called every Thursday, but after he got the job as regional sales director last fall, he started traveling so much that we stopped our regular weekends. That meant we didn't need to go over so many details. I'd talked to him last week, and he never called two weeks in a row.

The phone finally hushed. I carried my plate to the sofa, just as the television screen went white with bright sky and the plane took off the runway. The theme song had started: *This is my boss, Jonathan Hart, a self-made millionaire. He's quite a guy.*

"You need to be nicer," Mom said.

"I am nice," I said, but mostly I soaked in the credits and Stefanie Powers's magical hair. *This is Mrs. H. She's gorgeous. She's one lady who knows how to take care of herself.*

"Are you?" Mom sat next to me, sofa cushions tipping enough that my taco slid across the plate.

"You hear me talking to him most nights, Mom."

"Maybe he'll grow on you."

I wanted to watch my show. I wanted her to shut up about this boy she'd never even met, who possibly smoked pot and plus he was Catholic, so why was she his biggest fan?

"Why should I hope he grows on me?" I said. "Like, what, fungus? Is that a good theory of dating?"

Her lips clamped together, making wrinkles where there weren't usually any. Her eyes turned wet. She could do that so quickly.

She stood up, tightening her loose towel, and I stared at the television. Her footsteps were loud and heavy as she left the room. *It was a joke,* I wanted to say, but I didn't. I focused on Jennifer Hart taking off her fur in a train compartment, pouring champagne, smiling up at Jonathan, and soon there would surely be a charming sex reference. I thought of how I would love to ride in a train, the kind with beds attached to the walls. The kind where murders happened.

Mom banged around the kitchen, muttering. For someone talking to herself, her voice really carried.

I always say, she said. She used that phrase a lot with herself. *I always say there's no point,* she said, and a cabinet door slammed. *Margaret,* she said, *you know you do this every time, and you know how she is—*

"I'm putting your lunch money in your purse," she said, loud enough that she was clearly not talking to herself.

She liked to give me money when she was crying.

Then she was back in the room, pointing a pen at me, her face shiny and blotchy and hard. The pen had liquid inside, and when you turned it over, a Moxie-ish dog floated up through the liquid.

"Is this for Lucia?" she asked.

"That was in the bottom of my purse," I said.

"Is this a present for her?"

"Why were you going through my purse?"

"I was putting your money in. Is this for her?"

Now she was avoiding saying Lucia's name. Not good. Lucia racked up points in Mom's usual categories—attractive, well dressed, good manners. Nice-looking husband who wore a suit to work. But Lucia scored well, too, in a whole different system, and I still hadn't figured out how that affected Mom's calculations. I was never sure whether Mom wanted to take me away from Lucia or take Lucia away from me.

"Yeah, it's for her," I said, because I had stalled as long as I could.

Mom dropped the pen on the couch and spun away from me. She stopped in front of the television, swiped at the volume knob, and suddenly I could hear the moths hitting the window. She insisted that burglars didn't break into a well-lit house, but the floodlight brought the bugs by the hundreds.

"You never get me fun gifts," she said.

That wasn't true. On Mother's Day two years earlier I'd gotten her a hilarious oven mitt that said One Hot Mama. She didn't even smile when she opened the box. She stuffed it in a drawer and never took it out again, and so last Mother's Day I got her candy-covered almonds like usual and she was much happier.

I watched the flying bodies smack against the glass, one after another.

Mom said more stuff, following me as I put the pen back in the side pocket of my purse. I imagined handing it to Lucia and how she tipped her head back when she laughed, like there was something funny overhead. I imagined leaving it on her doorstep, and I thought of the dusty gasoline smell of her carport.

Eventually Mom went to her bedroom, and I finished watching my show. That was how our nights worked: I picked my words carefully, but never carefully enough.

It wasn't a bad ending.

Some nights were worse.

II.

The day before I met Lucia, my mother took her car into Mosely Brothers because the brakes were sticking, and she did that voice she does like, *Oh goodness me, what is this strange contraption they call a car? How am I ever to understand its complicated pieces? I think I have a problem with this part called, oh, the brake? Brakes? Am I saying that right? Giggle giggle shrug smile. I cannot even imagine how you know all these big words, you impressive man in overalls, and won't you please oh please fix it for me?*

That's a slight exaggeration.

But I said to her while we were sitting in the Mosely Brothers waiting room, with its light-up Coke machine and half-empty pot of coffee, "You're smart, Mom. Why do you act like you don't know anything?"

She cried. Right there in the waiting room.

Lucia had hot pink fingernails, shining, and my mother was big on never painting your nails brighter than a pale peach. Lucia's eyes were deep and dark, and all the women in my family except for me had blue eyes. She was like someone out of a fairy tale, only in a suit.

She talked to me and she knew about movies, and right there in her lobby

I wondered—I mean, I was only thirteen, so I didn't have the right words, but it was something like—

Is this how you can be?

Lucia wasn't afraid of anything.

You have to understand that on the day before a road trip, which usually meant visiting my grandmother in Huntsville, Mom always went to a full-service gas station to get the tires checked. I was unaware that women could use self-service gas stations. I had no idea that tire gauges were sold in stores.

Mom never drove on the interstate. She never drove at night.

My grandmother and aunt followed these rules as well. There were others. You never called a boy, even if it was to ask about a homework assignment. If you wanted to make a rum cake and you were out of rum, you needed to call up an uncle or a husband or a father, because a woman alone was not safe at a liquor store. (I imagined liquor stores as something out of *Mad Max*, with barbed wire and dust storms and men in spiked helmets whirring chains through the air.) You should never swim in the ocean because of riptides. Never leave your car without checking twice that you locked it. Never sleep on your face because you'll get wrinkles. Never wear your bathing suit into the front yard to get the mail, because what if Mr. Cleary next door sees you? Never go to Kmart in cutoff shorts, even if you're in the middle of gardening and only need more potting soil, because what if someone sees you? Never stand at the bar in a restaurant, even if you're waiting for a table, because what if someone sees you?

I always wanted to ask, What happens next? After they see you?

Once I stopped by to see Lucia on a Saturday, and she was weeding her flower beds without makeup. Not even foundation. I never saw my mother without makeup unless she was ready for bed.

Women in my family were afraid of everything.

An office lobby is a flat, cardboard kind of place, and an office lobby is all I had of Lucia at first. She changed for me when I saw her in her house. Like when you pull a Barbie out of her box, and for a while it's enough to stare at her tiny shoes and the blue slivers of her eye shadow, but eventually she's only a doll propped up on the carpet. But if you get her a Dreamhouse—and maybe a Corvette—then she has some substance. You can build her a whole life. You can sit back and watch her as she moves from room to room and turns on her record player and picks up the phone to make plans and solve problems. That was what Lucia's house did. It let me move my imaginary Lucia around, room to room.

I added Bard, and he was another helpful piece. Was that how it was to be married? Because it wasn't what I'd seen. They laughed. They talked like someone had written their lines for them, sharp and quick.

Where did the pile of dog towels go? Lucia would say.

In the washer, Bard would say.

In the washer with our towels? Where do you think the dog hair goes, Evan?

It gets washed, Lucia.

It gets washed right onto our towels! Do we really have to go over this again?

We don't have to go over it again. It's a washer. It washes.

They would go on like that forever. They argued about the longest street in Montgomery and whether you had to count only streets within the city limits or whether you could include Montgomery County. They argued over whether a wombat is a marsupial. They never argued about anything real.

Why can't you just try harder? I heard Mom ask Dad once, toward the end. *If you wanted to be happy, you'd be happy.*

I don't think I can be happy while I'm with you, he'd said, and I suppose that wasn't exactly an argument, was it?

Once I got my license, I came by more often than Lucia knew. My only rule was that I couldn't go by more than twice a week. She worked late a lot. Sometimes, when her car was gone, I barely slowed down. Other times I parked at the curb and went through the motions of knocking on the kitchen door. It was an excuse to look through the window. I could see the copper pots dangling from the hooks over the stove. I could see the spice rack. Her kitchen was nothing like ours—nothing of hers was like anything of ours. At home everything was too hard or too worn down, too clean or too grimy. Our couch and chairs were wooden armed, impossible for napping, and polish drenched every inch of wooden furniture. Once I had to set a piece of lemon cake on the coffee table for a second, and when I bit into it, the polish had soaked into it like sauce.

In Lucia's house, everything made you want to touch it. The cranberry-colored carpet was soft under your feet. The chunk of driftwood felt like an ancient bone. The den lamps had silver leaves with dangling crystals, and when you set a drink on the end table, the crystals swayed. Lucia cut flowers from the yard and put them in vases. She had wine bottles in a pyramid. I'd never seen anyone drink a glass of wine other than on TV. (Did it involve a trip to the liquor store? Did she go by herself?)

Mom liked Elvis, but we only listened in the car. Oldies 106.9. Lucia played the blues, and she always lifted the arm of the record player with one finger. The records had names I'd never heard—Muddy Waters and T-Bone Walker and Pinetop Perkins, and I tried to learn them but I never managed because how can you listen at the same time you're talking?

The music sat in the air, more like a smell than a sound.

The books took up one whole wall, with shelves from the floor to the ceiling. We had bookshelves at home, but they were filled with bowls of pot-pourri and Mom's endless figurines. Lucia gave me *Alas, Babylon* and *Animal Farm* and *The Fountainhead*. Before I met her, I mostly read Dad's old paper-backs with their covers of cowboys and sunsets and sword-holding men and women wearing fur and daggers. Robert E. Howard—oh, I spent a lot of nights with Conan, wishing I could slip into his world, and I would be the fiercest kind of woman warrior, riding horses and slitting throats and eating roasted mammals that I'd killed with my own hands. Lucia's books didn't have massive thews or volcanic blue eyes, but I'd open the pages, knowing she had read the same words, and I'd swallow them whole at night—or they'd swallow me—and Mom was a universe away, watching reruns of *Bewitched*.

III.

After Sunday dinner at Aunt Molly's, I pulled up by the curb at Lucia's. Evan's car was gone, and the house was dark. I was equal parts relieved and disappointed. I had suspected they didn't go to church, but maybe they went somewhere with late services? Maybe they were having lunch in a fellowship hall somewhere or waiting for the check at Red Lobster?

I hoped they'd gone to church.

I knocked on the door anyway, standing in the carport with my forehead against the window, staring past the reflection of my Laura Ashley dress with tomato sauced dripped down the front. I imagined some future version of myself inside Lucia's den, coming home and pouring myself a glass of tea— no, wine—and then falling asleep on the sofa. I watched my sleeping self, a complete stranger. I listened to the wind chimes making their fairy sounds. When I wandered back down the driveway, I did it slowly.

"Many will meet their doom," I heard myself singing, "trumpets will sound. All of the dead shall rise, righteous meet in the skies—"

It had been the closing hymn today. Even the part about eternal damnation was cheerful. I stopped at my car, keys in hand. The longer I stayed, the harder it would be to invent a believable excuse. As it was, I could tell Mom

I'd stopped for gas, although she had to work this afternoon, and there was a chance that she was already headed to flip around the OPEN sign at Barre None and sell leotards and toe shoes to a bunch of ballerinas.

I spun away from my car, heading down the sidewalk in the opposite direction from Aunt Molly's house. I had never turned right when I left Lucia's house. I had no destination. I was only taking one step after another, and within a few houses, the street seemed unfamiliar.

The sermon today had been about Noah and the blessings of righteousness, and I'd partly listened but I'd also figured out a long time ago that if I kept reading past the verses the pastor quoted, I'd find the good parts. Like the chapter about Noah starts with an announcement that in those days "Nephilim" were on the earth, and the "sons of God" had children with the "daughters of men," and those children grew up to be heroes. So what the heck was a Nephilim? It was like the writer got off track and started a fantasy novel in the middle of the Bible. There was an entire world buried in that verse, and—even when I asked—every Sunday-School teacher shrugged and skipped right past it.

They skipped past the part after the flood when Noah got drunk and passed out naked, and they skipped the part in Leviticus about how to deal with men's discharges and semen. (I wished someone would explain what men discharged besides semen.) Pastors loved to talk about how Lot's disobedient wife was turned into a pillar of salt, but what about the part where two angels visited Lot's home, and a mob of men demanded he hand over the angels to be raped? And then Lot offered up his two virgin daughters to be raped instead? Those same daughters later got their father drunk, had sex with him, and wound up pregnant.

"Are you reading your Bible every night?" my grandmother loved to ask me, and I wondered if she had any idea what was actually in the thing.

I could hear the martins in the trees. Away from my usual path, every step seemed sharp and clear and foreign. The concrete was mottled with leaf shadows and smashed crepe myrtle blossoms the pinks and purples of Hubba Bubba. A worm, dried out. Tiny volcanoes of anthills.

"Troublesome times are here," I sang, starting over from the beginning, "filling men's hearts with fear. Freedom we all hold dear now is at stake."

Today the pastor had stood in the pulpit and explained how God's deep disappointment in mankind forced him to flood the earth and obliterate nearly everyone on it. We taught toddlers about those cute animals walking two by two, but God wiped out, maybe, thousands of kids and parents and grandparents. Or was it millions? We never talked about the slaughtered ones. We talked about Noah and the blessings of righteousness.

"Aren't we lucky," the pastor had said, smiling. He was a gentle man, not like those angry preachers in movies. "Aren't we lucky to be born here? To be born into the right families at the right time and place? Think of some African tribesman, born in the dirt, who never even hears the name of Jesus. Who never has the chance to be redeemed. We are blessed, brothers and sisters. We are chosen."

It was a pleasant thought as long as you didn't think about all the people—tribesmen or otherwise—roasting in hell.

Everyone has their role.

It was one of the pastor's favorite lines. *A congregation follows its elders. Children obey their parents. A woman is a helpmeet to her husband.*

Alice and Gus Rogers sat across the aisle from me, shushing their six kids, who were all a little strange because they weren't allowed to watch television. The Rogerses had been missionaries in Africa for years, and if we believed everyone who was unbaptized would burn in hell, shouldn't more of us be like them, strange or not? Shouldn't we head out to convert all the Africans or Asians or Episcopalians or whatever? Instead we sat there, Sunday after Sunday.

Everyone has their role.

Was our role to be saved and everybody else's role to burn?

The whole church was lazy, like when adults find a chicken sandwich inside the Arby's bag instead of the Beef 'n Cheddar they ordered, and they eat it because it's too much trouble to take it back. The Rogerses sat behind my fifth-grade Sunday-School teacher, Valerie Springer, who couldn't teach my class after that year because once we turned twelve, a woman wasn't allowed to lead a class with boys in it. Did Mrs. Springer ever point out that women teach those same boys all day long every Monday through Friday? Did anyone ever say, hey, could we spend more time talking about these people condemned to eternal damnation? Lucia grew up Methodist, which meant she was sprinkled as a baby instead of being properly baptized, and it was impossible to imagine that she would go to hell, and yet I thought of multitudes disappearing into rising water, screaming and sobbing.

Sometimes my thoughts twisted down these paths until I rounded a corner and caught a glimpse of something so big that I couldn't make out its shape, and I'd have to turn away.

A squirrel circled his way up a pecan tree, claws scrabbling against bark. I breathed in the sweetness of flowers—camellia? Honeysuckle? The sun was warm on my face, and I let it soak in.

I took a right at a stop sign and tried to let the questions drain out of me. It was possible that I was confusing laziness with faith. On good nights, I could still close my eyes and feel God in the room with me as I prayed, and love would fill me like a balloon. In the moments between prayer and sleep I lost myself entirely, and I drifted up through the stars to him, floating away to a place I didn't know or understand, and everything made sense.

I wanted that feeling of floating.

The squirrels bickered in the trees. A concrete fountain bubbled in someone's front yard, and yellow roses curled around a fencepost. I stepped over a cracked handprint in the sidewalk, with a single yellow petal wedged into the thumb. There was nothing special about this street except that I'd never set foot on it. Now here I was wandering down the sidewalk alone, and not a single person had tried to stuff me in a van or tear off my clothes. All I'd seen were squirrels and petals and sun slashing through the leaves, and one day I'd be able to turn down any street I liked. I would take long walks and not know where I was going. I would roam for hours and get lost and find my way back, and—finally!—the thought of it was something like closing my eyes and drifting up to the stars.

A loud bark made me jump. The dog was just ahead of me, behind a chain-link fence that boxed off a wide backyard with a patio and tall grass. The dog bounded toward me, head as high as my shoulder, tongue hanging out, slobber spraying.

I knew her right away, but it took a little while for me to believe I was really seeing her.

"Moxie?" I said.

She sproinged, tail wagging her entire body. A couple of beagle-ish dogs came running up behind her, yapping, keeping their distance from me. I turned back to Moxie and saw her red collar with her silver tag jingling back and forth. I stretched out my hand toward her, and the beagles went nuts. I was trying to reason with them, scratching Moxie's head at the same time, when a man with a beard slid open the patio door. I nearly called out to him because this sort of thing happened in our neighborhood sometimes, especially with the Martins' cocker spaniel, who was always bolting out of their gate. Whoever found him would plop him into their backyard.

I'd always wondered why a dog as big as Moxie didn't jump the fence. Maybe she'd finally done it, and this guy had found her. I could see a water bowl on the patio.

I stepped back, though, as the man slid the door closed behind him. I didn't call out. No good reason why. I started walking like I was only strolling past. The man waved at me, and I waved back.

"Come on, Chewie," he called.

It took me a second to realize that he was talking to Moxie. He'd given her a new name.

This man had stolen Lucia's dog.

Lucia

1.

The drive to Andalusia took a little over an hour, and—in spite of herself—Lucia felt a rush of giddiness when she turned onto her old street: the Hoovers' magnolia trees, which she'd climbed so often, tearing off seed pods and pretending they were grenades. The dead end where she'd learned to ride a bike, with the ear-shaped patch of rough asphalt that still called to her with the *thunk-thunk* of front and back wheel; the fig tree at the Colliers' where she'd tossed pinched-off fig stems into the zoysia grass.

It was an illogical giddiness, like waking up and seeing snow out the windows—*no school!*—before remembering that she had to work regardless. She saw her parents at least once a month. This was no great homecoming. This was not even home.

Mr. Dorian's VW Rabbit, freshly waxed in the driveway.

Bright blue shutters on a chalk-white house. She'd seen skinny little Harold Stinton in that yard a hundred times, pestering someone to toss a grape, and he'd catch it in his mouth, braces flashing. His cargo plane had been shot down in Khe Sanh, and Lucia's mother had whispered the word "fireball."

Julie Bartlett, two years older than Lucia, was watering the begonias in front of the house where she'd grown up. If Lucia floated above the trees, she could point to the homes of a dozen girls who'd gone to school with her, who were all still here, more or less. Maybe a few miles away in Opp or Enterprise or Brewton.

Evan pulled into the driveway, holly branches scraping against the car as he parked by the side door. He got out and retucked his dress shirt: they always dressed for her parents as if they'd been at church that morning. Lucia was standing and straightening her belt when her mother pushed open the storm door, makeup fresh and hair well tended, bracelets and necklace coordinated, bare toes curled around the top step.

"Was the traffic bad?" Caroline asked. Her first question always involved traffic.

Lucia kissed her cheek.

"Not bad at all," she answered. Her mother smelled of Oil of Olay and White Rain hair spray, and Lucia inhaled.

"Not a single log truck," Evan said, which earned him a jab in his side from Caroline.

Her mother's obsession with log trucks had grated on Lucia for years—every time she got in a car, her mother issued some sort of log truck advisory. Lucia had long congratulated herself on muffling her annoyance, *No, Mother, I was not behind any log trucks,* and if there was condescension in her voice, it was surely justified because, really, how many deaths were caused by fallen logs each year? Then she brought Evan home to meet her parents, and eventually, after maybe the twentieth warning, he'd brushed a hand against Caroline's elbow and said, "So tell me about this relationship between you and log trucks."

Her mother had laughed and, in that moment, log trucks had become a joke. Evan had a knack for filing off the edges. It was an unexpected benefit of marriage: when confronted by some small blight growing in the family crevices, her husband could smile and lop it off, send it flying through the air, inconsequential.

The storm door closed behind them, the kitchen warm from the sun beating through the glass. Several empty serving dishes were lined up along the counter waiting to be filled, and the table was set.

"I like your hair pulled back like that," her mother said. "It's burning up in here, isn't it? I don't think the air's blowing right. I'll open a window."

Lucia hung her purse over a kitchen chair. "It feels fine. You're just hot from running around."

"Oliver!" her mother called. "They're here!"

"We'll go say hello," said Lucia.

"Well, it's not as if he's going to come in here, is it?" said Caroline. She drifted toward the stove, lifting the lid from a pot of field peas, which Evan loved. Her curls—silver streaking the brown—did not shift as she stirred.

Lucia nudged Evan, steering him down the dim hallway with a hand between his shoulder blades. As usual, he bumped into the phone shelf that jutted from the knotted-pine wall.

Oliver Roberts was in his recliner. His white hair, still thick, swooped over his ears. Behind him, the mantel was decorated with two etched-glass hurricane lamps and a poodle made of sweetgum balls. The television thrummed with a stagecoach chase scene.

"Here they are!" he boomed. "My two favorite lunch guests!"

Lucia crossed over the rope rug, red as a blood clot. Her father flipped down the footrest, making as if he would stand, but as usual, she reached him before he made any progress. She hugged him, his cheek scraping hers pleasantly, and he shook Evan's hand.

"Still feeling good about Coach Dye and that wishbone offense?" Oliver asked.

"I am," Evan said. His voice was always heartier when he talked to her father.

"He called us the University of Auburn," huffed Oliver. "Doesn't even know the name of his own college."

"That only happened once," Evan said. "You called me Edward at least five times on my first visit. Cut him some slack."

Oliver laughed. "I thought I called you Edgar."

"That, too."

"Hey, I got a new joke," Oliver said, arms stretching to the ceiling.

"Let's hear it," Evan said.

"It's a little racist, but—"

"No, Dad," Lucia said.

Next to her, Evan studied the carpet.

"It's not a bad one," her father said. "There's this black bus driver who makes the same stop every day—"

"Dad," Lucia said, and part of her wondered if she should just let him tell the joke. Because it hurt him. It actually hurt his feelings that she would not listen to him. "Come on."

"Lucia, it's a joke. You know that. It doesn't mean anything. Lord, the look on your face. You're so *serious*."

Evan looked away from the floor. "I'm telling you, if Dye can work miracles in one season at Wyoming, he can do it for us."

"Did we watch the same game?" Oliver said, diverted. "Auburn against Wake Forest? The smallest school playing in a Power Five conference?"

"He's changing the whole system," Evan said.

"I think," Lucia said, "that I'll go see if Mother needs any help."

Evan dropped onto the sofa, legs sprawling, and he gave her a look that said: *Once again you're abandoning me while I stay here and talk football because we are manly men and the kitchen is not our domain, and how the hell did you ever come out of this house?*

· Thank God he was an Auburn fan. A philosophy major, Ohio born, but the football redeemed him with her father. It opened the door to endless talk of post patterns and lob passes. Sitting across from her father, Evan never struggled with what to say next.

She was jealous sometimes.

She stepped back into the humid air of the kitchen. She opened the refrigerator, pulling out the pitcher of tea and nudging aside the Hershey's Syrup, which she could taste on her tongue just by looking at the can. Caroline was bending into the oven, pants slightly too tight, a bulge above her waistline. She would hate this view of herself.

"Do you want me to slice some tomato?" Lucia asked.

"That'd be nice," Caroline said. "Celery, too. Make sure to string it good."

"I know," said Lucia.

"The Jell-O salad is on the middle shelf," said Caroline. "And I need the Cool Whip."

Lucia pulled out the Jell-O—lemon, her favorite—and the Cool Whip.

"Do you know," said her mother, reaching for her silver mixing bowl, "that I've started adding almond extract? Can you imagine?"

"To the Jell-O topping?"

"Mm-hmm," said Caroline. She had the cream cheese softening on the counter, its silver skin split open. "A teaspoon."

Lucia cracked the oven, peering at the casserole and the dish under it— surely dumplings—both golden and simmering. The bubbles churned against the Pyrex.

"Do you remember Mavis Thorington at church?" her mother asked.

"I don't think so," said Lucia, thinking, *She's dead. Whoever she is, she's dead.*

"Her husband was Winston?" her mother prompted.

"She's dead, isn't she?"

"Massive heart attack. In her garage. Lucky she wasn't driving."

Lucia slipped on an oven mitt and turned the chicken casserole. "Do you leave out the vanilla when you put in the almond? Or add both?"

"I cut out the vanilla altogether," Caroline said, smashing cream cheese with a fork. "'Just a splash' of almond, as Mama would say. You know she never measured anything."

"'A splash and a dab and a shake,'" Lucia agreed. Her mother enjoyed sifting through the old familiar phrases, bringing her own mother back into the kitchen with them.

"'Stipple on some aloe,'" Caroline said.

That was a verb Lucia loved. She'd never heard anyone use it but her grandmother, who until the very end had kept an aloe plant by the sink, snapping a leaf for every scald and blister.

"Don't get sentimental over the Jell-O," she told her mother. "Granna didn't even miss her leg. She'd be fine with you letting go of the vanilla."

"Lu-cia," said Caroline, laughing soft and low. "How was Chicago?"

"Good."

"You flew?"

"I wouldn't drive to Chicago, Mother."

"How was the flight?"

This part of her life felt exotic to her mother, Lucia knew. Airplanes and hotels and taxis. She suspected that if she described each moment of the flight in detail—the stewardesses' uniforms, the chicken salad, how the man next to her hogged the armrest—her mother would sit enthralled.

"Same as usual," she said, knowing she should give her mother the chatter that she so obviously wanted.

"Did you order room service?" Caroline asked.

"I don't think so. No. We ate out."

"But you have, haven't you?" Her mother gave her a sly look. "You've ordered room service before."

"I have," Lucia said. She opened the oven door again, deciding the dumplings were ready. "Are these apple?"

"Pear."

"Last week I did them with chocolate and raspberries."

"Chocolate?" Her mother reached for a wooden spoon without turning her head. She had a pink burn mark across her wrist, the seared imprint of the oven rack. "You went to school with Mavis's nephew, actually."

"Tom," Lucia said slowly. "Tom?"

"Tom," agreed Caroline. "That boy had a head full of mayonnaise. Remember when that baseball cap flew off his head when he was driving down the highway, and so he put the car in reverse and drove backward to get it?"

"Yeah," said Lucia, laughing. "And the station wagon—it was a station wagon, right?—ran into him. Or he ran into it. I remember."

There was a reason that they talked in the kitchen—dumplings and Jell-O salads filled the empty spaces. The past could do that, too. It was as if the two of them were standing far apart, separated by a huge bedsheet, a wide flat expanse. One old story would fold up the distance, bring them close, corner against corner.

"Tomato," her mother reminded.

Lucia reached into the far-right drawer where the sharp knives stayed, and the lace curtains blew against her arm. Her mother had opened a window after all, and the familiarness of it washed over Lucia. She knew this place. She knew the cereal cabinet squeaked, making it dangerous to snitch Rice Krispies—which were kept not in a box but in a Tupperware cylinder—in the wee hours of the night. In the drawer under the toaster, you could find every possible variation of aluminum foil, Saran wrap, and sandwich bags. Bacon grease was collected in a Crisco tin by the sink. The view out every kitchen window was all leaves and branches. The curtains were tacky, but she loved how the hot air blew through the mesh screens and the green of the trees pulsed.

Most of the time she could barely remember the girl who had lived in this house, but there were moments—lace fluttering, wind smelling of honeysuckle and bacon and Barbecue Lay's—there were moments where she was right under Lucia's skin.

"I saw the piece in the paper," her mother said. "I saved a copy."

"About the counseling center?"

"The women who called had trouble with their husbands, I suppose? And you'd tell them if they should get a divorce?"

"I'd tell them what options they had," Lucia said. "If they wanted to leave, I'd tell them how to do it smartly. Like to take the children with them because judges don't like it when the mother leaves the children behind. That kind of thing."

"Such a fuss," her mother said.

Lucia finished peeling the tomato, focused on the narrow margin between peel and flesh. Her mother had, more than once, bought a dress she disliked because she didn't want to hurt the saleswoman's feelings. Her mother, asked by a teenage Lucia if it bothered her that women weren't allowed to speak in their church, had said *I don't really care for public speaking.* When that church had splintered a few years ago over the question of whether to let black people join, her father—despite his taste in jokes—came down on the right side of the issue and her mother would barely speak to him for weeks. *It's not worth all the hurt feelings,* she'd said. *Everyone mad at each other. Such a fuss.*

"I spoke to one woman whose husband had broken her thumb," Lucia said. "He bent it back until it snapped."

"Gracious," Caroline said, but Lucia got the feeling that she did not entirely believe it had happened. In her world, breaking a woman's bones was not a thing a man did, and if a man did do it, it reflected poorly on the woman for being with him in the first place. Really it was best not to think about it.

Lucia slid the tomato neatly into the glass dish already two-thirds full of cucumber slices and chunks of Vidalia onion. She had seen this particular dish filled with these particular foods her entire life.

"Moxie's gone," she said.

"What?"

It was a relief to allow the thoughts in her head to match the words coming from her mouth. "Evan came home two days ago and she was gone," she said. "We've driven around the neighborhood for hours."

"She'll turn up," Caroline said cheerfully.

Unless she was dead in the road somewhere, Lucia thought. Unless she was hurt and bleeding. The dog did not have good odds when it came to the survival of the fittest. As the days passed, Lucia was finding it harder to push back these sorts of thoughts.

"Go on and tell the boys to come help their plates," her mother said.

Lucia retrieved the men. They led the way as they all sidestepped along the counter, plates in hand, dipping into Pyrex and Corningware. Eventually they settled into their usual places with Oliver and Evan at the head and foot of the kitchen table. Their chairs squeaked against the linoleum as they pulled them out.

"I asked her about room service," Caroline said, still standing. She reached for the tea pitcher and topped off her husband's glass. Lucia had never seen her father pour her mother a glass of anything.

"She's ordered it, hasn't she?" said her father.

"I made him a bet, Lucia," Caroline said.

Evan unfolded his paper napkin. "You people know how to have fun."

"What's the big deal about room service?" asked Lucia. "It's a business expense."

Her parents laughed.

"A business expense," mimicked her father, not unkindly. Proudly even, as if she had suddenly spoken a sentence in French.

Caroline sat, finally. She folded her hands.

"Shall we pray, everyone?" Oliver said. "Dear Heavenly Father, thank you for this food, this day, and all your many blessings—"

You did it yourself, Lucia thought, behind her closed eyes.

She knew that beneath their sunny affection, her parents felt that she had gone off to college and come back a stranger. It wasn't true. In first grade, the teachers had laid out a box of multicolored reading sheets. You started at pink and worked your way to black. She got to black before anyone else was even past purple. Her parents had expected straight As, and she'd delivered. They told her she could do anything. She won trophies and ribbons and plaques.

Did they expect that her wiring would short-circuit when she got her high school diploma, all the momentum leeched out of her? That she would step into the real world and want nothing more than to find a man and have children and scour the mall for pretty dresses and hand towels?

They taught her to think and they taught her to want. She was exactly who they had made her to be.

"Everything looks delicious, Mother," she said, as she opened her eyes.

II.

Lucia peeled off the paper that was taped to her door, noticing that it was actually a receipt from Spencer's Gifts. *Call me at Molly's,* the note said, followed by Rachel's signature and a phone number.

The phone call did not take long. Lucia shouted down the hallway to Evan that Rachel had spotted Moxie and that she would be back in a minute with the dog. Then she was stepping out the not-quite-closed door, still in her striped dress and wedge sandals. Moxie. Filthy snout and big wet tongue and wiggling, crushing weight on your lap, and she had missed the dumb dog so much. She was pacing up and down the driveway when Rachel pulled up to the curb. She shifted into park a little too quickly, her feet hitting the pavement while the car was still rocking. She slammed the door, then yanked at the handle a couple of times before heading toward Lucia at a trot, pastel-flowered dress flapping.

Lucia hugged her. "I've been so worried. Did she look all right? Did you talk to the people who have her?"

They were already moving, turning onto the sidewalk.

"She looked fine," said Rachel. "Her normal self. But the guy was calling her Chewie. Isn't that strange? She still has her red collar and tag around her neck, so why hasn't he called you?"

Lucia stopped. With a little prompting, she got a more thorough account of what Rachel had seen and heard, and her relief shifted into something darker. Had the man stolen Moxie right out of the yard?

"I don't think you should come with me," she said.

"I have to show you the house." Rachel headed off at full speed, as if she could outrun an argument.

Maybe she could, because Lucia fell into step. Her anger was overpowering anything else. He had stolen her dog. A dog as trusting as any animal could be, not an iota of self-preservation in her. If this fool of a man thought that she wouldn't rip him apart to get Moxie back, he was mistaken.

She crushed a pinecone underfoot.

"We take a right up here," Rachel said. "It's on that street."

"Thomas Street."

"I guess," said Rachel. "Hey, I saw that story about you in the paper."

Lucia looked over. The girl was a fast walker, thank goodness, not a stroller. And did everyone in the entire city read the *Alabama Journal*?

"They think you're a 'pretty little blonde,'" Rachel added. She seemed to believe the phrasing was flattering.

"That is what they wrote," Lucia said.

"And you're a feminist."

"I am."

"Why," said Rachel, "would you kidnap a dog that lives a couple of blocks away?"

Lucia abandoned thoughts of discussing women's equality.

"Because you're not that bright," she said, but that was likely not the whole of it. She thought back to her vandalized car years ago, and she thought of the occasional nastiness she got in the mail. It was possible that she had represented this man's wife or ex-wife, or maybe she had refused to represent him. It was possible that he was a nutcase who believed women should be obedient and homebound. It was possible that this was some elaborate attempt to meet her. *Pretty little blonde.* This option would not have occurred to her before Judge Musgrove told her—in open court a few years back—that he would have dismissed any case just for the opportunity to sit and watch her sweet ass walk out the door. Before Garrison Langley had admitted that he'd offered her that short-lived partnership because he'd hoped that she'd sleep with him. *Amenable,* he'd said. *I hoped you'd be amenable.* He'd had a couple of martinis, but no question he was telling the truth.

Sometimes she wondered at her sex appeal. Maybe it was the strangeness of her—a woman lawyer—that drew them in. Like a woman with three breasts. Bizarre but intriguing.

If this man had stolen her dog hoping to sleep with her, it was a stupider plan than offering her a partnership.

When they pulled even with the chain-link fence, Rachel pointed to where she'd seen Moxie, but there was no sign of the dog. They turned the corner to the front of the house, and the yard was all shadows and dirt. The roots of a huge pecan tree spread out in winding spokes, and thick branches rubbed against the roof, creaking against the rain gutters.

As they walked up the front steps, Lucia again had a pang of uncertainty about bringing the girl with her. She knocked three times, angling herself more squarely in front of Rachel.

The man who answered was about her height, maybe in his fifties, with silver hair and an untrimmed beard. He wore a T-shirt airbrushed with a sunset. She recognized him: she'd seen him walking his beagles past her house.

"Hey there," he said, smiling.

She did not smile back.

"I'm Lucia Gilbert," she said. "I live on Avalon, and I believe you have my dog."

The man rubbed a hand across his beard. "Do I?"

"I think you do," she said. "My friend saw her in your backyard. An Airedale. With a name tag that says Moxie."

She kept her eyes on him, ready for him to push back at her.

"All right," he said, even keeled. As if she'd asked for a drink from the garden hose. "You want to go see her? She's in the back room."

In a few steps, the three of them were standing in a laundry room, the smell of dryer sheets filling the air, Moxie bouncing in her four-footed fashion, beagles running in circles around her, yipping. She reared up, paws landing on Lucia's shoulders, which was always forbidden, but now Lucia let the sharp claws sink into her collarbones.

"Moxie," she said. "Sweet girl. Such a sweet girl. Did you miss me? Oh, don't lick up my nostril."

"All right," said the man, standing behind her. "I'm Marlon Reynolds. Did I say that already? That's a good dog you've got there."

Lucia elbowed Moxie gently until she thudded back to the tile floor.

"Didn't you recognize her?" she asked. "Surely you'd seen her in my yard."

The man shrugged. He looked, she thought, like one of the Oak Ridge Boys. "I saw a dog walking down the street. I didn't want her to get hit by a car. I took her in and fed her and made sure she was safe."

"My phone number is right there on her tag."

"Is it?"

Lucia couldn't read his tone, which was no tone at all. She slid her fingers around Rachel's wrist, pulling her from the laundry room. Moxie followed, pressing close and drooling. When they were out of the small room with an open path to the front door, Lucia turned back to Marlon Reynolds.

"I thank you for taking care of her," she said. "But you didn't call me. You didn't make any attempt to contact me. It looks more like theft than a rescue."

"You think I stole her?" he asked in that same calm way.

"Yes," she said, taking a step closer. He took a step back. "You took a dog that did not belong to you. That's the definition of stealing. You—"

"I found her," he repeated. "Her mouth was all mud. You might check your backyard. My guess is she dug under the fence."

"The mud doesn't mean she dug a hole," she snapped. "She just likes the taste of dirt. And why didn't you contact me once you found her? If she goes missing again, I'll let the police know about this. I want you to stay away from my dog. Do you understand?"

He took another step backward.

"I do," he said, giving a two-fingered salute. "As subtle as you're being, I think I got the message."

"All right then," she said.

She turned and walked toward the front door without looking back, steering Rachel in front of her. For once, Moxie actually heeled. With one yank of the doorknob, they were all spilling back into the shaded yard. Overhead, the branches still clawed at the eaves of the house. The whole visit hadn't taken more than five minutes.

"Come on," said Lucia. "Let's get a little distance from Marlon, why don't we? Come, Moxie. Come, Moxie. Come."

The heeling had been short-lived. She tugged at the dog's collar, wishing she'd thought to bring a leash. Usually if you could start her momentum, she would follow.

"You don't mind it, do you?" Rachel asked.

"What?"

"Fighting. Having someone angry at you. It makes me sick to my stomach when someone is mad at me."

The girl looked more exhilarated than anxious. She ran a hand over Moxie's back, then veered onto a shaded lawn, taking a short leap into a half-raked pile of leaves. She landed with both feet, bits of leaves flying around her, swirling.

Adrenaline—Lucia felt it, too.

The wind was already full of things. White camellia petals blew around their ankles, skimming along the sidewalk then out into the street. Petals and leaves, a piece of plastic bag, an insect wing. A ladybug landed on Lucia's throat and then ricocheted away.

"A therapist once told me that I use the conflict in my work to fill my need for conflict," Lucia said.

Rachel roped her tangled hair over her shoulder. Her dress was flecked with pieces of leaf. And some sort of red stain. "You have a therapist?"

"I tried it once."

Rachel brushed at the leaves. "You have a need for conflict?"

"I think her point was that we all have a need for conflict."

"I don't," Rachel said.

Lucia rolled her shoulders, which were starting to ache from her hunch-backed position. Her fingers were deep in fur.

"It was like a Jedi mind trick," Rachel said, her words speeding up. "Like he was powerless to resist you. You know, back when I first met you, Mom said you were the first lawyer she called because people are scared of you."

"People say that. Among other things."

"Doesn't it hurt your feelings?"

"Yes," said Lucia.

Two squirrels ran across the street, twisting up a pine tree, chattering and ecstatic. Lucia barely held on to Moxie as she lunged.

"I suppose it doesn't hurt my feelings that much," she admitted. "I've known lawyers who hated a fight, and the stress melted them down eventually. I accept the need for conflict. You have to decide what you'll let in, and you keep the rest out. Sometimes, you know, kindness isn't effective. And when that happens, I can play whatever role is needed."

III.

A few weeks after she'd retrieved Moxie, Lucia was checking the mail when she saw Marlon walking up her driveway. The beagles were at his feet, silent and perfectly in sync. She wondered how he managed it.

"Hey there," he said.

He wore denim shorts and a faded T-shirt with enough holes that she thought moths might have been involved. He held a banana, half eaten, in the hand that wasn't filled with dog leashes.

"I'd wanted to say something to you," he said. "First of all, I'm sorry."

"For taking my dog?"

"Well, now, I didn't take her. She was out already, and I let her in. But I did keep her. I admit that. You're not around much, you know? She barks. She barks all day long, and I can hear her from the sidewalk."

"I didn't know that," said Lucia.

He took a bite of the banana. The beagles stood there.

"I thought I'd take her in," he said. "I thought maybe it would give you an easy out. Some people don't really want their dog. I didn't know if you'd come looking. I only wanted to make sure you were good to her."

Lucia nodded, wondering. Was she good to Moxie? Was it wrong to leave a dog at home for nine or ten hours by herself? She felt a rush of guilt, but she'd learned that guilt came too quickly: it needed parsing. Why should only her long hours matter? Evan was gone, too. And wasn't solitude the lot of most dogs? When she was growing up, hadn't she left Barnie—round black face, moplike body—for the entire school day? Her mother had been there in the house, but her mother hardly spoke to Barnie. Did it count so much just to have a human moving through the rooms, banging pots and pans occasionally?

"Anyway, I apologize," Marlon said. "I know you love your dog."

Lucia wished that she did not feel a rush of pleasure at that. She wished she didn't care what anyone thought of her or her dog. She watched as Marlon folded up his banana peel, one handed, and tucked it into his pocket.

"So you're a lawyer, I hear?"

"I am," she said.

He rolled a small black shape—some part of the banana stem?—between his fingertips.

"How come?" he asked.

"I had a roommate who was going to medical school," she said, wondering how long the beagles could stay frozen. "We were competitive."

It was the truest answer she had. It did not make for a satisfying narrative arc, but it was accurate. She'd coordinated her law school interview with her roommate's visit to Vanderbilt, and then she'd sat across from the dean of the law school and he thanked her for coming and asked her why she was worth taking a slot away from a man. Her fingers had gone slightly numb as she yammered out an answer, unsure how to justify herself. It was the first time she understood that her gender needed to be offset. Neutralized. Later she wondered if the question was supposed to test her ability to argue persuasively while stunned and hurt, but if so, surely she would have heard of men being asked some similarly insulting question. Although what could they be asked that would compare? At any rate, when she visited Cumberland Law School, the dean didn't ask her that. He looked at her LSAT scores, and he told her if she'd come there, she'd be the queen of the law school. She made her decision before she even climbed back into her dinged-up Cutlass.

When she started classes, she had to look up the definition of "plaintiff" and "defendant."

Marlon kept rubbing the banana remnant between his fingers. "You like divorce cases, I guess?"

"I seem to be good at them," she said.

She did not especially like divorce cases. Back in those first years, if someone handed you a case, you didn't ask what kind it was. Torts, contracts, civil liberties, a little bit of criminal—she had done them all, and this was where she had ended up. She had taken a series of steps, each one logical, and they had taken her to family law, without her ever aiming for it. The truth was that when she thought of what she loved about law, she thought of sitting in the White Tortoise, that old head shop downtown, the walls full of bongs. She'd been on retainer with the ACLU, and they wanted to challenge the state's new paraphernalia law.

She'd reached out to a dozen law enforcement agents, telling them that they were invited to their first-ever deposition in a head shop. Once they got there, she sat them down at one long table, where she'd spread her props: a bong, a glass pipe, a Coke can, an empty toilet paper roll, a razor blade, a mirror, that plastic spoon from McDonald's that was good for cocaine snorting. A few other bits and pieces.

She'd neatly labeled each item, and then she'd gone through the list with each deputy, one by one. *Is this paraphernalia? And this?* Out of those ten deputies, not two of them had the same answers. She knew before she left the shop that the law would be overturned. She could almost hear a clicking, like the turning of a Rubik's Cube, bright squares sliding into place. That was what it felt like when you found the answer—where there'd been a jumble of colors, you started to see a pattern. You began shifting the pieces into place. That was what she loved: the moment three or four moves before the case was won—the moment when she saw it coming.

"Do you hire detectives?" Marlon asked.

"No," she said. "I do not."

"Because this is the second thing I wanted to say. There's a car that comes by your house."

That struck Lucia as funny. "Why are you casing my house, Marlon?"

"I'm dead serious," he said. "When I'm out with the dogs, I see a Black Buick pull up and sit there. I've seen it three or four times over the last week."

Lucia stepped sideways, poking at the hostas planted under the front window. The leaves were flattened, and she wondered if Evan had accidentally stood on them when he mowed the yard.

"Rachel drives an old Buick," she said.

"It's not the girl," he said.

Lucia wondered how many times a day Marlon walked his dogs, and she wondered how many of those times took him past her house.

"Who else would it be?" she asked.

"That's my point."

She was not positive that this man was completely sane, but she was starting to like him. Her mother might do the same thing: construct private eyes or hit men out of lost deliverymen.

"Well, Marlon," she said, "if they want me, I imagine they'll come to the door."

IV.

Saturday afternoon, her hand on the hard line of his jaw, bone and skin and bristle. His knees clamping her hip bones as she leaned forward, her hair falling around his face. Juicy Fruit on his breath. His hands on her waist, fingertips biting, as he flipped her to her back.

The flat of his tongue on her collarbone. His sweat dripping onto her throat.

Moxie, barking from the hallway, furious, as if mujahideen were storming the house, gory death imminent.

"She's been hallucinating strangers at the front door," Evan said, pausing above her. "She's determined someone is out there."

Her hands sliding over his shoulder blades. "More," she said.

He moved against her. His teeth clamped onto her upper arm, fastening only for a moment.

Her hands in his damp hair.

"Anytime," he said.

V.

As she did every morning when she got to the office, Lucia picked up the mail from the basket where Marissa weeded and sorted it. Her various reflections went through the same motions along the lobby walls. She carried the stack down the hallway, bumping her office door open with her hip.

At her desk, she ran a finger under the flap of the envelope with the Jackson & Price return address, fairly sure it was Paul Price trying to set up a meeting about the Woodruffs. She scanned it—*As you likely know, my client and yours recently discussed the details of their divorce. If you'd like to meet . . .*

The next letter was a request to cohost a fund-raiser for George McMillan, which she would obviously do because she liked the man and also, Lord, if George Wallace won the governor's nomination—it didn't bear considering. She opened the third envelope. The lack of a return address should have made her cautious, but it had been months since she'd had one of these. *Dear Lucia Gilbert*, it started quite professionally. *I hope one day you understand the damage you've done, how you ruin things and people. You reap what you sow, that's the truth. I look forward to you rotting in hell sooner not later. Even if you get on your knees and pray and I bet that's not what you do on your knees, you will burn and scream and you'll deserve it.*

It was typed and unsigned. She ripped it in half and tossed it in the trash can. Once upon a time she wondered who would go to the trouble of typing and mailing such a letter, but now she didn't wonder about any part of it.

Her thoughts drifted instead to Bequeatha Long, a girl from her family court days who had been taken from her addict mother and placed with an aunt. Out of view of the courts, the aunt kicked Bequeatha out of the house when she was thirteen. There were only so many ways for a girl to earn money, and by the time the courts rediscovered the child, she was fifteen years old with one prostitution charge and a thirty-eight-year-old boyfriend. That boyfriend shot the assistant manager at an Exxon station and stuffed the body in the trunk of his car. Bequeatha—such a doll-like face—had been waiting in the car during the robbery; at her own arraignment, her eye had been swollen shut. The boyfriend had punched her not long before the robbery, and she'd driven the car like he told her. What was she supposed to do—let him kill her, too? She was poor and she was black, and they tried her as an adult and sent her to prison for twenty years.

You reap what you sow, the judge had said to her, his gold tooth flashing, and Lucia had imagined ripping it out with needle-nose pliers.

Let that be a lesson to anyone who said men and women weren't treated equally. People might scoff at the idea of a woman astronaut or Supreme Court justice, but when it came to punishing that girl just as harshly as a grown man—well, justice had been completely blind.

No one ever mentioned that sometimes you reaped what other people sowed.

"Here you go," said Marissa, inches away, holding out a cup of coffee.

"Thanks," Lucia said.

"Gladys Plexico just called again about her late parents' house—"

"I meant to get back to her yesterday," Lucia said. "Call and tell her she's free to put the house on the market. The court eliminated that restriction on married women four years ago—she doesn't need her husband's signature anymore to sell her own property. No need to wait until the divorce is final."

Marissa gave the trash can a light kick. "So what did the letter say?"

Lucia remembered her first firm, where the secretary had plopped herself on the edge of her desk and announced, "Just so you know, I don't work for women." And yet she'd managed to find Marissa, who knew her well enough by now to interpret her paper ripping.

"Rot in hell," Lucia said. "In summary."

"No signature?"

"Why do you still ask that?"

Marissa pushed her dark curls out of her face. "You should *have* to sign a letter like that. You should have to put your name and phone number at the end, in case someone would like to continue the discussion."

"I don't want to continue the discussion," Lucia said.

"You're telling me that if that lowlife was standing in front of you, you wouldn't have a response?" Marissa was already through the doorway, headed back to her own desk with its stash of Tic Tacs and thermos full of Coke. "You've got a potential at eleven. The outline is on your desk. Then you've got the luncheon at twelve thirty, as you know."

Lucia eyed the rest of the mail, then pulled her Dictaphone from the drawer. Marissa was wrong. A response required thought and she refused to waste any. She settled the Dictaphone into her palm, running a thumb over the buttons that felt as if they'd been worn into the shape of her fingers. She propped an elbow on her desk and began her response. "Marissa, this is to Paul Price at Jackson and Price. Dear Paul, I'd be happy to meet about the Woodruff case."

VI.

Beverly Leles was a woman who would radiate old money and fine china even if she were in overalls, not that she would ever own a pair. Collarbones sharp and hand trembling slightly as she pulled at her pearls, she had the look of a Gothic heroine.

Hopefully a heroine, thought Lucia, and not a madwoman in the attic. *If you feel the need to cry,* she had told Beverly, *don't hold back. It's not bad for the judge to see your emotions.* But sometimes a woman misunderstood that concept and cried the whole damn time, and there was such a thing as overkill.

"Didn't you hope to be an architect yourself?" said Arnold Dobson, standing too close, his belly brushing against the stand.

Beverly's hand dropped into her lap.

"No," she said, leaning into the microphone. "Well, yes."

"When was that?"

"When I was an undergraduate. I was never serious about it."

Arnold cocked his large square head. His white hair scraped his collar. "You hoped to design office buildings," he said. "You hoped to leave a mark on the world."

Lucia caught Beverly's eye. That exact line had come up in the deposition, and while Lucia considered objecting—could Arnold never remember to ask an actual question instead of preaching at them all?—she let Beverly handle it.

"At some point I did," Beverly said, smiling slightly, exactly as they had practiced. "I liked the idea of building something that would last."

"And you stopped wanting to leave your mark?" Arnold asked, too incredulous.

"No. But I realized there were other options that appealed to me more. I think I am leaving a mark."

"Of course. You dig up marigolds and your husband has designed six different buildings from Atlanta to Mobile. Did—"

Lucia half stood. "Object. Your Honor, counsel is testifying. That's not a question."

"Sustained," said Judge Harrison, eyelids at half-mast. His sleepy look was deceptive.

"Did your resent your husband's success?" Arnold asked.

"No," said Beverly. Not a hint of tears.

Arnold shook his head in what he surely imagined was a fatherly way. The man was a complete dick. Once Lucia had gone to his offices for a meeting, and she'd overheard him telling his secretary to hide the Tab because she would want one. As if having to drink a Coke would crush her soul.

"How many clients have you had so far this year?" Arnold asked.

"Two, but both are extensive projects. I'm currently redesigning the gardens at the F. Scott and Zelda Fitzgerald House."

"Well," said Arnold. "Isn't that impressive."

Lucia stood. "Your Honor, Mr. Arnold is not asking a question."

"Sustained," said Judge Harrison.

"Move to strike," said Lucia.

Arnold barely paused. "The truth," he said, "is that you stayed home with the children, and your husband continued to grow more famous."

"Your Honor, there he goes again," said Lucia. "We're not in court to hear Mr. Dobson's lecture."

A slight raising of Judge Harrison's eyelids. "That's correct, Ms. Gilbert. But that's not a proper objection."

"I'm sorry, Your Honor," said Lucia. "I object on the grounds that counsel made a statement rather than asking a question."

"Sustained."

"Has your husband grown to be an architect of some renown since you've been married?" snapped Arnold, his temper showing.

Go on, thought Lucia. *Turn up the heat. See who burns.*

"Yes," said Beverly. "In the South, I'd say."

"You hate him for it, don't you?"

"No," she said.

"In fact, you want to punish him by taking his children away from him?"

"That's not true," Beverly said, voice steady. "That's not true at all."

Lucia wished for a Kodak: she'd love to offer up this moment the next time someone asked why she left Legal Aid or the D.A.'s office and switched to private practice. The question always held a certain condescension.

I'm sorry. Those were the first words Beverly Leles had spoken to Lucia. Marissa had waved her into Lucia's office, and Beverly had apologized for walking into the room. The husband had stripped her of every bit of value, like a thief coming back to the same empty house night after night, ripping out the copper and marble and hardware, bit by bit, until the place was gutted. The husband—he was sitting there now, big eared and bony—had told her that she was too heavy and that her laugh was too loud and her vegetables were too soggy. Bit by bit. Eventually her daughter and son started telling her the same thing.

At times Lucia grew furious with clients who seemed eager for court, but the truth was that some landed here through no fault of their own: they happened to be married to a narcissist or sadist or what have you. She'd watch amazed as a client sat there listening to a litany of their worst sins—real or invented. Nothing could be worse than looking across these scratched parquet floors at someone you had loved, someone who had stripped you naked and soaked up your secrets, and who had then brought you here to be stripped naked again.

Such a weapon, intimacy.

Arnold crossed his hands over his belly, making Lucia think of Rooster Cogburn. "You've been in therapy for quite some time, haven't you?" he asked.

Enough, thought Lucia.

"Objection, Your Honor," she said. "Privileged. Move to strike."

She was sustained, of course.

"You're depressed, aren't you, Mrs. Leles?" Arnold tried again.

Dick.

"Your Honor," Lucia said, "you just ruled on this issue."

"Sustained."

"I move to strike," Lucia said.

Arnold shot her a look, and she held back a smile. It was amazing how a few interruptions could rattle someone.

Arnold rubbed a hand over his slicked-back hair. "Don't you want this divorce—despite your husband's desire to remain married—because you—"

"Objection," said Lucia. "Your Honor, we have not heard Mr. Leles's wishes. That question presumes a matter not in evidence."

The husband stared openly at her now. The sad look he had kept pasted on his face slipped long enough to let the rage show. *It stings, doesn't it,* she thought at him, *to be shut up over and over again.*

He fixed his face. But she could see under the table where his hands were in fists, pressing his thighs so hard that his pants were a mass of creases.

Lucia smoothed her skirt and enjoyed her view of his knuckles. She had not been honest with Rachel—she did not merely accept the need for conflict. She did not play some halfhearted role. When she saw a fight coming, she ran at it, landing with both feet, waiting to see how the pieces flew up around her and what shape they might take.

VII.

The days and the meetings and the faces did not exactly blur, but the edges overlapped. The shaking of hands. The settling into the chairs. The questions and answers and regret and resentment. The man now in front of Lucia had fired his lawyer and asked to meet with her directly, which was unusual, but he was a high school principal, soft-spoken, and she'd seen his paycheck stubs. They had left her sympathetic.

He was a tall man, knees touching the front of her desk and elbows overhanging the chair.

"I know my wife," he said. "I know what she wants, and I know what I'm willing to do. So, as I said, I think I can save us all some time."

"All right," Lucia said. "Why don't you tell me what you think she wants?"

"She wants me crucified," he said. "She wants me to suffer, and there is no amount of money that will satisfy her."

Lucia straightened a pen on her desk. He was not wrong. His wife would rather have his bloody pelt than alimony.

"Affairs do make people angry," she said.

"I know," he said, running a hand over his thin hair. "I was angry when she had her affair, too. But she's not mad about my cheating. She's mad because I left, which is the strange part. I don't know how she can possibly want our marriage to continue."

Again, Lucia couldn't find a flaw in his thinking. "So far," she said, "you don't seem to feel very accommodating."

"Kelly is not my favorite person in the world," he said. "But I'd like to think I can be fair. I've drawn up a budget showing what I need to live. I'll give her the house. I've listed a child support figure that I think is generous. I can't magic up money where there is none. If she insists on going to court, that will eat up money, and she'll get less. She needs to decide whether punishing me is really worth the financial loss."

Lucia took the folder he passed to her. She hated to admit it, but he was more reasonable than his wife. More fair-minded. You didn't like to think that sort of thing—you needed to stay firmly on your client's side— and maybe that was why these meetings were meant to be between lawyers. You wanted to keep your focus narrow. Too much perspective could paralyze you.

A DIFFERENT DAY.

Donna Lambert's main liability was her face, which brought to mind Bo Derek, all gorgeous cheekbones and eyes. Her hair was a problem, too, dark waves of it past her waist, although she could pin it up for court. Still, no judge would look at her and see a victimized woman. A judge would see a woman who was used to hearing "yes" more than "no," and the judge would be right.

"I wanted to ask you about Jerry," Donna said, hair falling over her shoulder.

Lucia had wondered why she wanted an appointment now when her court date was three months away. "The man you met at the barbecue? The one from Atlanta?"

"Yes. I wondered—"

"You can't see him," Lucia said. "Not if you want this to come out in your favor. The last thing you should do is start another relationship in the middle of a divorce."

"I visited him last weekend," Donna said. She smiled, and it was well practiced. "We'd been talking on the phone every night. It's not—it's not casual."

Lucia lay her pen down. She let the silence expand.

"I told you not to see him," she said at last. "I told you that you could talk by phone occasionally. You told me you wouldn't see him. You lied. I told you that if you lie to me, we're done."

"I only—"

This is what it's like to hear "no," Lucia thought.

"We're done," she said.

A DIFFERENT WEEK.

"I want them," the man said. "Is there any way—any way at all—that I could get custody? I take them to school most days, and I help them with their homework. More than she does. I'm a good father."

Lucia sighed. The same answer, always, no matter what man sat in the chair.

"I'm sure you are," she said. "But unless your wife has some very problematic behavior that leaves her unfit, she will get custody. The courts believe that children are better off with their mother."

He ran a hand over his forehead, pulling his eyebrows high, skin stretched tight.

"You believe that, too?" he asked.

"I don't," she said. "Not universally. I don't think your legal rights should be based on your sex. If a woman makes more money than a man, she should be the one asked for child support. If a father is the more involved parent, he should be considered for custody. But that's not the way the courts work right now."

He'd dropped his hands to his thighs. His fingers tapped against his khaki pants so lightly that it seemed more like trembling.

"I'd hoped," he said, "that with a woman lawyer, it might help—"

"I'm sorry," she said. "I'll do what I can, but the courts are very set in their ways, unfortunately."

"You ever read *Hop on Pop?*" he said.

"Pardon?"

"We read it every night. Maybe a hundred nights in a row at this stage. I've been begging them to let me try something new, not to make me read about Mr. Brown and Mr. Black one more dang time, and I'm getting my wish, aren't I?"

He dropped his head so that she couldn't see his face, and she was glad.

Rachel

1.

I had ten minutes before the homeroom bell would ring, and I was passing my old middle school. I was going forty-five, maybe fifty, and it took me a few seconds to realize that the police car was following me. When I pulled over, the policeman called me young lady and lectured me about school zones. He said I could run over some little girl and it would haunt me forever. I wanted to say, hey, I spent three years at that school, and trust me, most of those girls would not be a huge loss.

I wound up avoiding a ticket and getting sixteen hours of community service at Oak Park. Two Saturdays. Eight hours each.

I wasn't concerned when Mom dropped me off that first day. (We'd driven over the day before, making sure that she was comfortable with the route.) The park was green and leafy and familiar. As a kid, I'd fed stale bread to the ducks here, and I still remembered the big slide, and how if you didn't put your hands down to brake yourself, you'd land on your butt.

I stopped by the information booth, and soon enough a soft-bellied, gray-haired man with matching navy shirt and pants came walking across the grass toward me. When he got close enough, I could see his badge. A security guard. I smiled, but he didn't smile back. He only asked for my name, and then he led me down a dirt path, thick with trees on both sides, until we hit a sidewalk. He didn't say a word. We wound up at a picnic pavilion with a concrete floor and benches attached to the tables. Another man, balding and tanned, was inside the pavilion, wiping down tables with a gray rag.

The security guard stopped.

"Now then, Rachel," he said, looking at me, finally. "This is—what's your name again?"

The man with the rag looked up, still wiping. "Luther."

"So Luther will be doing the men's bathrooms. You'll do the women's. There are three sets of bathrooms at the park, and Luther can show you where they are. You'll empty out the trash cans every two hours, plus wipe down the toilets and the sinks with the cleaner—you tell her about that." He jerked his head at Luther, and I was pretty sure he'd forgotten his name again. "You'll mop the floors once in the morning and once in the afternoon. Wipe off the tables in the pavilions. There's eight pavilions, and don't miss any. Pick up any litter. Don't just stand around. Look like you're working."

"Yes, sir," I said. I wondered if he'd told me his name and I'd missed it.

Luther nodded.

"I'll be in the guard shack," the man said, pointing vaguely behind him. "You come get me if any issues come up."

He walked off, and I was left with Luther, who was about my height and probably about my weight. I was sure his waist was smaller than mine, and I thought of how girls at my school liked to say, *If he can fit in my pants, he can't get in my pants,* although I could see several reasons why this man would never get in my pants. He'd kept his head turned while the security guard was standing there, but now he faced me, smiling, and he was missing a tooth. His skin was all leather.

We said hello, and he pointed me toward a broom propped against one of the wooden pavilion posts. The bristles of it curled to each side like an old-fashioned mustache, and it didn't seem to make any difference to the pollen and dust on the concrete, but I felt better with something in my hands. I swept my way across the floor as Luther wiped the benches, dirty water trickling on the concrete from his wet rag.

"How much time you got here?" he asked me.

"Sixteen hours," I said. It occurred to me for the first time that maybe he wasn't an employee.

"What did you do?" he asked.

I told him about my speeding.

"I got three-hundred and twenty hours," he said.

That made me lose my rhythm. "What did you do?"

"Littered," he said, and he made a clicking sound like he was encouraging a horse.

I kept sweeping, he kept wiping, and nothing seemed any cleaner when we finished. Eventually we carried the bucket and broom to the closest set of bathrooms, where Luther unlocked a closet full of mops and spray bottles and toilet paper. He stepped inside and pushed himself against the wooden shelves so I could fit in, too, and my arm brushed against his arm. It was all shadows in the closet, with only the sunlight coming through the trees for light. It smelled like the old lawn mower shed at Molly's. Luther held up the glass cleaner for the mirrors and the multipurpose disinfectant for the toilets, and his fingers brushed against my thigh as he reached down for the toilet paper.

He didn't seem to notice.

He talked me through the list of chores, and then I was inside the women's bathroom, starting with the mirrors. The sinks were rusted around the drains, one of them clogged with wet paper. None of that was too bad. The toilets, though. You don't normally look too close at a toilet—not at the creases where the metal bolts fasten to the concrete, not at the curve of the bowl, inside and out. No matter how I tried to keep my eyes unfocused, I couldn't help but see the spattered stains. Dark blotches. Hairs, swirled and dried. A bloody tampon tossed on the cement. My hand was only a wad of paper towels away from all of it. My hair, even in a ponytail, kept falling forward. I had a sense that this was not me. I wasn't someone who cleaned public toilets. I wasn't someone who needed to wash my hands three times to make sure I wasn't contaminated with a stranger's diarrhea.

I stepped back outside the bathroom, nose full of chemicals, and Luther was waiting there, wiping his hands on his jeans like he hadn't bothered with a paper towel. I was almost glad to see him. He could give me instructions, and I could follow them, and that didn't require any thinking, and we'd go along like that and then the day would be over.

"How old do you think I am?" he asked.

I did not want to be offensive.

"Go on," he said. "You won't hurt my feelings."

"Forty-five," I said, thinking surely he was nearly sixty.

"Shit," he said. "Excuse me. I'm thirty-six."

"Sorry," I said.

"Ain't your fault," he said. "I know how I am. You see this?"

He yanked up his T-shirt sleeve and pointed to a white jagged line of a scar on his bicep. I nodded.

"Bullet," he said. He held out his hand, and I handed him my cleaning bottles. His sleeve stayed hitched up, showing the bottom inch of his scar. He set the bottles, one at a time, back into the open closet, and then he closed and locked the door.

"I've been through it," he said, turning back to me. "I've been shot, stabbed, cut with a bottle, run over, and pushed off a building."

Even though I wished he would keep his distance so that his elbow wouldn't keep touching mine, I couldn't help being curious as we walked back into the open air, trees spreading over us. The day was warming up, and I felt the first sheen of sweat on my face.

"Nearly died from a car wreck, too," he said.

"The one where you got run over?"

"No, that was being run over. The wreck was when I ran my car into a telephone pole. That was before they took my license. And then they give you community service eight or nine miles from your place, and they know you have to walk, so what does that tell you?"

"You walked here?"

"No choice."

We cut through a wide field, bordered by oaks, as much dirt as grass. Old acorns covered the ground, and they disintegrated with every step. Eventually we reached another pavilion, this one in view of the playground. A few kids were swinging, and a mom was sitting on a bench, reading a *People* magazine. The sight of them settled me. As we scrubbed the tables, Luther kept up a steady patter, telling me about dogs he'd owned and how he liked his hamburgers cooked and how good the fishing was at Lake Martin. He asked me questions about where I went to school and if I had brothers and sisters and if I had a boyfriend. I kept my answers short.

"You like camping?" he asked.

"I guess," I said. "My dad took me once."

"He doesn't take you anymore?"

"He travels a lot," I said.

He nodded. "My dad didn't do much neither."

Even though I had my eyes on my broom, I could hear the sympathy or pity or whatever it was in Luther's voice. I didn't bother correcting him. I didn't see my dad often, but when I did, we talked books and movies, and he told me about his job and I told him about school and he listened. He always listened. It wasn't a bad thing that he had a life outside of Montgomery: it was a gift. Dad didn't require a single thing from me. I never had to worry about him. He enjoyed me, but he didn't need me, and that was what I loved most about him.

"I know this place up on Smith Lake," Luther was saying. "Perfect place. I could take you. Your dad, too. Nothing untoward. We'd have a nice time."

He'd stepped closer to me, and I stopped sweeping.

I could smell him. I could see a fleck of maybe pepper wedged in his gums as he smiled.

I thought of a conversation between Mom and Aunt Molly after Aunt Molly had let the yardman—a white yardman, granted—come in and use the restroom, and both of them were wondering whether that had been smart, whether it was all right to let that kind of man into your house, even when that same man had cut your grass for seven years, because you never knew, did you? I could picture Mom pressing her lips together at Luther, even though he had done nothing more than lose a tooth—and a driver's license—and try to make conversation.

"Thanks," I said.

"You'll tell him I asked?"

"Sure," I said.

Two more hours, steadily working. A little past noon we each got a pack of crackers from the vending machine and sat on a bench—a solid two feet between us—eating them. I drained a Fanta. The breeze turned the day from hot to pleasant.

"So what did you do to get all this community service?" I asked. "I know it wasn't littering."

He folded up his empty cracker wrapper, creasing it carefully. *Lance Toast Chee Peanut Butter,* it read, and I'd never noticed that the cracker people didn't use the word "cheese."

"It wasn't what I did," he said. "It was what they said I did."

"Okay," I said. "What did they say you did?"

"They said I raped my sixteen-year-old niece. Or sexually assaulted her or some bullcrap."

He kept folding that piece of plastic. *Chee Chee Chee.*

"But you didn't?" I said.

"Nah. She just told them she'd said no."

He stood, taking three slow steps to the trash can. He said more, but I faded in and out. He and his brother didn't get along, and his brother was always looking for an excuse to get back at him. And the girl, well, he wasn't nearly the first—

When he finally faced me, he held a hand over his eyes, blocking the sun.

"You scared of me now?" he asked.

"No," I said.

"'Cause you're easing away from me," he said. "I ain't gonna do nothing to you. I don't do that sort of thing. You hear me?"

"I know," I said. "I know you're not."

I made myself walk to the trash can and stand next to him as I threw my wrapper away. I watched it fall into a paper cup full of soft drink and rainwater and dead gnats.

I smiled at Luther, reassuring him. I wondered how to find the security guard's shack. I'd gotten turned around, not paying attention, and now, obviously, I needed to get out. I needed to tell the guard that I was squeezing into closets with a rapist, and someone needed to drive me home.

"Ready?" said Luther.

"Ready," I said, and we walked on to the next bathroom. When we got there, I pulled one paper towel after another from the dispenser, and they filled my fist until they looked like a dead flower, brown petals blooming.

It was another hour before we passed the security guard's office, a small wooden building with a single window. I needed to make up an excuse to talk to him privately, I thought. It wasn't that I was afraid that Luther would stop me—I could scream at any point, I'd told myself several times. He had not threatened me or propositioned me, and he had been very subdued since he told his story. Now that I had pushed through the first wave of panic, now that the words—*rape, rape, niece, niece*—had stopped playing through my head, I wondered if I might be overreacting.

But I wanted to explain everything to the security guard. I didn't trust myself. I didn't feel like I *was* myself.

I told Luther that I needed to fix my hair, and I made a big show of leaning over and rearranging my ponytail, and he said he'd meet me at the bathrooms. When he'd trudged out of sight, I knocked on the guard's door. The old man opened it quickly and—miracle of miracles—smiled at me.

"Hot day, huh?" he said.

"Yes, sir," I said.

"You can call me Maxwell," he said. "You want to come in and have a coke and cool off?"

It was as if he had just remembered that I was a teenager who drove a little too fast, not some hardened criminal. Or maybe he'd been trying to scare me in the beginning. Maybe that was the way it worked—try to scare the teenagers enough so they'd never speed again, and if you threw in a rapist, well, all the better.

I told him that I would like a drink. His office was air-conditioned, icy, and the sweat on my face evaporated as I stepped through the doorway. The room held a desk, two chairs, and a small refrigerator. The walls were empty except for a cheap plastic clock and a shellacked fish on a plaque. Maxwell opened the refrigerator, and it had drinks stuffed from top to bottom, including a few beers. I asked for a Dr Pepper, and when he handed it to me, I noticed that instead of a wedding ring, he wore a class ring, dark gold and ruby-stoned.

He waved me toward the chair that wasn't behind the desk. I'd taken my second sip when someone banged on the door.

"Hello," called Luther. "Hello, sir?"

Maxwell went to the door, opening it only a crack. "Yeah?"

"She in there?" said Luther, clearly not remembering my name. "I was wondering where she went."

"She's in here," said Maxwell, his voice not warm. Like a different man than the one who had offered me a soft drink, and this park was a different world entirely, some *Twilight Zone* kind of set. No one seemed real.

"Can I come in?" Luther asked. He peered around the door, half his head appearing over Maxwell's shoulder.

I smiled at him and wondered why I did it.

"No," said Maxwell, a hand on his thick brown belt. "She'll be on in a minute."

He closed the door.

I held the Dr Pepper can against my forehead, and it felt beautiful. I had an immense affection for Maxwell all of a sudden, who finally seemed like what I expected from an old man.

"He okay?" Maxwell asked, easing himself into the chair behind his desk. "He bothering you at all?"

"He's fine," I said, trying to think through the question. Was it possible that Maxwell knew about the niece? Had I been right earlier—did they—whoever "they" were—like to use rapists as a deterrent to speeding?

"You don't sound so sure," he said.

"He says he's here for raping his sixteen-year-old niece," I said.

Maxwell pushed back in his reclining chair, staring down at the floor with his chin tucked against his throat. "He said that?"

"Yes, sir."

"He told you that? That exact thing?"

"Yes, sir."

"Well." He pushed a drawer closed with his knee. "But he hasn't done anything to you?"

"No," I said.

"Well. You come on in here anytime you get too hot, okay? It's hard work for a young thing out there on a day like today, and you don't want to overdo. I got plenty of Coca-Colas."

He stood.

I stood, too.

"Thank you," I said, and I opened the door and walked back into the heat, and, no, none of it was real. Luther was waiting. I let him lead me to the next bathroom and the next and the next, and he asked me if my mother could give him a ride when she came to pick me up, and I said that ever since she'd been made manager at the ballet store, she was bone tired at the end of the day and surely would want to go straight home.

When Mom got there, I slid in the car fast, my thighs slick on the seat. I slammed the door and locked it. I was not entirely sure that Luther wouldn't come ask her for a ride himself.

"So how was it?" she asked, cheerful. "Are you exhausted? Were there other kids there? Did you plant flowers?"

Yes, I said, to all of it. I wanted to keep her smiling. I always wanted to keep her smiling.

"You want to stop by Kmart on the way home?" she asked. "They've got blue raspberry Icees today."

No, thank you, I said.

While Mom was taking her shower that night, I called Lucia. She didn't like to talk on the phone, so I tried to be brief.

"I have something to ask you," I said.

I could hear music in the background. Evan said something, but I couldn't make out the words.

"You still there?" she said to me.

She was always so efficient.

"I got a speeding ticket," I said, "and so instead of paying a fine, I got community service at Oak Park. There's a guy there with me—he cleans the men's bathrooms and I clean the women's—but he's there for raping his sixteen-year-old niece, and I wondered if you could come to the park next Saturday?"

I heard a small sound, like she set something down. A glass? A book?

"Raping his sixteen-year-old niece?" she said slowly.

I was calming a little. Her voice—her voice alone—made everything seem fixable. It had the opposite effect of my mother's voice. Mom could ask a question and my shoulders would hunch, but with Lucia, a question would let me breathe out all the things I wanted to get rid of.

"He hasn't done anything to me," I clarified. "He asked me to go camping, and he's been shot and stabbed and run over, but he hasn't been, like, inappropriate."

She was quiet.

"Let's back up," she said. "When did your community service start?"

She did not seem concerned about efficiency. I talked a long time. When I hung up, I did it slowly, because the phone line was another way of pressing my face to her window, and when the receiver settled into the cradle, I was jerked away from her puffy sofa and the lamp with dangly crystals. I was back inside my house and nowhere else. I wondered if I had been silly to call her and I wondered if really I only wanted to see if she was mine enough to sacrifice a Saturday and I wondered if she would bring bread so we could feed the ducks.

II.

It was nearly ninety degrees the next Saturday, an unusually hot and humid October day. Even the birds were lethargic. As Lucia and Evan circled around the pond toward me, two ducks tipped upside down, heads disappearing into the algae. They didn't seem to have the energy to right themselves.

Lucia and Evan both gave me a hug as they said their hellos, our damp arms brushing. Evan was in shorts, which I'd never seen him wear.

"I need to get back to the bathrooms," I said. "I was hoping you could head in the same direction, and, you know, just be around and—"

"Which way?" asked Lucia.

"Popcorn?" asked Evan.

"Yes," said Lucia. I loved that about her. How she liked food. How she ate it, unafraid. She looked from Evan to me. "But let's wait. Will he be there at the bathrooms, Rachel?"

"Luther?" I asked.

"The security guard," she said.

"Wait," I said. "What?"

"Will the guard be at the bathrooms watching you? Or do I need to go to his office?" she said.

"I don't know if he's in his office," I said, which was true. "I haven't seen him yet this morning. But you don't need to say anything."

She turned away, not answering.

I should have expected it, of course. Had I really thought she would be content to meander through the flowers? Had I secretly hoped she would do this—storm through the park, Jedi-mind-tricking anyone in her way?

I did not feel like I had hoped for it.

"Seriously, Lucia—" I started.

She was scanning the gray gravel path behind us, where an older couple had started tossing handfuls of Corn Flakes into the water. "Excuse me," Lucia said, talking over me. "Do you happen to know where the guard shack is?"

The old couple didn't happen to know. But the two girls on the other side of the water pointed us in the right direction after Lucia called to them loudly enough that a duck scuttled across the pond.

She did things like that. She asked strangers questions. They gave her answers. I had once walked around the Galleria in Birmingham with my mother for almost an hour looking for the Things Remembered monogramming store, and she refused to ask a single person for help. If I wanted to get my hair done for prom, she'd pace around the house, practicing the phone call for days. *I want to make an appointment with Mildred,* she'd whisper, circling the kitchen. Clickety-clack of heels. *It's for my daughter. No. Hello, I'd like to make an appointment for my daughter with Mildred. Hello, this is Margaret Morris, and I'm calling about an appointment for—Hello? May I ask who this is? I'm Margaret Morris calling about an appointment for my sixteen-year-old.*

Circling circling. Clickety-clack.

Lucia's sandals crunched on the gravel. She wore sandals when she wasn't at work, even in the winter, and her toenails were perfect and red. Evan held her hand, and I walked slightly behind.

"What are you going to say?" I asked.

She paused, dropping Evan's hand. "I won't embarrass you."

"I'm not worried about that."

She set a pace faster than I could think. I could not form the right words, not even in my head, and I had no choice but to follow along, duckling-ish. I had just spotted the guard shack in its open clearing when I heard footsteps coming fast enough that it made me spin around.

"Hey," Luther said, stopping a couple of feet away. "I was looking for you."

His white T-shirt was wet at the armpits. He had a tattoo on the inside of his wrist—blurry and dark—that I somehow hadn't noticed before.

"Maxwell was asking where you were," he said. "I told him you didn't feel good. I told him that."

"Thanks," I said.

"You better come back with me, though. I don't want you to get in trouble."

Lucia had stepped closer to me, shoulder to shoulder.

"I'm Rachel's friend," she said.

She held out her hand, and there was nothing about her tone that could possibly be considered threatening. Only she wasn't smiling and she never looked away from him, not once, and was that all it took, I wondered? Eye contact and no teeth?

Because Luther wouldn't look at her. He shook her hand but stared past her shoulder the whole time.

"I didn't want her to get yelled at," he said.

Behind him, crossing through a bed of pine straw, I saw a familiar figure in navy blue approaching. Maxwell came to a stop when he reached us, and the look on his face was not grandfatherly.

"Where you been?" he asked me. No one here remembered names.

"I—"

"We distracted her," said Lucia, holding out a hand again, but this time she was smiling. "I apologize, Officer—"

"Maxwell," he said. "Just Maxwell."

"Rachel," Evan said softly to me, "come get that popcorn with me now, why don't you?"

I shook my head, stepping away from Evan. Lucia frowned, but she turned back to Maxwell.

"I'm Lucia Gilbert," she said, and she let her hand hover above his arm. Jedi strategy. "You're in charge of the community service placements here? I had a little experience with that back when I handled juvenile cases."

"Lawyer?" said Maxwell.

"I am."

"I handle the placements all right," he said, shifting his feet. "Keep them organized, give them a schedule, check to make sure they're on track. I've been doing it, oh, six years now. You got a good, hardworking girl here."

He assumed, I realized, that she was my mother.

She didn't correct him.

"Do you know he touched her?" she asked.

Maxwell twitched. "What?"

"A child rapist placed in a park," she said. "You know what he's charged with, correct? And he's assigned to a place that's swarming with children. It defies explanation. On top of that, he's paired with a teenager. Who he invites to go camping. Who he touches—her elbows, her thigh. Without her consent."

Maxwell looked down at me. I could feel Luther watching me, too, but I hadn't looked at him since Lucia said the work "rapist." She was moving too fast for me.

"Is that right?" Maxwell said, and he had hairs growing from a mole above his left eyebrow. "You didn't tell me he touched you."

"No, sir," Luther answered. "I never—"

"I think it was an accident," I said, and Luther nodded, but no one else seemed to hear me.

"This is not acceptable," Lucia said. "Surely you can fix it. Surely you can move this man to a more appropriate location."

As uncomfortable as I was, I could appreciate her. She was not accusing Maxwell. She was letting him be the one who could fix things.

"The court people will think I did something wrong," said Luther, looking only at Maxwell now. Stepping farther away from me, putting the whole pathway between us. "If you make me move. I'll get more hours or—I don't know. It's not right. I didn't touch her. Not once. I only invited her and her dad—"

"You come on in the office with me," Maxwell said to Luther. He looked back at Lucia. "Ma'am, we can take care of this quick and easy."

"I appreciate that," said Lucia.

Luther ran a hand over the curve of his skull, his T-shirt sleeve pulling up so that I could see his bullet scar, pale and crooked.

"Rachel," said Evan, stepping closer. He blocked my view of Luther, exchanging a look with Lucia in that mute language they had.

"Popcorn," Lucia said, and I felt Evan's hand light on my shoulder blade.

"Come on," he said.

I let him lead me away, and I could hear Luther murmuring, and I wondered what would happen in that office. Lucia might be a part of it, but I wouldn't be, apparently, even though I'd made it all happen. I had not meant to make it happen. Lucia had never asked me, and she'd never asked Luther anything, either, and he had never threatened me and never hurt me, and if I'd set some punishment in motion, I wanted to undo it. Lucia would not undo it, I knew. Not when she had won. That was what this was, I supposed. Winning.

Lucia

1.

"Natalie Wood died," said Rachel, toeing off her shoes in the kitchen before following Lucia through the dining room and into the sunroom.

"I saw the headline," said Lucia.

Rachel stopped in front of the wide window that faced the street. "We never come in here. It's nice."

With the sun vanishing behind the trees, the whole room was golden. The light spilled into the dining room, but this space soaked up most of the glow. A dozen cacti decorated the end tables, rounded shapes covered in needles and fangs and fuzz. Lucia climbed onto the futon so she could reach the hook she'd already screwed into the ceiling. It needed a few more turns.

"It gets too hot," she said. "I just need one more minute with this."

"Has it ever seemed strange to you," Rachel said, "that Robert Wagner would be married to someone who wasn't Stefanie Powers?"

Lucia bent down and picked up the Christmas cactus Marissa had given her, stretching to hang the planter on the hook. "I hate to tell you this, but Robert Wagner is actually a different person than Jonathan Hart. *Hart to Hart* is not a documentary."

She let go of the cactus, watching it sway.

"I know that," said Rachel. "But isn't it better when it's real? Like Bogart and Bacall?"

"Maybe," admitted Lucia.

Rachel flopped onto the futon, feet flying up. Her hair was falling from her ponytail, and she swiped it from her mouth. It was always the hair over the ears, Lucia thought, that would not be contained. Back in her own ponytail days, she had hated those uncontrollable bits—they'd had the look of sideburns.

"I feel guilty about this," Rachel said, "but when I heard about Natalie Wood on the news, my first thought was *finally*! Finally, he can marry Stefanie Powers. I mean, I'm not actually glad his wife died. That would be terrible. But don't you think there must be something between them, in real life, for them to seem so in love?"

Sometimes Lucia forgot Rachel's age entirely. Other times it seemed like the girl still believed in Santa Claus.

"How can you fake it that well?" Rachel went on, lifting a throw pillow onto her lap, jamming her elbows into the cotton. "Do you ever wonder that? Why do we want to believe them? Why does acting even work? Why do I feel anything at all about Stefanie Powers and Robert Wagner?"

And this was why Lucia liked to let the girl keep talking. Just when you thought she was blathering, she'd spin off in some interesting direction.

"A need for escape?" Lucia suggested, sinking onto the cushions.

"How did you know? With Evan? That he was the one?"

"Well," said Lucia, and it was actually shocking that the question had never been asked. "It was a complicated beginning. I was nearly done with law school, and I was dating someone else. I didn't want to start anything with Evan. But—soul mates."

It was not a term that divorce lawyers tended to use.

Still. She thought of Perry Jones, tall and killer dimples, and he was a good guy, but as he talked—even as she talked—she'd felt herself, so often, floating away, a part of her distant and contemplating. When she'd met Evan, there was no part of herself floating. No part of her that he didn't reach.

"So you knew right away?" the girl asked.

Lucia groaned silently. *Yes,* was the answer that came to her.

"I don't think it's that easy," she said instead. "I felt like he was different right away. But I don't think that you can know for sure, 'Aha! This is the man I'm going to spend the rest of my life with.' You're sixteen—you really can't know it at sixteen. And here's a better answer—I think you can feel sure and still be wrong. Sometimes you think there's a click, and really it's just sex or neediness or a thousand other things. A lot of people get it wrong."

"I know," said Rachel.

Lucia heard the refrigerator door open and close, and Evan came into view briefly, Moxie at his heels. A moment later, he stepped through the kitchen doorway.

"It looks good," he said, nodding at the cactus. He reached out and straightened a dining-room chair. "Geez, it's a furnace in here, Lucia."

"I know," she said. "Come on, Rachel. Let's move to the den. I can't take it anymore."

She held out an arm, waving Rachel toward the doorway, and she could see the wet marks on the back of the girl's shirt as she stood. Those stray pieces of hair at her temples were damp.

Lucia was still looking at Rachel's head when the window behind the futon shattered. The sweaty stray strands and the frizzing curls against the nape of her neck.

The pale curve of her neck.

The bite of glass against Lucia's bare calves. Chunks of glass on the cushions, geometric.

A gunshot. The thought was so clear Lucia could almost see the words. It came to her after standing there for hours, and also it came to her before the shot was even fired.

She wrapped one arm around Rachel, shoving her down and landing next to her, her chin slamming against the girl's shoulder hard enough to make her teeth ache. The second shot came then, a sharper, clearer crack with no glass involved. She didn't see where it hit. She had a hand over Rachel's head and she was trying to inch them both under the dining-room table, away from the window, and, God, her jaw ached.

Evan. He had been right there at the doorway to the kitchen, and now there was an empty space. She called his name as another bullet went into the doorframe. Shards of wood fell to the carpet.

Rachel moved underneath her, not making a sound other than breathing. They were pressed against the dining-room chairs, and when Lucia craned her neck, she could see something shining and black on the den floor. Evan's shoe. His pants leg hitched up past his knee.

Another shot. A cactus hit the floor, dirt spilling, black. Moxie was barking madly from somewhere. Another shot—the fifth?—then silence. The sound of an engine outside?

Lucia lifted her head. Rachel was still partially underneath her.

"Evan?" she called again.

"I'm okay," he said, and the shoe jerked out of her sightline. His face came into view, and he crawled toward them. "You?"

"Rachel?" Lucia asked, and the girl turned her head just enough that the curve of her cheek and ear were visible, along with one brown eye. Everything else was covered by hair.

"Yeah," Rachel said.

"You're sure?" said Lucia.

"Yeah," Rachel repeated, showing all of her face, pale but whole.

"I'll call the police," Evan said. "Keep away from the window."

"Obviously I'll keep away from the window," Lucia said, getting to her knees, though she looked back at the window, considering trajectories.

"We're going to crawl into the den," she told Rachel. "Keep down until we're out of view. Okay?"

They crawled. Moxie bounded into the room, her tongue lapping at every inch of skin she could reach. Lucia herded her forward, wanting to keep her away from the glass. When Lucia finally stood up, she had a long scratch from her wrist to her elbow, smooth and straight like someone had tried to dissect her. Evan was on the phone, his back to them, checking the lock on the carport door as if that mattered when someone could just climb through the front window. *It's 5285 Avalon,* he was saying. *Someone in a car shot through the front window of the house.*

Rachel leaned against the bookshelves. She skimmed a hand over the driftwood. She touched one fingertip to the milk-glass chicken.

"You're sure you're all right?" Lucia asked, laying her hands on the girl's shoulders.

"I'm fine," Rachel said. "I promise."

"Nothing hurts? Nothing at all?" Because sometimes it happened, Lucia had heard, that shock set in and kept you from feeling injuries.

"Someone just shot at your house," Rachel said, shifting under Lucia's hands. "Someone just shot at your house."

Lucia felt the hard knobs of the girl's shoulder bones, the slight rise and fall of breath. "Yes," she said. "But we're all okay. It's all fine."

Fine. No one bleeding. No one dead. Standing here, the dog slobbering over their feet.

"Were they shooting at you?" said Rachel. "On purpose?"

Lucia smoothed Rachel's hair back from her face. Her pupils looked slightly dilated. Lucia remembered how a woman on the battered women's hotline had talked about having her ribs broken, saying she'd never even felt it. The woman had said it was like she'd lost her glasses, like everything around her went blurry, and even the paramedics' questions seemed unreal. Lucia had wondered if maybe shock wasn't the right explanation, if maybe the blur was a coping mechanism you developed when you had a husband who beat the crap out of you. Maybe you told yourself nothing was real.

If the woman had been right, though, it helped to assure Lucia that she herself was not in shock. Nothing was blurry. She could see so clearly. She thought about an old Spider-Man comic where Peter Parker suddenly realized his superpowers. She could see and hear more clearly than she ever had. The molding along the doorway had seven distinct edges. The tendrils of the carpet stood up in formations like coral. Evan had a small hole in his sleeve, no bigger than a pencil eraser. The pork chops he'd planned to grill were marinating by the sink, and orange juice had splashed over the side of the pie plate onto the counter.

Glass broke, quietly, in the sunroom. Probably a stray piece falling from the window.

"We need to get you home," she told Rachel.

"Surely she'll need to talk to the police," Evan said. He'd hung up the phone and was walking toward them, headed past the doorway that led to the sunroom.

"Stay back," said Lucia.

"They're gone," said Evan, although he sped up his steps.

"I don't know why Rachel has to stay," Lucia said. "She didn't see anything."

"Still."

"Fine," said Lucia, turning back to Rachel. "We need to call your mom. She should know what happened. You might be in shock, so you probably shouldn't drive home. I could drop you off or she could pick you up. I'll explain what happened."

Rachel let out a long breath. "Don't call her. You should not call her."

"She's your mother. I can't not tell her—"

Rachel laid a hand on her arm, her grip tighter than Lucia would have expected.

"I'll drive home, Lucia. I'll tell her when I get there. It'll be worse if you tell her over the phone. It'll be worse if she comes by. Do you know what she'll do if she sees that window blown out?"

"I have some idea."

"I'll be fine," Rachel said.

"I should drive you home," Lucia repeated.

"Then I'll have to deal with coming back for my car," Rachel said. "I'll tell her when I get home, and she'll see I'm safe, so she won't be able to hallucinate any terrible things. I'll tell her—I don't know, but, Lucia, seriously—someone was shooting at you. Why are we talking about me?"

Every word came out clear and calm. Rachel did not seem to be in shock, either.

"Don't worry about Lucia," Evan said, stepping closer to them. "She comes from strong stock. Did she ever tell you about her grandmother?"

"Her grandmother?" said Rachel.

"She got her dress caught in the tractor she was driving," he said. A breeze pushed past, lifting hair and shirt tails, like a whole wall had vanished instead of a window. "No one was around. She managed to cut the engine, but her leg was mangled and they had to amputate."

"She was eighty," said Lucia.

"A year later, she was back driving the tractor," Evan said. "Strong stock."

The familiar rhythm was a relief. Evan had always loved this story, and Rachel had her head tilted, soaking up every word. If they could all keep playing their parts, everything would settle.

"You always use that phrase," Lucia said. "It's like saying I have good birthing hips."

"Your grandmother drove a tractor?" Rachel said.

"Hell, yes," Lucia said.

She wouldn't normally say "hell" in front of the girl. She wondered if Evan and Rachel had the same thought, because the silence thickened like custard, a few seconds changing the texture entirely. They remembered. They stood, unmoving and dry mouthed, until sirens cut through the quiet. The wails seemed to be coming from miles away, but it took less than a minute before the police car slid to a stop along the curb.

Lucia rushed to the not-there window. One police car. She had expected more.

Two men in blue, in no hurry to get out of the car. Adjusting the visors, reaching toward the floorboards or the glove compartment, and what might they be doing—Spitting out gum? Pulling out paperwork?

Lucia watched the one on the passenger side climb from the car, his every movement careful. She watched his black shoes ease onto the pavement. The way he boosted himself with a hand on the door. The way he ducked his head down, saying something to his partner, who was still inside the car. The two of them strolled up the driveway at a comfortable pace. Still, they'd arrived here very quickly.

She wondered if she was judging time poorly.

She stood by the door, aware of Evan tugging Moxie toward the guest bedroom. She waited for the policemen to knock and then she could not wait any longer, and she yanked the door open before they'd reached the welcome mat. She answered their hello and studied their faces: she didn't know them. She'd had a passing thought that she might. In the old days, she'd spent plenty of time with policemen. These two looked to be in their early thirties, soft-faced and unfamiliar.

Everything picked up speed.

The patrolmen came inside and looked through the sunroom, picking their way through the glass, and they called out a question every now and then but not many. They ran their fingers over the bullet holes in the wall and door-frame. They nodded and said they'd take a look outside the house and then come back. When Evan asked if he and Lucia could come as well, the men waved them forward. Lucia asked Rachel to stay inside with Moxie and, shockingly, the girl agreed with hardly a word. She curled up on the den sofa before Lucia had even closed the kitchen door.

Six bullets, the policemen counted. Lucia hadn't remembered that many shots. One lodged in the fence around the backyard. One stuck in a wooden column of the carport. Three in the wall of the sunroom, and the one wedged in the doorframe.

Did you see the car?

No.

Do you have any reason to believe someone would be targeting you, Mrs. Gilbert?

No.

Do you have any guess about who might have done it?

No.

Because it feels personal.

Well, yes, it did.

Lucia felt a burst of interest when they said they would go question the neighbors: she should have thought of it herself. She watched the officers cut across her yard, and then she went inside, washed her hands, and poured three glasses of ice water. Evan and Rachel took their glasses and went to check on Moxie, and Lucia wandered through the den, finishing off her water.

When the policemen came back, they stood in the driveway and told her that Mrs. Jackson across the street had looked out her window and seen a large, dark car, probably navy blue or black. It was a four-door, she said, but she wasn't good with car names. She'd seen it driving away, only from the back, and she had no idea who was driving. One person? More? She couldn't say.

No one else had seen anything, although several people had heard the shots, including Marlon, who came by with the beagles. At that point, the policemen were talking through the science of bullets.

"Was it the Buick?" Marlon yelled from a good twenty feet away.

"That's Marlon Reynolds," Lucia said quickly, taking in Marlon's less-than-pristine beard and ragged shorts. She did not want anyone to shoot him accidentally. "He lives down the street."

Both policemen signaled for him to come closer. One of them reached down and patted a beagle. Inside, Moxie went nuclear.

Marlon told them exactly what he'd told Lucia a few weeks earlier. One of the officers took notes, and the other one—the beagle petter—flexed and unflexed his right hand, like maybe he had some arthritis, even though he was surely too young for it. Lucia watched his hand curl and straighten, and something about the movement pulled at her. His face was familiar after all. A hallway started to coalesce, and she tried to bring the setting into focus.

There.

She'd been passing a defendant in the corridor before his arraignment; he'd gotten hold of a box of Junior Mints, shaking them into his mouth straight from the box. His aim had not been good, and chocolates had bounced from his chest onto the floor. A policeman had yanked the candy away from him, and that policeman had been doing this same thing with his hand. He'd caught her eye and they'd shared a moment of silent disbelief over the candy, and she'd seen him a few other times after that in the hallways. She thought he'd mentioned saving up vacation time for a honeymoon in Mexico.

She looked at the policeman in her driveway, curling and straightening his fingers. He wore a wedding ring.

"I know you, don't I?" she said.

"I was wondering if you'd remember me, Mrs. Gilbert," he said. "Matt Atkinson. It's been a long time."

"We met back—" she started.

"Honestly," he said, stretching out his fingers. "I don't remember the details. I do remember you, of course."

She hadn't remembered him, though, and that shook her. These men had asked questions and she had answered them, but she had little faith that their questions were the right ones, and now she wondered if she could even trust her answers.

Evan's hand at her back, between her shoulder blades. A solid touch.

Marlon touched her shoulder, too, as he left. The beagles' claws clicked on the concrete.

"What happens next?" Evan asked.

"There's a chance that the bullets will tell us something," said the policeman Lucia didn't know. He had mentioned his name and she had already forgotten it. "We'll see if they lead us to someone who's been in trouble before."

"You'll leave some sort of guard here, right?" Evan said. "In case whoever did this comes back?"

Both policemen shook their heads.

"There's no reason to believe they'd come back," said Matt Atkinson. "That's not how this sort of thing usually works."

"You said it felt personal," said Evan, and he was furious. Lucia doubted the policemen could tell from his tone, but his overpronounced words were as good as screaming. "If it's personal, there's a very good chance he'll come back, whoever he is. I don't understand why you're acting like this happens every day."

The officers said a patrol car would be circling the neighborhood. They said the presence of the car would certainly be a deterrent. They said Lucia and Evan should call if they saw anything out of the ordinary.

By the time the men climbed back into their cruiser, Evan was nearly shaking with anger. Lucia, too, was ready for them to leave. They had nothing else to offer. What she most wanted, at this moment, was for the details of the shooting not to appear in the newspaper the next morning. As the patrol car veered around a pothole, brake lights flashing, Evan kicked at the splinters flecking the carport. She thought of Chris Sanderson with his Tom Selleck mustache and meticulous handwriting. He'd been a police sergeant when they first met during an assault case years ago, but he'd been promoted to lieutenant this past spring.

She turned toward the door, wood bits crunching under her sandals. She checked her watch and hoped that Chris was at the station. She likely had his direct number at her office, but she'd just call the front desk—

"You getting a broom?" asked Evan as she brushed past him.

She nodded. Yes, a broom would be good. She'd get one after she called the police station. But first she would check on Rachel—the officers hadn't asked the girl a single question, so there'd been absolutely no reason for her to wait around this long. If she still couldn't convince Rachel to accept a ride home, Lucia would at least walk her to her car. And then she'd call Chris Sanderson, who had always exuded competence. No whining or excuses—he just did what needed to be done, and she'd always appreciated that.

II.

She couldn't sleep. At 1:00 a.m. she was pulling the Yellow Pages out of the drawer, turning to *W* for "windows," then switching to the *G*s for "glass." Glass repair? Or would that only involve windshields? She smoothed down the pages, centering the phone book on the counter. She'd leave it open, and that would be one less thing for the morning. She'd at least caught Chris Sanderson at his desk, and he'd promised to keep the incident out of the papers.

On the couch, Moxie snored, back legs twitching.

Lucia jerked at a quick, dark movement just inside the sliding doors, expecting a roach. It was only the shadow of her arm, stretching.

She had kept out of the sunroom for as long as she could. Now she gave in to its pull, swatting at the overhead light switch. The duct tape and tarp had been more successful than she'd expected: although the tarp rippled slightly with the breeze, the tape held firm. The effect was to make the room seem not so much damaged as under construction. Neither sweeping nor vacuuming had gotten rid of all the glass on the carpet and sofa. When she ran a hand over the cushions, invisible shards pricked her palm. She backed away, pressing herself against the wall, not so far from bullet hole number one, which had been stripped of its actual bullet.

A little plaster would fix the holes. And she'd need to repot the chin cactus, which was dented, but all in all, the room did not look like near murder.

She heard footsteps.

"Lucia," said Evan, the floor creaking under him as he came toward her. His boxer shorts were off-kilter, rucked around the crotch.

"I'm going to call someone about the window first thing in the morning," she said.

"Lucia."

He leaned against the wall next to her. She slanted into him.

"You really have no clue?" he said.

She shook her head.

His hand skimmed up her leg, then slid under her T-shirt. "I love this thigh. It's the most perfect thigh in the universe. Your right thigh, I mean. The left one—it's adequate, I suppose."

Even now, he could make her laugh.

"We do have to actually talk about it," he said.

"I don't know what to say. I don't have an answer."

"I'm not looking for an answer."

"What are you looking for?"

She saw Rachel's hair, frizzing at the neck, copper curls. A spill of dirt, gray and dry, the chin cactus round and red like her mother's ancient pin cushion. The groove of Rachel's button carved into her arm, dog hair like a tumbleweed. The dry skin of Evan's naked knee.

"Thoughts," he said. "Any thoughts at all."

"I couldn't sleep," she said.

"It doesn't have to be right now," he said, and God, she loved this man.

The tarp rattled like paper, the sound of someone searching for the right page.

"I know I have this ability," she said. "To, you know, close the door when something is too hard. To block it out."

His fingers curled around hers. "I had no idea."

They stayed against the wall for several quiet minutes, and then he asked her if she'd like him to make coffee and keep her company. She told him to get some sleep, and eventually he disappeared through the doorway and she was left alone with the tarp and other things.

She had nearly forgotten the feel of 3:00 a.m., how the streets and the skies and even the insects were silent, how your arms were heavier and your head was thick. During law school and the first years of her career, she'd been well acquainted with this syrupy time of night. One year at Legal Aid. Two years in the district attorney's office, first with family court and then with juvenile court. She hadn't lasted long. She—pretty little blonde—would lie in bed and discover that some child had burrowed into her brain, maybe Bequeatha Long with her doll's face and swollen eye. Maybe Alicia Redmont, who shot her father after he kicked her pregnant mother in the stomach, or maybe Jed Louis, who robbed a man at gunpoint but still slept with a Winnie-the-Pooh bear in tenth grade—and how was she supposed to have known those sorts of stories existed? She would sit at this same dining-room table and think of how she might make a difference—such simple, stupid, nursery-rhyme morality, a near impossibility with the children, who—before she ever met them—had been broken into so many pieces that neither she nor all the king's horses and all the king's men could have put them back together again. She'd tried. She'd listened. She'd remembered the names of their sisters and mothers and best friends, and she'd carefully explained their options, and she'd always shown up when she said she would. She'd played a silent game as she walked through the county jail—*Who would kill me?* And she'd look at face after face and think, *He would. He would. Maybe not him.* And sometimes then and sometimes now she cringed at herself, wondering if she should have done it all differently, because she had not turned into a crusader, at least not the kind who could have helped those children. She did not work for the Southern Poverty Law Center, which was walking distance from her office. If she had aimed for that path, she could have made it happen, surely. But she hadn't, so what possible use was there in wondering?

She could sleep at night now. Normally. Her clients wished for things that she—and the courts—could possibly grant. When she flipped through her stacks of paper, she found answers in them.

She had no desire to relearn this time of night.

She had a good view of the partial wall between the small foyer and the sunroom. The cream-colored molding that set off the gold walls did not look as pristine from this angle. She stared at the decades of paint. How had she never noticed the pockmarks and bubbles? The molding looked fine from a distance, but up close, it was all flaws. The paint had peeled away completely in some patches, and Lucia could see down to the naked wood, the old iterations of paint exposed, archaeological.

She might as well make a call to a housepainter after she called the window repairmen.

III.

On Saturday, three days after the shooting, Lucia's father called to ask if she and Evan would be home that afternoon. Her parents had visited once already: her father had run his finger down the splintered post of the carport, and her mother had started many sentences she didn't finish.

Lucia wasn't surprised that they needed more shoring up. She was standing in the kitchen when her father opened the door. He was inside so fast that Moxie never made a sound.

"It's not locked?" he asked, incredulous.

"I saw you pull up," Lucia said, wrapping her arms around him and kissing his rough cheek. How did he always smell of grass, she wondered, even when he'd just showered?

"You keep it locked, though?" he said.

"I'm not an idiot, Dad," she said.

"I know that."

Her mother pushed in, too, and her hug was longer than usual.

"Are you all right?" Caroline asked, breath in Lucia's ear. "Are you doing all right, really?"

"I'm fine, Mother," Lucia said. "I promise. It's all over with, and the police are checking on us, making sure nothing else happens. It was just a fluke."

"Oliver," Evan called out, rounding the corner of the hallway. "Come have a seat."

"No need," said her father. "This won't take long. I tell you, though, I still can't get that game out of my head. I hate to admit it, but he's the best that's ever been."

It took Lucia longer than it should have to realize that he was talking about the Iron Bowl. The Auburn-Alabama football game had been two weeks ago, but both her husband and her father were still talking about Bear Bryant, as if there were anything left to say that had not been printed a thousand times.

For once, she would be thrilled for the conversation to stay on football.

"Y'all want a glass of tea?" Lucia asked.

Her parents both shook their heads. Caroline stepped up to the kitchen counter, straightening the pile of mail. Oliver reached into his back pocket slowly, and Lucia somehow knew by just the motion of his arm that he'd brought a gun. He laid it flat in his palm and held it out to her.

"I want you to take this," he said.

Evan was already shaking his head, but Oliver kept his eyes on Lucia. His hand was steady, and the gun was dark and polished. Attractive, even, if you thought of it as a sculpture.

"It's just a little twenty-two pistol," her dad said. "Good for a woman. Not too heavy. Not much recoil. It only holds six rounds, but it'd still be my choice. You can keep it in your purse. Go on. Just hold it and see how it feels."

"Is it—"

"You think I'd hand you a loaded gun?" he said. "Didn't I teach you anything? I've got the magazine in my other pocket."

She took it from his hand. The metal was cool and smooth, light in her palm. Her father had taken her target shooting when she was younger, wooden circles hammered into trees, squirrels jumping through branches. She'd never particularly liked the idea of guns. This one, though, felt comfortable.

"Why do I need a lady gun?" she said.

She was playing her part now, and as she expected, her father snorted slightly. She expected Evan to laugh, but he didn't.

"I've been warning you," Oliver said, as he double-checked the deadbolt on the door.

Lucia shook her head. "Please don't—"

"This is what happens when the blacks move in," he said.

She set the gun on the counter, turning it so that the barrel pointed toward the wall. "Black people are not the issue. The neighborhood is perfectly safe."

"It's not their fault—I'm not saying that," said Oliver. "It's the way it is. Violence follows them, even the good ones. They bring it with them. You look at Martin Luther King and what happened everywhere he went. You can't deny that's the truth."

Lucia stood at the spot where the kitchen linoleum gave way to den carpet. She kicked at a scrap of gnawed rawhide and, across the room, Moxie lunged to her feet.

"I can deny it," she said.

"Honey," said her mother. No more than that. It was not clear who she was chastising, but Lucia's father pivoted, rubbing his hands together hard enough that it seemed possible he would start a fire.

Lucia watched him pace around her kitchen. She could picture him when he was dark haired and lean, driving her down country highways with cookie crumbs all over the front seat. He'd taken her past old sharecropper shacks, planks of wood barely stuck together. He'd pointed to two black children playing on a splintered porch, and he'd told her, *Maybe you'll pass one of those kids on the street one day, and maybe they won't talk like you do or act like you do. You remember this. You don't ever know what people come home to.* She'd watched through that same car window as he changed a cavalcade of flat tires: he was incapable of driving past any woman, black or white, stranded on the side of the road. He'd taught her to stop and help strangers.

He'd taught her that Mexicans would cheat you if they could. He'd taught her that a husband was the head of his wife just as Christ was the head of the church. And so what was she supposed to do with all of it, looking at him now scanning her cabinets for some loose knob he could tighten?

"It has nothing to do with the neighborhood, Oliver," said Evan, falling onto the sofa. "It wasn't random. Tell him who you think it was, Lucia."

"I have no idea," she said, puzzled. "It could have been random."

"Really?" Evan said. "No idea at all?"

She understood then. He was desperate enough that he was willing to bring her parents into this. She had refused to hypothesize, and now he was hoping to have numbers on his side.

"Really," she said. "I have no idea."

She did not really believe that the shooting was random, but why burden her parents with that detail? She'd tried to convince Evan: there was no solving this. So many names and so many faces. These past few nights, lying awake, she'd assessed every person she'd encountered in the past week. The past month. Surely she averaged a dozen new people a week, and that was if she hadn't done any public speaking. If she stretched back further through the years, back to the *would-he-kill-me?* days, she might have met hundreds a month. Those names and faces were gone, most of them, wiped clean from her mind.

But she didn't have to delve that far back. Divorce drove people crazy. When your family fell apart, it stripped you down to your most primal self, which was why divorce lawyers tended to get assaulted more than, say, estate attorneys or intellectual property guys. How many people might hate her? Maybe none. Maybe a thousand. There was no keeping track. If she tried—if she pictured a maniac behind every face she passed on the sidewalk or smiled at from behind her desk—she'd never make it through the day.

"You think you know the person?" her father asked her. It obviously hadn't occurred to him. He propped an elbow on the counter, nearly mirroring her mother's pose.

"Won't y'all please sit down?" Lucia said to them both.

"We're fine," said Caroline. "Do you? Do you think you know whoever did it?"

Lucia stepped backward until she felt the wall. She pushed against it, easing the ache in her shoulders.

"There's no telling," she said. "It could be anyone I've ever met over the past decade or more or it could be someone I've never met. It's pointless to start going down that road. The police will see what they can find out. That's their job."

"What about that fellow who ran the bulldozer into his wife's bedroom?" her father asked.

That case had been in the papers. The photos had been compelling.

"It wasn't a bulldozer," Lucia said. "It was a backhoe. And the wife's sister had some internal injuries, so he got sentenced to five years. It's not him."

Her father rested his chin on his hand. She could feel him warming to the topic. Her mother was scraping away with one fingernail at something on the countertop.

"You've had nut jobs," Oliver said. "You don't talk about them, but we know you've had nut jobs."

Lucia was not, legally speaking, allowed to talk about the nut jobs. She'd never mentioned the man whose wife had found him tied up with extension cords, with their real estate agent naked on top of him, rubbing his chest with a Brillo pad. She hadn't told them about the woman who emptied her children's college savings account. She hadn't told them about the man who executed his son's gerbil or the grandmother who set her daughter-in-law's car on fire. All of those stories involved their own ugliness, but it was assessable. It was contained inside a single house and limited to a couple of people, maybe a handful, if you counted children and grandmothers and real estate agents. In court, there could be a reckoning, and she could be part of it.

Some things did not have a reckoning, and waiting for one would drive you crazy.

"What about the black man who killed that woman at Sears?" her mother said.

"That man's in prison, Mother," Lucia answered. "When you kill people, you wind up in prison. Can we please stop doing this?"

"You've overdone yourself," Caroline said. "You've just overdone yourself."

Lucia watched as her mother toed off her shoes, nudging them against the wall, toe to toe and heel to heel. She needed things in their appropriate place. Shoes and dishes and cereal in Tupperware and men and women and black and white, and she believed that if you never veered outside the lines, nothing bad could happen to you. Like a lasso laid on the ground, warding off the snakes. And if something terrible did happen, that surely meant you had stepped over a line.

Lucia picked up the gun, letting it rest in her hand. Hollywood made up that story about lassos. Westerns were full of nonsense. Snakes could go anywhere they wanted.

"Thank you, Dad," she said. "I'm not sure I want this, but—"

"Why wouldn't you want it?" asked her father.

"I don't know. A gun in the house? A gun in my purse?"

"I have one," said her mother. "There's no harm in being safe."

"You have a gun?" Lucia asked, and she could not have been more surprised if her mother had announced that she had voted for Jimmy Carter.

"Of course I do," said her mother. "In the bedroom closet. Although if I'm driving by myself, I keep it under the seat just in case."

"Is it in case of a log truck problem?" asked Evan.

It was well-timed. Lucia smiled along with the rest of them, but she was thinking of when she was a teenager, already cringing at her mother's talk of well-folded napkins and no chewing gum in church. She'd pulled into the driveway and felt a thump under her back tire. When she got out, she saw the squirrel, its back broken. Bloody and skull-mangled, dragging itself away from the car.

She had screamed like some bimbo in *Friday the 13th,* and she'd run to get her mother. Caroline had marched to the lawn-tools rack in the garage and then, as Lucia had covered her eyes, she'd bashed the squirrel over the head with the shovel, and Lucia had felt like she was watching a stranger.

"A woman alone," Caroline said. "Things can happen."

"What things could happen, Mother?" pushed Lucia, out of habit.

"A maniac could shoot through your window, for one thing."

"And you'd shoot back?" Lucia said. "And kill him in a hail of bullets with your sharpshooting skills?"

Her father opened his mouth, making the slightest breath of a sound, but her mother laid a hand on his arm.

"If you're working late in your office and a man is coming toward you," Caroline said, "don't you think pulling out a gun would make him pause?"

Lucia considered her mother, standing there with her immovable hair and her bare feet.

"It will make you feel safer," her mother said.

"But will she actually *be* safer?" asked Evan.

"Than if she had no defense at all?" Oliver said. "Yes."

Lucia looked from her parents to her husband and back again. They'd arranged themselves on opposite sides of the room, so the only way to carry on this conversation was to twist and turn.

"I have mace," she said. "I keep—"

"I got it for her years ago," Evan interrupted.

"Why are you two still standing up?" Lucia said. "Would you please go sit down?"

Oliver at least stepped from behind the counter, venturing onto the carpet. "I know you think you're the same as a man, Lucia," he said. "I'm not even disagreeing with you. Fine. But even a man—"

Lucia lifted a foot and brought it down hard, aware that the movement was perilously close to a stomp. It was easy to slip into old patterns with her parents, but they had their own patterns and they were still standing up instead of sitting on the sofa like reasonable people and everyone was talking too much.

"Dad, I don't think I'm the same as a man," she said. "Okay? You know why? Because Arnold Dobson, the jackass, does not walk into a courtroom thinking, oh, since I'm a man, I need to make sure that what I do reflects well on any men who might come after me. If I make a mistake, it hurts all men everywhere. No, Arnold Dobson walks into a courtroom thinking 'I'm Arnold Dobson. I'll do whatever the hell I want and it will be brilliant.'"

Her father walked to the sofa. He backed up until his legs hit the cushions, but he did not sit.

"Who's Arnold Dobson?" he asked.

"A man," said her mother. "A lawyer."

Lucia ran a hand over her face. They were only trying to help, and she knew that. She looked back at the gun, dark metal on the white Formica. The truth was that she had liked the weight of it, and as she stared at it, her hands felt empty. She thought of bloody squirrels and shovels.

"All right," she said.

"What?" said Evan, standing. Now everyone in the whole damn place was standing.

"I want it," Lucia said.

"You're not taking the gun?" Evan said, somewhere between a statement and a question.

She suspected that the look on his face was the same one she had worn when her mother announced she kept a gun in the car.

"They have a point," she said.

"Good girl," her father said.

"I'll certainly feel better," said her mother. "If that matters to you."

A flash of red streaked past the glass doors. A cardinal, which Moxie would probably try to eat.

"Everyone can feel better," Lucia said.

The cardinal circled back, winging past the wind chimes.

Soon her parents left, happy.

She was left with Evan, unhappy.

She locked the door behind her parents and turned back to the gun, still biding its time on the counter. She needed a place for it. Obviously, the bedroom made the most sense—the bedside drawer would be closer, but the top shelf of the closet would be safer.

She could feel Evan watching her.

"It makes sense," she told him, moving his keys from the counter to the wicker basket. He always forgot and tossed them on the counter. "You're the one who wants me to do something. Now I've done something. So tell me again why you're angry?"

"I don't have a particular problem with the gun," he said.

She waited for him to finish, and when he didn't, she turned to face him. He stood still until she came closer, both of them in the middle of the den, an empty patch of carpet between them.

"I have a problem," he said, "with you pretending that the gun solves anything. You can't just carry a gun around and assume that if someone shoots at you, you can shoot back. You can't let this into our lives every day and every minute."

She agreed with him completely.

"Evan," she said, "I could get killed every time I walk from this house to my car. You think I don't know that? You think I'm ignoring it? Every time I walk from the parking lot to my office. Every time I walk past a window. Every time I go to the grocery store. What do you expect me to do? Shut myself in the house? Hire bodyguards, who, by the way, wouldn't be able to stop a bullet? At some point you have to accept that there is risk and that you cannot eradicate it. I am getting up in the morning and going through my day, and I'm doing everything in my power not to let this into our lives."

He took several breaths before he spoke.

"You're going through your day? So the past two mornings when you went to work, you just walked to your car, pulled out of the driveway, not worried at all?"

"As much as possible," she said.

"Well, I think about it," he said. "I think about it plenty. Did you even notice that I was at the door on Thursday and Friday, watching you pull out? Trying to look for some man hiding with a gun, hoping that if you did get shot, I could at least get to you quickly. I'm beginning to think that I might do that every morning forever. Wait for bullets. Wait for a phone call from the hospital."

He lifted his hands, flexing them in the air, like he was going to catch something that never came. He turned his face away from her.

Moxie finally spotted the cardinal and threw herself at the glass door, leaving a swathe of drool. She barked, insistent, and the cardinal twitched. Lucia laid a hand on the dog, buying a few seconds of quiet. The barking and the wind chimes and Evan would start again any second.

"I worry about you," Lucia said. "Of course, I worry about you."

"Me?"

"You or Rachel could have been hurt just as easily as me. It's not like it was a precise sort of attack. But, Evan—there's no point to it. There's no end to it. If we start—"

Moxie growled, low in her throat. Evan thumped on the glass, scaring away the bird.

"You know very well that there are steps we could take," he said to the patio. "But you don't want to discuss them. Here's the thing: you don't get to out-argue me. This isn't court. There's no winning. No one wins if we're both miserable, and you know that better than me."

IV.

Lucia pulled into Rachel's driveway, stopping just past the sidewalk. The front curtains were drawn, and she couldn't see any lights, but both cars were parked in the garage. Her watch confirmed that it wasn't quite 6:00 p.m., so unless Rachel and her mother ate early—which seemed unlikely given Rachel's leisurely evening visits—she wouldn't be interrupting supper. She wouldn't have been forced to stop by unexpectedly if only someone would have answered the phone. She'd called half a dozen times since Rachel had left her house, and no one ever picked up. Weren't they ever home?

Well, they were home now.

She walked up the cobblestones toward the front door, the rosebushes snagging her skirt. Ivy clung to the stonework, and she had to nudge the leaves aside to ring the doorbell. As she waited, she pulled a soggy advertisement for lawn service from the storm door. She was reaching for the doorbell again when the doorknob turned. The door made an unsettling sucking sound as it swung partially open. As Lucia was wondering whether anyone ever used this entrance, Margaret stepped into view, a ring of keys in her hand. She kept hold of the door, blocking the view of the room behind her.

"Hello, Lucia," she said.

She did not offer any invitations.

"Margaret," Lucia said, "I'm sorry to bother you. But I was wondering about Rachel. I wanted to make sure she was all right. I've called—"

"When?"

"Excuse me?"

"When did you call?"

"Today. Yesterday. The day before."

Margaret let her hand fall and the door inched open. Lucia could see white carpet and stiff-backed chairs covered in pale green velvet. Figurines on a glossy end table. It seemed like the sort of living room that no one ever sat in.

"I see," Margaret said, and her voice was like a stranger's. Formal. "We've been having dinner with my sister these last few nights. I'm sorry you went out of your way to stop by, but this saves me a phone call myself, really. I'd prefer you not see Rachel anymore."

"What?" Lucia asked. "Is she okay? She said nothing was—"

Margaret shifted her keys, rattling them against her thigh.

"She's not hurt. But she's a mess. Poor thing, she stayed in the shower for nearly an hour last night, just paralyzed. She does that when she's scared."

No, thought Lucia. *You do that when you're scared, like when you thought Rachel's Key Club adviser had invited your ex-husband to the Christmas party. Rachel stays in the shower when she's pissed off at you, and she collects all the stray hairs and stuffs them down the drain and hopes that the pipes will back up, and it worked at least once after you told her she was getting heavy through the hips, because you had to call the plumber.*

"I hate that she was at the house when it happened," Lucia said. "I hate that it happened, but I especially hate that she was there."

"Someone shoots a gun into your house," Margaret said, "a millimeter from her head, nearly killing her, and you don't even call me to explain? You can't show that much consideration for me? For her?"

Lucia considered that. *A millimeter from her head* seemed overly dramatic.

"I did call," she said.

"You called after days had gone by," Margaret said. "You left it up to her to tell me everything."

This Margaret bore no resemblance to the eager-to-please woman who spoke in question marks and structured entire conversations around department stores. Her confidence rattled Lucia.

She had known from the moment Rachel drove away that she'd made a mistake. Of course she should have taken her home. Of course she should have called that night, in part to check on Rachel, but also to flatter her mother's ego. No, that was unfair. She should have called and talked to Margaret because it was the right thing to do. But she hadn't been able to face that conversation, and so she would pay for it now.

"I'm sorry," she said. "I should have called earlier."

"As I said, I'd prefer you not to have any more contact with her," Margaret repeated. "I've told her not to go by your house. I've told her not to call you. Surely you don't want her to get a bullet through the head next time?"

A movement behind Margaret. A bare foot on the white carpet.

"Mom?" Rachel said.

Lucia couldn't see her face. She leaned forward, but the door blocked her view.

"Go back to the den," Margaret said, still facing Lucia.

"But—"

"Now."

And that was all. Rachel disappeared, never more than a quiet voice. Lucia remembered her own mother's voice and how a single word would draw a line that could not be crossed. She was surprised, though, that Margaret was capable of drawing those lines, and she was shocked that Rachel would not step over them. Children were supposed to crave boundaries, though, weren't they? It was comforting, on some level, to be told what to do.

"Margaret," she said, "do you think I don't lie awake at night thinking about what might have happened? I love her like family. I understand if you

don't want her coming by the house for the foreseeable future. I can understand if—"

"She's not your family," Margaret interrupted. "She's not your responsibil-
ity. I don't want her anywhere near you. There's no telling where the lunatic
might show up next. He could be anywhere. He could follow you anywhere,
and if he sees her with you, he might come after her."

"You're talking to me right now," Lucia said sharply, because she couldn't
stop herself. "Doesn't that mean you're making yourself a target?"

"I don't care about me," Margaret said.

Something about that sentence felt more real to Lucia than anything else
in the woman's monologue.

"I apologize," said Lucia. "I didn't mean to be rude."

The apology seemed to soften Margaret. Her shoulders lifted and fell.

"I'm sorry this is happening to you," she said. "I hope they catch whoever
did it, but the truth is that you're not my job. Rachel is."

Lucia leaned back, and her heel caught on the step, sending her stumbling. She grabbed at the doorframe to steady herself, fingers digging into ivy
and scraping against stone. She let her hand rest flat against the rock. She
thought of how wooden walls splintered so easily.

She had replayed the scene in the sunroom endlessly, and she would have
been willing to bet that she'd thought about bullets through the head—
copper curls frizzing, the fragile feel of a skull under her fingers—every bit as
much as Margaret had. But maybe that wasn't true. Maybe her flashes of
bloody what-ifs—Evan never stopping in the doorway, never prodding them
to leave the room, Rachel still sitting on that sofa when the first bullet smashed
through the glass, Rachel dead, brain and bone everywhere—maybe the
thoughts that haunted her were nothing compared to Margaret's imaginings.

It was possible that Margaret was right. Caught up in the rhythm of their
argument, Lucia would have been slow to acknowledge it, but now she worked
a piece of gravel loose from her shoe and let herself contemplate the other
woman's words. She thought of Rachel tucked away somewhere inside the

house, barefoot and agreeable. This girl was not Bequeatha Long, ambushed by race and poverty and history and bureaucracy. It would take very little to make sure that she was safe.

"You're her mother," Lucia said. "Of course, you want what's best."

"You agree then?" said Margaret.

"I do. Can I talk to her, though?"

"Why?"

"To explain. To let her know that—"

"I don't think that's necessary," Margaret said. "It would only complicate things, don't you think?"

Lucia lay a hand on the stone again, pushing. The pressure loosened something in her shoulder.

"If she disobeys me," Margaret said, "I hope you'll do the right thing. You know how she is."

"I do," Lucia said.

V.

Rachel knocked on the door the next day. As Moxie galloped down the hallway, Lucia opened the door.

"I couldn't get away until now," Rachel said. "Mom was calling in the afternoon to make sure I came home straight from school and finally today she—"

"You heard us talking, right?"

"Yeah. I'm so sorry she talked to you like that. I'd told her that—"

"She'd like you to keep your distance from me," Lucia said. "I can't blame her."

"Why won't you let me finish?" Rachel said, flapping her hands. "She's *wrong*. That's what I'm trying to say. The way her mind works—she overreacts. She can't tell me to stay away."

"She *can* tell you," Lucia said. "She's your mother."

Rachel shook her head frantically. "Do you think it's, like, your fault? It wasn't. And I'm fine. Totally fine. Look, I told her that I'd keep away from your house for a while, and if we just come up with a compromise, I'm sure she'd agree to it. You just have to help me. Maybe I don't come by here for the next month? Two months?"

"Your mother thinks it should be more permanent," Lucia said. "And she's not wrong. I couldn't—"

"Permanent?" said Rachel.

"I couldn't stand it if something happened to you," Lucia said.

Rachel kept shaking her head. "You mean I should stay away until they catch whoever did it, right?"

"I promised your mother that I wouldn't see you."

She'd had the words planned, anticipating this visit, and it was easier to say them than she'd expected. As she spoke, she noticed a swirl of inked words on Rachel's hand, a cursive message from some friend, surely, maybe Tina or Nancy, and how was it that she'd never met either of them after all the stories she'd heard? She took in the ragged shorts, frayed like all the girls were wearing them, and she wondered if all the girls wrote on one another's hands and wore shorts in December. She wondered if all the girls refused to carry umbrellas and ran bareheaded to the car in pouring-down rain, and she wondered if all the girls lapsed occasionally into bad Katharine Hepburn impersonations. The last one, she thought, was only Rachel. No one else.

She reached out, wrapping her arms around Rachel. She kept it efficient. This was one thing she could do, and she would finish it and it would be done. She stepped back inside and closed the door. As she turned the deadbolt, Rachel was still talking.

Rachel

I.

As I pulled into our garage after leaving Lucia, I saw Mr. Cleary next door watering his pansies. I waved, hoping that would be enough, but when I checked the rearview mirror, he'd put down his hose and stepped onto our driveway.

I was going to have to say hello, and I dreaded it. The tears had dried on my face, and I was drained and empty and also I'd rushed over to Lucia's house wearing cutoffs that Mom thought were too short even for yard work, and everything was wrong and it was hard to fake rightness.

"Hey there," Mr. Cleary said, as I slammed my door.

I tugged at my shorts. "Hey, Mr. Cleary."

He wasn't normally social; I couldn't remember him ever going out of his way to speak to me. His wife and their little son used to live with him, but after the divorce Mrs. Cleary and the boy moved in with her parents, while Mr. Cleary kept the house. Mom thought that was inexcusable.

"You have a wasp nest," he said, pointing. "I thought you'd want to know. Winter's a good time to take care of it."

I looked up, and there it was: a big, cardboardish honeycomb globbed on to the eave of the garage. Someone should spray it, but that someone would have to be me. So actually, no, I did not want to know. If Mr. Cleary wanted to be helpful, couldn't he have taken care of the nest without ever telling me?

The hose was laying there in his yard, gushing. His sweatshirt was too tight, and his jeans were too loose, and he was the kind of not-tall man who puffed out his chest to compensate.

"Thanks," I said.

I was aware I didn't sound thankful.

"Something wrong?" he asked.

Over his shoulder, through his chain-link fence, I could see the turquoise rectangle of his swimming pool. It was the only interesting thing about his house, which was red brick, flat, and long, decorated only with gray shingles and white gutters. Compared to it, our stone cottage with its brown-and-white Tudor top looked even more charming. Instead of a cheap fence, we had a stone wall that ran from our garage to the side of the house, blocking off our backyard entirely.

I liked the solid castle feel of our house. Stone was good, too, because it did not need repairing. Even my mother could not worry about rotting or peeling or termites.

Mr. Cleary's pool was too turquoise, and I turned away from it. I imagined once upon a time he had thought his boy would enjoy swimming and now there was only a boy in the house for four days out of the month. I had never seen him or Mr. Cleary or anyone else in that pool. It was a waste, having a pool when you didn't even swim, and it was more of a waste to spend time scooping out all the leaves and bugs, and why would anyone keep their pool filled up in December?

"Nothing's wrong," I said.

"You keep pulling at your shorts," he said. "It's not a wasp, is it?"

"You're a little obsessed with wasps," I said, and he seemed to think that was funny.

"At least I don't have one up my shorts."

It was a stupid joke.

"I don't have a wasp up my shorts," I said. "They're just too short, and if Mom sees me wearing them in front of you—"

"In front of me," he repeated. He nodded once, and then he turned away, reaching for his garden hose.

"I just mean my shorts are too short," I said.

I was aware that I had implied something I didn't mean to imply, and I wasn't even sure what it was.

"I'm not what you would call a fashion critic," said Mr. Cleary, drawing up the slack on the hose and looping it over his hand.

"I know," I said. "Mom just thinks—"

"I know what she thinks," he said, not looking at me. "She thinks you should be careful. Like every mother before her. And you think she's unfair and doesn't really love you, like every teenage girl before you."

"I don't think that," I said. The man didn't even know how to work a garden hose.

"No?"

"Did they teach you that in grown-up man school where every man your age sits in a row and thinks exactly the same thing?" I said. "The seven commandments of girls? No teenage girl shall trust her mother? All teenage girls shall have the same brain?"

It was not, actually, me who said any of that. I was sure of it as soon as the words left my mouth. I yanked at my shorts.

"Were you just referencing *Animal Farm*?" Mr. Cleary said.

"No," I said. "Kind of."

"Well, you're right. I was unfair."

I backed away, feeling for the latch on the iron gate. Overhead, I thought I saw a movement in the wasp nest.

"Sorry," I said. "I've had—I didn't mean to be rude."

He shrugged. "I wouldn't call it rude as much as—"

I didn't hear the end of his sentence, partly because he took a long time finishing it—if he ever did finish it—and partly because I had hurried through the gate, waving over my shoulder. I was full of too many things, and I wasn't sure what might come pouring out next.

The gate clanged behind me, and then there was no more Mr. Cleary. There was only stone wall and crispy brown grass and ivy. The cobblestones stretched from my feet to the back door, and I leaped across them. For as long as I could remember, I'd made a point to avoid the grass growing between the cracks. I landed on stones and only stones, and I avoided the far right one that had split down the middle. I reached the single brick step, and I stood there with my hand on the screen door. Even on the best of days, I felt a shift when I took the first step inside our house: I spun myself, like a Lazy Susan, and the person I was in the outside world moved out of reach. I became a Rachel who looked for signs and portents. A Rachel who studied her mother's face and plotted her next move.

I could feel myself spinning, as familiar as the rhythm of hopping the cobblestones, and I hated it.

I did not want to watch my step.

I pushed through the door, and the tinsel rippled on the Christmas tree in the corner. The colored lights were woven too deeply into the branches, weak flickers of blue-green-red-yellow. Mom sat on the edge of the sofa, one knee bent, toes resting on the coffee table. She didn't even look up. Her legs were slick with lotion, and she pulled her plastic orange razor steadily up her calf. Ankle to knee, ankle to knee.

I turned down the volume on the TV, and that made her look at me.

"What are you doing wearing those?" she asked. "It's fifty degrees outside, for heaven's sake, and those shorts—"

"She won't even talk to me," I said.

"Rachel, you look like—"

"Why did you tell her to stay away from me?"

Mom lifted her razor. She held it in the air.

"You need to ask me why?" she said. "You must have heard every word I said to her. You went by anyway, I guess? After I told you that you were not allowed. You lied directly to me and told me you were going to Tina's."

She pumped more Vaseline Intensive Care into her hand, slicked up her leg, and started over. This was part of her routine. Every night she shaved each leg at least four times. Sometimes she did it for an hour or more; she said she found it relaxing, even though her skin would streak red. I preferred when she did it in her bedroom behind a closed door.

"You don't get to tell me I can't see her," I said.

"I do get to tell you that."

"No," I said. I took a step closer. "You can't lock me inside the house and slide food under my door and keep me from seeing anyone. I have a car. I'm not some little girl you can drag around."

"And that's why I spoke to Lucia," she said. "I knew she'd respect my wishes, even if you don't. I'm your mother. It's my job to protect you."

It was the first time I'd ever thought my mother and Lucia sounded alike.

The lotion had soaked in completely, and the razor scraped against her skin. I could hear each hissing stroke. It was getting dark outside, and the moths thudded against the window.

You can't do this, I thought, only it was not a thought. It was a pounding in my head. This was worse than gunshots.

"You're not doing it to protect me," I said.

The blade sliced into her. She sucked in a breath, but she didn't move her leg. I watched the blood drip into the dent of her ankle, splattering on the polished wood of the coffee table and on the floor.

"Look what you made me do," she said.

Her nightgown had slipped off one shoulder, and I could see her nipple. This was a woman who practically hung upside down in front of a mirror before she left the house, making sure not the least bit of cleavage showed, not that she had cleavage. I could see her rib bones through the V of her gown. She hated even the slightest curve of her breasts to show through her blouses.

She spent all day covering herself up, but at home she'd wander naked from the shower to the den, not even bothering to wear a towel. As if I weren't even there.

I made sure never to be naked in front of her.

"*You* did it," I said. "You cut yourself. Why do you always make it someone else's fault? Why are you always just sitting there, some poor pitiful thing who has things happen to her?"

She straightened her knee then, more blood running down her long pale leg, and it was hard not to stare. Her legs were pretty, of course, and you could still see that she'd done ballet all through college, but there was also something beautiful about the blood.

"I am your mother," she said, finally tugging her nightgown back into place. "You do not speak to me like that. Do you hear me?"

"Yes," I said, raising my voice. "I hear you."

"You will not speak to me like that."

I thought of what Lucia once said about everyone having a need for conflict. I wondered if when he lived in the house with us, my father had filled my mother's need for conflict. I wondered if anyone else living in the house might at least spread the conflict around. Because most of the time it felt like Mom was waiting for me to hit a hidden trip wire, like in a war movie, only she's the one who would explode. Usually my anger couldn't match hers—no emotion of mine could ever match hers—but at this second I thought it might.

She picked up the razor again, and I heard it rasp along her thigh, and I hated the sound. I hated the sound of her razor and I hated the smell of her nail polish remover and I hated how her hair spray got in my eyes, and she did all of it right in front of me, no matter what I said, and it turned out that I did have a need for conflict.

"Well, why?" I asked. "Why do you get to be my mother? I didn't have any say in it."

She stood up in one smooth motion and threw her razor. I felt the wind of it across my cheek before it bounced off the television set and landed in the red basket full of magazines, and it was such a flimsy, tiny thing that it would have been funny, except it wasn't.

Her arm hung there in the air, frozen after her throw. She looked like she was casting some terrible spell. I watched her stiff arm, the bulging veins in her hand, and I thought of the last time she'd tried to hit me. I'd been ten years old, and she'd grabbed the hairbrush from the counter and raised it to smack my knuckles, always her favorite spot, but I'd caught the brush instead, jerking it away from her. We'd stared at each other, breathing hard, and she never hit me again, but I could tell she missed it.

"We can't pick," she said. "I love you more than anything in this world, and if something happened to you, it would kill me. You don't care about that, I know. But I would do anything for you and you know it. I will not let you run around with someone who has an assassin after her. You could die. Do you even understand that? Lucia did. She didn't even argue with me. Do you understand that you could have gone over there and never come home and laid there bleeding on the floor and I wouldn't have been there? I wouldn't have been able to do anything?"

Her eyes were wet, but her face was dry except for the Pond's. She stared at me, her arm still reaching, fingers splayed.

I thought I had seen every possible feeling on her face, but I was slow to recognize this one. Terror. She hadn't moved her arm yet because she couldn't. She didn't look like a magician. She looked like my grandfather after his last stroke, when he was lying in the hospital bed and couldn't even roll himself over.

"Mom," I said.

She dropped her arm and it slapped against her smooth leg. Now the tears were falling.

"I would do anything for you," she said again, her voice shaking. She swallowed. "It doesn't matter if you think I'm stupid or pathetic. It doesn't matter."

Every time I was close to hating her, she made me hate myself instead.

I thought about what Mr. Cleary had said about girls thinking their mothers didn't love them. I hadn't been lying to him. I knew Mom loved me. She loved me more than anything. She loved me too much.

She grabbed her lotion and her towel and her plastic tumbler of water, which sloshed all over the carpet. She marched into the kitchen—again, almost funny—and I heard the tumbler land with a clatter in the already full sink. I waited for her to come back into view. I was staring at the kitchen table, cluttered with mail and receipts and boxes of Lipton tea, when something blurred through the air and smashed against the lemon wallpaper. I knew it was glass by the sound of shattering.

A juice glass, I guessed. Hard to tell, unless I stepped closer to the broken pieces.

I could hear the air coming through my nose. I'd been having trouble with loud noises. I watched the kitchen and waited to see if there would be more. I was always waiting to see if there would be more. It had been a while since the last explosion—nearly a year ago? A ceramic potted plant that scattered soil and roots all over the patio. Once it had been a gravy boat, and, as Mom swept up the pieces, she'd said that we never used it anyway.

Now she strode into the den, empty handed, straight backed.

"Don't go in the kitchen barefoot," she said as she brushed past me, keeping her face turned away.

I watched her walk down the hall, talking under her breath, nightgown slipping off her shoulder again. My head was full of words, and maybe that's why she talked to herself, because she had to let the words out somehow. But as I whispered there in the middle of the den, the smell of lotion around me, it wasn't my mother I was talking to. It wasn't even myself.

You don't understand, I said. That's what I wished I had been able to say to Lucia. *You don't know her at all. You think she's the person you see in your front yard, but you can't see her when the moths come. You think she's scared, and she is, but that doesn't mean she's weak. You think she's powerless, but she's got all the power in this house and sometimes I think if I don't get out of here, there won't be anything left of me.*

I thought of Mom's face, terrified. Her arm, paralyzed.

And I was just like her. Frozen. I looked at the blood on the carpet, and I knew I should go grab a paper towel or maybe a broom, but I only stood there.

※ **1982** ※

Rachel

I.

I didn't exactly dislike Tamara Vance, but I avoided her if possible. She was round and soft and big chested, and while I didn't hold that against her, when the boys asked her to jump up and down, she accommodated them, pretending she didn't understand why they asked.

When I saw her at Tina's party, "Rock Lobster" was playing too loud on the stereo, and there was that *down, down, down* part where everyone wiggled themselves to the floor. Tamara jumped off the sofa, giggling.

"What?" she asked, falling onto one knee, her jean miniskirt barely keeping things covered.

"Going down," said a boy named Travis, and everyone laughed, including Tamara.

Several other boys were dancing, holding their noses and swimming down to the floor. One of them jumped off the coffee table.

"Why did the Auburn fan get fired from the M&M factory?" Travis called out over the music. "Because he kept throwing out all the Ws."

Tamara climbed back onto the sofa. It made me angry how hard she tried to please them. Did she think that because the boys liked her boobs, they liked her? Because they didn't even like her boobs. They just liked the physics of them.

"Go-o-o-o-iiiiing down," I heard Tamara say, and I turned away before she jumped.

"What's faster than a black guy stealing your television?" Travis said, barely pausing. "His brother with your stereo."

I usually reached this stage of disappointment at a party. I started out having a decent time and then everyone got drunker and then some people got naked and some people got stupid and some people got unconscious, and I started regretting going to the trouble of lying to Mom in the first place.

The lying was a new experiment. No other eleventh grader I knew had a 10:00 p.m. curfew on the weekends, and I was done with it. I was done with plenty of things. The dishonesty had gone well so far: on this particular night, I'd told Mom I was having a sleepover with Tina, and that was true. Granted, Tina was on the patio doing Jell-O shots with a couple of her brother's college friends, but eventually she would be asleep and so would I.

I headed down the hallway, careful not to nudge open any doors. You did not want to glance inside a bedroom at this time of night. I was aiming for the end of the hall and the room that belonged to Tina's oldest brother, the one who'd graduated college last year. He'd moved his old bed and dresser to his new apartment, so his empty bedroom had turned into the place where everyone dumped their purses and jackets.

The door wasn't closed. I stepped into the quiet room. The purses were lined up against the wall, and the coats were piled in the corner in a way that made me want to jump into the middle of them. I'd borrowed a black halter top from Tina, which possibly made me look like a stripper, and besides that, I was freezing. I missed sleeves.

I was studying the coats when John came in. Even from the corner of my eye, I recognized the dark-green shirt he'd been wearing. I wondered if he'd followed me, but that was ridiculous.

"Do you ever get tired of being the only one who doesn't drink?" he asked.
I turned toward him.

He wasn't wrong. I'd had a sip of someone else's beer a couple of times, but
nothing more than that. I didn't drink. I didn't swear. I didn't do anything.
I'd never let a single boy put his tongue in my mouth or his hand up my shirt,
although that was possibly related to the lack of beer. Mom had taught me
well. Once you started something, there was no telling where it might go.
What if something happened? What if someone saw?

"Do you?" I asked. He sometimes had a beer or two, but for a guy that was
the same as not drinking.

"It's more fun to watch everyone else," he said, leaning against the doorframe. "Why are you staring at the coats?"

"I'm bored," I said, and thought about our English teacher's instructions
for writing a college essay. She told us to do more than convey basic information. She said that if we wanted to be chosen, we needed to be distinctive.

"I was thinking of how they're like a pile of leaves," I added. "It would be
a soft landing."

"Huh," he said, rubbing his chin. His jaw looked like it could have been
drawn onto a cartoon superhero. "I feel like the purses have more potential.
We could build something. Like a maze."

He picked up a small, neat bag, shiny blue and zipped.

"A purse maze?" I said. "Not very challenging. You need high walls for a
good maze."

He did not seem to mind the criticism. We discussed purse pyramids and
purse juggling, and we landed on purse bowling. It happened so quickly, the
shift from communing with coats to holding up my end of this unexpected
weirdness. We arranged the purses into a triangle, and the whole time I had
to keep one hand across my chest to make sure I stayed inside my halter.

Once we had all the purses standing on their sides, precarious, we counted
our paces and marked a starting spot with someone's plaid scarf. We kept the
rectangular blue purse for our bowling ball. John waved for me to go first,

and I took two steps back and sent the purse tumbling through the air, skimming the carpet before it smacked into a denim, an Esprit, and one massive gold lamé.

I got a spare.

He got a split.

A few throws later, I managed to bounce the blue purse under the one remaining piece of furniture in the room, a small bedside table with a flower-patterned ceramic lamp like something my grandmother might have. I could see why Tina's brother hadn't taken it with him.

I dropped to my knees and reached under the table, and as the carpet nubs came close to my face, I remembered lying on Lucia's floor with her elbow against my spine, her hair in my face. My cheek had been pressed into the carpet, my hand under the dining-room table. I'd felt only carpet at first, but then I'd latched onto something hard, and it was a pencil, the small eraserless kind you use to score putt-putt, and I'd been thinking, *Wait, Lucia and Evan play putt-putt?* as more glass fell from the window. I was still holding the pencil in my hand when the shooting stopped. I didn't let go of it until I got in my car.

After that first shot, Lucia had reached for me and pushed me down, and her hand curved around my head and her body covered mine.

It had been nearly three months, and I never thought about Lucia anymore. I didn't wonder whether she liked the B-52's or whether she'd ever worn halter tops. I didn't imagine her response to Travis and his racist jokes. I didn't construct entire conversations where I told her about my history teacher kissing boys on their birthday or about Aunt Molly setting her kitchen on fire. I didn't ever replay that afternoon when we'd stood in a laundry room facing a man who could have been a murderer or worse and how she'd looked at me across the linoleum, of how something joyful flashed across her face like *Watch this* before she forced that man backward through his own kitchen. I didn't think of how she'd slashed and burned at Oak Park, like I was the only thing that mattered, but how clearly I didn't matter at all.

I didn't think about any of it.

At first I had thought about it. I had thought, maybe, a phone call. I had thought, maybe, a letter. Some nice words for me to fold up and keep. For weeks I checked the mailbox before Mom got home, but after a while I stopped checking.

My cheek on the carpet, her hand on my head. I told myself that if she'd been killed, it would have been on the news.

"You okay?" said John, and I stood up, the blue purse in my hand. I sidestepped to the scarf, lining up my toes.

"You fouled," he said. "You don't get your second shot."

"There are no fouls in bowling."

"Well, there are in purse bowling, sweetheart," he said, and I was sure he had never called me sweetheart.

We wound up sitting on the floor, backs against the wall, sweating. He sat close enough that our elbows touched. Then his knee fell toward me, landing against mine, teepee shaped.

I felt a sort of carbonation run through me. Happiness, I thought, and I had not felt much of that in a long while. I'd escaped my house—oh, the transformative power of lies—but the parties were not so much better, and everything still felt wrong, and I didn't fit, quite.

But this.

It turned out I had been hoping for his knee against mine. I had hoped for some scene exactly like this, and now it was happening, so what I was feeling was surely excitement, only possibly it was nausea. Mom was always eager for me to procure a boyfriend, but she was emphatic that you did not let boys touch you, that if you did they would think the wrong thing, and what was he thinking and also what was I thinking?

John leaned toward me, and I had a moment to choose, but was I really choosing? I didn't move. He put a hand on my thigh.

His face, close. Stubble I'd never noticed on the hard angles of his chin.

His hand on my thigh, tightening, and he would think I wanted sex, surely, he would think—he would think—I would have to tell him no, and would he expect it—would he hate me—was this the time to tell him no?

Was there a right moment? Had I missed it, like missing that one beat where you can catch the double Dutch jump ropes just right?

I hadn't said a word.

He smiled, and I didn't even know this boy, did I? But dimples and purses and his hand on my thigh, moving higher, and this was not excitement, this was terror. Paralysis.

I lifted my hand and grabbed his head, too hard probably. I pulled him closer, and his lips smashed against mine. His mouth opened, so mine did, too. I was a thinking, moving part of this, whatever it was.

Too much thinking. I was expecting more lips and less tongue and teeth. His tongue felt like an oyster, room temperature, wet and thick. Sliding. He turned his head, and I turned my head, and his hand landed on my waist. I liked the heat of that hand, and best of all, it distracted me from his tongue. He leaned over me, pushing me sideways, my elbows digging into the carpet. My head tilted. John latched on to my lip, and then there was less tongue and the angle changed, and the kiss became less oysterish.

Good. It became good. He made a sound, and I liked it.

My thoughts turned off, for a while. I enjoyed the weight of him as he settled on me, one leg between mine. His hand slid down my naked back and over my butt, grabbing hold of it and pulling me against him, and I liked that, too. I could hear both of us breathing. I could feel his penis against my thigh. Penis. The word whirled me away into my head again, thinking of synonyms, of other girls who had talked in whispers, and I thought again that this was a language I didn't know, that I might answer some question the wrong way. I had been led to believe that boys transformed once a penis got involved. They lost control. I imagined werewolves, fingers curving into claws and chins contorting into snouts. John's hips shifted against me, and I worked my hands between us, pushing at his chest. It took two shoves, but he rolled off me partially, his hip settling on the floor.

"Okay?" he asked, smiling. He still looked like John.

"Yeah," I said. "But I don't want to, you know, do a lot more than—"

"Bowl?" he asked.

I laughed. It made a difference.

"Maybe more bowling?" he said.

He was a nice boy, and I nodded. He pressed himself against me again, his lips on mine. His hand slid under my silky shirt, up and up, barely grazing the bare underside of my breast, because obviously I couldn't wear a bra with this thing.

This was not terror. I pushed back against him. I felt his back flex under my hands, and I wanted my hands under his shirt.

The door banged open. I jerked away, and John moved, too, but much more slowly than I did. Tamara and Taylor stood in the doorway, a bottle of something clear between them. They had red Solo cups in their hand.

"At least you had your clothes on," said Taylor, his arm around Tamara, squeezing. I could see her pale-blue bra strap, too tight, cutting into her skin.

I felt my face heat up, and the blush embarrassed me as much as being wrapped around John. And cutting through the embarrassment, I thought, *Taylor Boatwright is making out with Tamara in front of everyone? He is so going to regret it tomorrow.*

Taylor held out the bottle. "Want some?"

"I put it in Seven-Up," Tamara said, looking at me, her face round and pretty and needing to please. "You'll want to mix it with something."

I shook my head.

"I don't know," said John, his hand still on my thigh where everyone could see it, and I wasn't sure if that was good or bad.

What if something happened? What if someone noticed?

"Rachel?" he prompted.

"What?" I asked.

He scooted me closer to him, his arm lifting from my leg and settling around my shoulders, and I had seen endless boys do this with endless girls, and I had wanted it. More than I wanted the kissing. I relaxed against him, and I thought about what I wanted.

"I will if you will," he said. "One shot each?"

Tamara giggled. She was propped against Taylor, unsteady. John ran his hand down my bare arm, and goose bumps rose all the way to my wrists. The pleasure of that touch knocked the fear out of me.

The purses were scattered across the floor, like they'd hailed down from the cottage-cheese ceiling. I thought of Lucia, her feet hitting the sidewalk, crushing pinecones, never a pause. I thought of the ducks in Oak Park, startled, as she called out to strangers. Never afraid of anything.

"Yes or no?" said Taylor, and his voice was slurred.

"It's up to you," John said.

He nudged me, jarring me loose, and that was a good thing. Taylor held out the bottle, and John reached for it. I put my hand above the waistband of his jeans and felt the muscles of his back stretching, and I could do anything I wanted.

11.

I wasn't an idiot.

I settled behind my steering wheel, letting my head fall back against the headrest. Eventually the overhead light went off, and I was left in the almost-dark and the almost-quiet: I could still hear the stereo playing inside Tina's house.

I had never been so happy to shut myself inside my hideous old-lady car. It had been smelling inexplicably of bananas, but now the familiar, sickly sweet smell was almost welcome. The pattern of my seats reminded me of ice cream sandwiches, and I ran my finger over the shallow holes. I did not want to drink whatever was in that bottle, and I did not want to get naked with John, at least not in the middle of an empty bedroom surrounded by purses and jean jackets. Really, if he wanted to get naked with me, he could at least ask me on a date, and why hadn't he done that anyway?

I could do anything I wanted. I had no one to ask me where I was going or what I was doing, and I didn't want to waste that time drinking awful liquor or trying to decipher John Henderson. So I'd left.

I was going to Lucia's. Maybe she would be asleep, and maybe she would be watching TV or reading a book, and maybe I would tap on the window and she would wave me inside and she would be so glad to see me.

I didn't think that would happen. It was nearly midnight.

Still. I had not looked into her den in months. I could at least look. That would be enough. And if Lucia were sitting there on the sofa, it would be a sign, wouldn't it?

The streets were nearly empty, and it must have rained earlier because the roads were black and shining wet. I had never driven this late at night, and the city looked different with the houses dark, the shadows dense, and the streetlights reflecting off the pavement. I'd found a new world hidden behind the old one, like Narnia inside the wardrobe.

By the time I reached Lucia's street, I was assessing logistics. More than once she'd heard my car door slam, and she'd spotted me through the front window before I made it up the driveway. I didn't want to give her a warning tonight—I wanted to be the one deciding what to do. I parked several houses down from hers at a rose-brick ranch where every window was dark. My winter coat spent most of its time wadded up in my backseat, but I didn't want to face Lucia with my cleavage on display, so I grabbed the coat and buttoned it over my halter top.

The air was cold and electric as I eased the car door shut. I didn't rush. If anyone was looking, I didn't want them to see a suspicious girl running down the sidewalk. I moved slowly enough that I couldn't hear my own footsteps. The stars were bright overhead, and the street was completely silent. Even the leaves on the trees were still.

I was two houses away from Lucia's when headlights flared along the pavement, and at the same time I heard music thumping. I glanced behind me, and I could see the headlights coming toward me fast. I couldn't make out anything about the car, but the music was so loud—"Elvira"?—that the windows must have been rolled down. The car veered into the other lane, and quickly corrected, but that swerve left me nervous. Who was out at this time of night, playing loud country music and drifting into the wrong lane?

The headlights came closer.

They'll drive by, I told myself. They'll drive by. And yet I thought of a few months earlier, when Tina had been bringing me back to my dad's after we'd gone to a late movie—Dad never gave me a curfew—and some guys in a pickup truck started honking. They pulled up next to us and shouted through the window, but we didn't want to know what they were saying. Tina sped up, and the truck dropped behind us, riding our bumper all the way down the Southern Bypass to Dad's house, even pulling into the driveway behind us. We ran to the front door, praying it was unlocked, which it was. The truck backed into the road and sped away, but Tina and I kept wondering—What if we hadn't gotten inside? What then?

I thought of my mother. *Anyone could be out at this time of night,* she'd told me in my roller-skating days. *You could be kidnapped or crammed in a van or who knows what.* It had been the things she wouldn't name that scared her.

As the light from the headlights spread across the street, I lunged behind a Jeep parked in the closest driveway. Hunching over, I balanced on the balls of my feet and told myself no one ever had to know that I'd thrown myself to the ground just because of a car coming down the street. Or maybe they would know: maybe tomorrow I'd tell everyone about how I'd been such a baby, terrified of headlights and a few *giddy-up-a-oom-poppa-oom-poppa-mow-mows,* and it would be hilarious, this picture of myself.

I couldn't see anything but the Jeep, the dark glass of the taillights and the grimy rubber of the bumper. I could see light, though, spilling under the car.

The car had slowed down, and I knew they'd seen me. The music shut off.

I heard their voices. Boys. They were still in the car, and one of them was laughing. I waited for a door to open. I waited for them to get out. I waited for them to come for me. My breath caught, and I choked on nothing but air.

"I thought she—" one of them said.

"Did you—"

I couldn't make out all the words. It was worse because I could only imagine how to fill in the gaps.

More laughing.

I peeked around the bumper. The car was stopped in the middle of the road. Surely they would pull over and park. I was no more than ten steps away, so easy to find, and it was foolish to stay here, practically trapped between the Jeep and the garage door.

I could run. If they were going to come for me, I should run, and I should scream, and someone would help me. Lucia and Evan would help me, even. But the boys were still in the car, and once I moved, they might catch me before anyone could come, or too, they might drive off and I would be running and screaming through people's front yards for no reason and everyone would throw open their doors and see me, and that was a whole different kind of fear.

I did nothing.

I kept my head down, and my thighs started to tremble. Maybe the boys suspected I'd gone inside the house. Maybe they'd seen my shadow, but they'd thought I was a fox or a deer or something else worth spotting, and now they were sitting there, harmless, hoping for a flash of yellow eyes in the dark. A thousand things were possible, and some of them were terrible and some of them were fine, but all I could do was wait and keep quiet. Was this how my mother felt every single day?

The music came back, full volume. One of the Oak Ridge Boys singing about how his heart was on fire.

The engine revved, and the driver hit the gas hard enough that the tires squealed. Then the driveway went dark again, and they were gone.

I stayed where I was for a little while. Breathing. When I stood, I watched the road. They had probably been my age, I told myself. The worst they would have done was to make some comment about my butt. They'd have asked if I wanted to go for a ride and they'd have hooted at me when I said no.

That's what would have happened.

The streets were empty again. I was steps away from Lucia's. Now the idea of peering through the glass and seeing her there, sunk into the couch, seemed so necessary that I was sure I would find that exact scene. I would tell her what happened, and she would bring me a ginger ale.

I didn't get to the window. I didn't get to the carport. I only got as far as the edge of the yard, which is when I saw the FOR SALE sign.

I stared at it for longer than I should have, as if there could be some explanation other than that Lucia and Evan were going to move. The sign said FOR SALE, not SOLD, but there wasn't much difference. She was leaving. She would leave and I would have no idea where she was going, and she would be gone.

Lucia was not longing for me to knock on her door. She was, actually, arranging it so I would never knock on her door again.

Lucia

1.

As usual during the first rounds of March Madness, every chair and stool in Rhonda's was filled. Glass bowls of peanuts and pretzels lined the bar. The lights were low and the smoke was heavy. The TV screens flashed above the liquor shelves, reflecting off the gloss of the bar. It was a massive slab of blond and dark wood, which conveniently matched beer and pretzels almost exactly.

"Settle down," said Evan, raising his palms to the television. "Still plenty of time."

Lucia didn't agree. It was looking like Ohio State was going to crash and burn in the first round, and James Madison was miraculously going to head to the Sweet Sixteen.

"They need bigger TVs," Evan said. "You can't hear worth a damn in here. Yes! Did you see that? Did you see it?"

Clark Kellogg had hit a shot, but it was surely too little, too late. Neither he nor the other guy—Campbell—showed any signs of getting hot, and it was the fourth quarter.

"I did," Lucia said. "I'm sitting right here next to you. And you can never hear anything in Rhonda's."

Evan was doing that thing he did with his palms, rubbing them against the bar, back and forth. Lucia supposed he found it soothing, but she had seen the rags that the bartender used to wipe down the wood, and she hoped Evan didn't intend to put his hands on her next.

She looked down at her napkin, where she had sketched out various squares and words and diagonal lines. None of it meant anything, but sometimes a pencil in her hand helped her think. Sometimes a crowded bar helped her think. You could never tell. Sara Conway was sure that her husband was having an affair, and she didn't seem like the hallucinatory type. But the bank statement and credit card records didn't show any of the usual red flags. No large sums of money being withdrawn. No secret credit card or unexplained trips for two.

Still. It was possible that she hadn't gotten the angle quite right yet.

The couple sitting next to her stood, the wooden legs of the chairs squawking. The woman bent down for her purse, and her elbow caught Lucia in the thigh.

The woman apologized profusely, and Lucia resituated her own purse in her lap. She felt the distinctive weight of the pistol shift, so different than the heft of her wallet and checkbook. She watched Evan's hand slide across the pretzel-spattered wood, reaching for her drink.

"Not your usual," he said, taking a swallow.

"I know," she said. "For some reason I wanted something sweet. Diet Coke and rum sounded good."

"It's not Diet Coke," he said, turning back to the screen. Or maybe he'd never turned away from it. "It's regular."

"What?" she said. "No, it's not. I ordered Diet."

His head bobbed slightly in time with a dribble down the court.

"Well," he said, "the bartender must've heard you wrong, because he poured you regular. I watched him. You were drawing on your napkin."

She tested her drink, letting it roll around her mouth. She tasted rum and melted ice and who knew which kind of Coke it was?

"Why didn't you say something?" she asked.

At the end of the bar, three large men and one large woman in matching Tennessee T-shirts screamed in harmony.

"I thought you must have ordered it," Evan said.

"I never order regular Coke," she said.

He watched the screen.

She tried to end it there. She had learned one of the great lessons of marriage during their first month. Her parents had come for dinner, and she was cooking and setting the table. All that was needed was for someone to ask them if they'd like tea or water when they walked through the door, and Evan hadn't done it. So she'd had to stop simultaneously stirring pasta and slicing tomatoes and buttering the garlic bread, and she had fixed the drinks while he sat chatting on the sofa as if he were a guest, too, and she was so angry she could hardly unclench her hands from the tea glasses. She didn't turn on him then only because her parents were in the room, and by the time they left, she wasn't angry anymore. The next morning she told him, "Do you know how I was running around cooking and you were sitting there with my parents? It would have been really helpful if you'd offered them drinks." And he'd said, "Oh. Sure. I can see that. I'll start doing drinks when people come over."

She'd told herself, ah, this was good to know. Wait until the anger passes. Don't attack.

"Evan," she said now, "I have never ordered a regular Coca-Cola in the whole time you've known me. Not once. I only like Diet."

"I figured that's what you wanted this time."

"I have never ordered one," she said again.

He did not seem to realize what he had revealed. Was it possible that—all these years—he had paid so little attention? She had always felt so sure that no one had ever known her as deeply and as well as he had, but could that be true if he had these sorts of gaps? Had he never bothered to know her at all?

It would make these past months make so much more sense.

"It's just a Coke, Lucia," he said. "Order another drink."

She shoved her drink away. It sloshed over the sides, and she blotted at the spill with her napkin.

Another missed shot by Ohio State. The far corner of the bar groaned, bottles slamming against wood. On screen, the Buckeyes trudged back down the court, clearly knowing it was over.

"Campbell needs to get his head in the game," said the play-by-play guy. "Right now James Madison just wants it more."

Lucia hated that kind of stupid talk. As if a player's main flaw was a lack of desire. As if simple wanting made a thing happen. She imagined Campbell wanted to win this game desperately. She imagined he was thinking about nothing but making his shots, and yet the shots weren't falling, and sometimes you had days like that, and thank God in real life announcers didn't follow you around rendering judgment.

Evan rubbed his palms against the bar.

She wanted to get her head in the game. She wanted to feel what she used to feel.

II.

It was one of the first jolts of true spring, a spike to seventy degrees when the winter coats were still hanging by the door. The weather wouldn't last, but it was the sort of tease that made Alabama a good place to be in March.

Lucia stretched her legs, her toes touching the grass. She could feel the wrought-iron pattern of the chair embossed on the backs of her thighs, but she didn't mind it. She listened to the leaves gossip.

"We could go out," said Paula, slicking more baby oil on her smooth brown arms. Evan's sister had the skin Lucia had always wanted. "Seriously, you don't have to cook."

"It's all done," Lucia answered. "Just finger foods. Nothing fancy. Watson's fine with cheese and crackers, right? Apple slices?"

"He eats anything," Paula said. "Except blueberries. And onions."

"No pretzels," said Watson.

The three-year-old looked up from his place in the grass, where he had been hunting a grasshopper. He laid a hand on his mother's knee, then let it trail down her oil-slick calf.

"You're wet," he said accusingly.

"I don't like pretzels, either," Lucia told him.

"They smell like gym floor," Watson said.

He turned back to his bug, sand-colored hair falling over his face. Soon enough he jerked, toppling backward, catching himself on his elbows. He'd had the same reaction every other time the grasshopper hopped. He hunched over again, his face low to the ground. The grasshopper would probably blind him next time.

Lucia slid down farther in her seat, watching. Watson recoiled again. Paula shifted, her rickety lawn chair squeaking: the plastic bands of the seat were frayed, dipping under her weight. Lucia hoped it held. The martins were in the trees, chattering, and the Chapmans next door were outside. The parents stood by the grill, dickering over some charcoal issue, while the two high school girls batted a volleyball back and forth without a net.

"Sharks can have fifteen rows of teeth," said Watson. "They lose teeth every week."

"He has a book," Paula said. "Where's Evan? How long does it take to give the dog some food?"

"He probably misplaced his glasses," Lucia said. "Or his glass of water. Those are the big two."

"Remoras suck onto sharks like hitchhikers," Watson said.

The lavender blooms on the Japanese tulip tree were like cupped hands raised to the sky. Elegant geometries. Evan once told her that tulip trees were actually a type of magnolia. That had been back when this house was bare except for cardboard boxes and Hefty bags, and she'd been standing on this same patch of grass swigging ice water from a coffee cup because the glasses weren't unpacked yet. She hadn't believed him at first. She was well-acquainted with magnolias—*genteel,* her mother called them. *Don't they just make you picture those beautiful old plantations?* Lucia had grown up loving the density of their branches: they were good climbing trees. Now she looked at the tree in front of her and remembered Evan's pronouncement. Sometimes your idea of a thing did not match the reality of it. That could be a welcome surprise or not so welcome. At any rate, there was nothing genteel about this magnolia. It was exotic. Unexpected.

The most beautiful tree she had ever seen happened to be in her own yard.

The sun and the breeze and Watson's ramblings were lovely, too. The azaleas were exploding in pinks and reds all along the back fence. She waved at the girls next door, who had come close, chasing their ball. They waved back, but then they spotted Watson and waved much more enthusiastically. He noticed.

"Why are those girls looking at me?" he asked loudly. It made the girls double their efforts.

"What girls?" asked Paula, turning, nearly tipping over her ancient chair. "Oh. Hey there!"

"They think you're cute," Lucia said.

"I am cute," Watson said.

Paula laughed, but Lucia didn't. She looked at his wide feet and his smooth curved cheeks—everything on him soft and round, perfectly designed to elicit affection. He knew that he was smart and good and loved, and that was not as common as she once thought it was.

She wished that she could shake the feeling that Evan had an agenda. That he had wanted to bring the child here to sway her.

"Maybe Evan's started getting the food together," she said. "I'll go check."

She unstuck her thighs from her chair and headed inside, making sure to close the sliding door behind her. The warm weather brought gnats. She heard cabinets opening and closing, and she knew she had been right.

"You think we're ready to eat?" she called.

"I thought I'd set out the cheese and crackers," Evan said.

She rounded the corner into the kitchen, and he was at the sink, washing off a cheese knife. "If we're doing that," she said, "we might as well do all of it. I've got the fruit in the fridge."

He wiped the knife with a hand towel. She didn't point out that the dish towel was hanging on the oven door.

"You don't have to do anything," he said. "If you'll tell me where stuff is, I can do it."

"I don't mind," she said.

She opened the refrigerator, pulling out the right bits and pieces of Tupperware.

"Can you believe he knows the word 'ophthalmoscope'?"

"I know," Lucia said.

"He's getting to the fun stage," Evan said. "Where he's not just a blob anymore. I don't like them as blobs as much as when they turn into actual people."

Lucia dropped bread into the toaster: she'd cut it into triangles to go with the shrimp spread. She spotted the tomatoes still crammed in their wooden basket—she would slice them. She had onions, too, and maybe a cucumber.

"Why did you ask them over?" she asked.

Evan had his back to her, reaching for a platter on one of the higher shelves. "What do you mean?" he said. "We haven't seen them in weeks."

"It feels like you're trying to—" She had gotten this far, and she was committed now. "Sell me. It feels like you're trying to sell me."

"Sell you on what?"

"Watson."

He pulled out the Desert Rose plates one at a time, slower than necessary. She heard each one clink as it joined the stack.

"It feels like you're trying to convince me," she said. "Like you're hoping— you're hoping—"

He finally turned toward her, and she realized she had misread him. He was not ignoring her. He was not trying to draw her out more by keeping quiet. He was furious.

"Like I'm hoping you'll tie on an apron and stay home and have babies?" he said. "You think I invited our nephew over here as some sort of ploy?"

"Are you telling me it didn't cross your mind?"

The toast sprang up, and Evan reached for it, tossing both pieces onto an empty plate. He blew on his fingers.

"It's like you're looking for a reason to be mad at me, Lucia," he said. "Like you're mad at me before I say a word."

He was not wrong about the anger. She knew that.

She had agreed to put the house up for sale. She had agreed to it even though there had been neither hide nor hair of the shooter. For all she knew, the psychopath had put a bullet in his own head as soon as he left their house. Regardless, if he had planned to follow up, surely he would have done so by now. And yet she had agreed that if a reasonable offer came in, she and Evan would relocate to some unknown destination, their names and number unlisted. *If it happened once, it could happen again,* Evan had said. *You're making it way too easy for someone to find you.* She had agreed to it—to all that needless effort and thought and expense—and yet she could still feel her husband holding himself back. Or maybe she was the one holding herself back. Sometimes it was impossible to tell.

"I feel the same way sometimes," she said.

"Like I'm looking for a reason to be mad?" he said. "I don't have to look. I have a reason. I want to keep you alive. And you seem less interested in that than I do. You're just—pretending."

She grabbed for a paper towel. Since they met, he had been the other half of her just like the movies promised. With other men, there'd been a part of her tucked away, watching, but Evan had reached every part of her and they had melted into a new thing.

Lately she had felt herself reforming again, separate.

"What do you want?" she asked. "What else do you want, I mean?"

"You know," he said.

"You asked me to think about it," she said. "I'm thinking about it."

"You're not really thinking about it."

"I don't want to join another practice," she said. "I don't want to go back to a bigger firm. I made my practice from scratch. It's mine. It took years, and you know all that."

"I don't know why it's such a huge difference if you join another firm. You'd be more secure in one of the buildings downtown with a front desk and a security guard. You'd still keep your own cases. You've had enough of-fers. You could go in as a partner."

"Like Garrison Langley offered to—"

"Don't do that." He dropped an elbow to the counter, and the toaster rattled behind him. "You're good at what you do. You know damn well that Garrison is the only one who ever offered you a job because he wanted sex."

She stared at him. The innards of the toaster were fading like a tuning fork.

"Okay," Evan said. "Not all of them offered a partnership because they wanted sex."

The laugh came out of her on an exhale. And just that quickly, the dis-tance between them almost vanished. There was always this moment in their fights—tightness and tension and then something like an orgasm without the lust. A release. It was almost worth the fight itself.

Evan reached for her, his hand heavy on her hip bone.

"I am good at what I do," she said.

"I know," he said. "We're saying the same thing."

She nodded, even though she knew it wasn't true.

III.

Lucia sat in the lobby, a green folder with the Conway deposition tucked under her arm, a vodka tonic in her hand, deciding whether to eat in the hotel restaurant or order room service. She was in no hurry to decide. The hotel had constructed a fake wilderness between the check-in desk and the restaurant, and she had chosen a seat in the shade of a rubber tree. Flower beds sprang from the carpet. A few inches from her feet, the turquoise water of an indoor stream wound all the way to the elevator bank, and ducks splashed nearby. Barry Manilow was playing on the hotel speakers. Every bit of it was false, and yet it was a scene well set.

A man stood underneath a different rubber tree. Dark haired and towering, gray pants and a white shirt unbuttoned at the throat, holding a glass of red wine. He caught her eye—she thought he caught her eye. Before Evan, she'd never dated a blonde or a man under six feet. With Evan she got the dark hair but not the height, not that it ever mattered.

She got this feeling in hotels occasionally. A remnant. She still—especially after a drink—could look across the potted ferns, see a man approaching, and remember when that sight set the gears into motion. It was distinctly different, the imagined relationship from the actual. That man walking toward you wasn't real, not in those first few seconds of forward motion. He was anything and everything, fill in the blanks, and then you married and you filled in the blanks. You never knew anyone as well as you knew the man you married, and that specificity was beautiful and deadening all at once.

The man with the red wine smiled at her. She appreciated the breadth of his chest.

She looked away, noticing the shamrocks sparkling along the front desk, each decoration as big as a basketball. She thought of how Rachel's St. Patrick's Day earrings hung nearly to her shoulders, green clovers glittering. It was a wonder that the girl's earlobes weren't stretched down to her chin. Last Halloween, Lucia had bought her a pair of light-up pumpkins that promised one hundred hours of battery life. Hopefully, they would still work this year.

A goldfish flashed through the stream at her feet.

She took a swallow of her drink, and she appreciated that it was more vodka than tonic. The man with the red wine had not moved.

She did not want or need a different man. Yet still she pictured him walking toward her. He would say, "Do you think the ducks are real?" or he would say "I wouldn't interrupt you if you were reading a book, but that looks like work." She would know that it was a line, but it would be a reasonably smart line, and he would bring up, oh, he would keep with the jungle theme and ask if she'd read any Jane Goodall, and they'd talk about *In the Shadow of Man*. At some stage he would mention grabbing a drink together, and she would say, "No, I'm sorry. I'm married." He would ask her to go for the drink anyway.

A hotel lobby opened up some sort of portal, a different life entirely.

She never fantasized about going up to a man's room. But she did imagine the drink. A brush of hand against hand, accident or strategy? In this alternate lobby world, she would slide her finger up the stem of her glass, and she would watch his eyes follow the movement. She would cross her legs, and her knee would touch his, and if the scenario managed to play through fully, it ended with her saying good night and leaving him there.

Even in her fantasies, she could not imagine anyone but Evan.

Still.

She sank more deeply into her armchair, and a duck, emerald headed, floated past. A second and third duck followed. She watched the flash of their orange feet as they paddled. She sipped away half her drink, and she did not think of unknown men but of the Conway case, which nagged at her because she still hadn't come up with any evidence of the husband's affair. She had come to Louisville to depose a former nanny who had seen both parents with their children. This nanny had helpful things to say about Sara Conway's warmth as a mother. She'd had nothing negative to say about Earl Conway, and that was fine.

Maybe there hadn't been an affair. Maybe Sara Conway had imagined it. But the truth was that her husband had left her, and when the man did the leaving, he usually had some other woman waiting.

Lucia glanced over, seeing a space where the tall man had been sitting, and even as she turned her head, a shadow fell across her lap. The shadow belonged to someone neither dark nor handsome. A round woman, waist overflowing her khaki slacks, stood by the arm of Lucia's chair. She wore a pin-striped shirt that identified her as staff, and her lipstick did not quite match the outline of her mouth. The woman held one arm close to her side, cradling several dinner rolls.

Seeing her, a duck sauntered up the concrete bank of the stream, teetering for a moment on the edge.

"They'll peck if you try to touch them," the woman said. "They're skittish."

"I wasn't going to touch them," Lucia answered.

The woman maneuvered a roll into her hand and began to break off bits of crust and toss them into the water. The duck slid back into the water, and others from all over the lobby started making their way toward the crumbs.

"You want to toss some?" the woman asked, offering her a roll.

"Okay," Lucia said, accepting it.

"They know me," the woman said. "I'm the only one who feeds them. I feed the koi, too. They love grapefruit. Did you know koi have back teeth?"

"You feed them grapefruit?" asked Lucia.

"I'm not supposed to feed them at all."

Another duck—pure white—scaled the concrete wall of the creek and stomped toward the woman's smudged Keds.

Lucia watched the ducks climb over one another, and she thought about diet. The nanny had mentioned that Earl Conway's mother was a nice old woman, good with the grandkids, and this was meant as a mark in Earl's favor. The nanny was a chatty sort of girl. She'd offered up that the grandmother had an ulcer, and almost everything upset her stomach. She ate a lot of cornbread and milk.

Lucia threw her bread, and it fell on the ducks like manna.

Earl Conway had started dutifully visiting his frail mother a few months ago, spending the night with her once a week. There were no hotel rooms charged on his card for those nights, so Lucia had assumed he was telling the truth about the visit. But there were also restaurant charges, high-end ones, and was a woman with stomach ulcers really spending time at steak houses? Was he spending those nights in his childhood bed or in some other bed altogether?

"So you're not supposed to feed them?" she asked the duck woman. "Do they have, oh, an official feeder?"

The woman shredded half a roll before she answered. "No one is supposed to feed them."

"What are they supposed to eat then?" asked Lucia.

"Algae off rocks!" The woman looked at Lucia head-on for the first time. Her lips held the shape of each word for a split second too long. "Isn't that horrible? You shut up a living thing for its whole life and you tell it that it has to suck its food off a rock? No, I don't think so. I won't stand for it, no ma'am."

Lucia had never seen such rage channeled by way of ducks, and it amazed her still how fascinating people could be. She listened to them talk all day long, and they could be cruel or dull or stupid, but often they were mesmerizing.

"So you take care of them," she said. "Even though you're not supposed to."

The woman nodded. "Some of the other staff say, 'It's against the rules, Sheila, you can't do that.' And I'm, like, 'I'm nearly seventy years old and I don't give a rat's patootie if it's against the rules.'"

She—Sheila—pointed to the scrum of ducks.

"That duck there is a male chauvinist," she said. "The brown one with the white splotch. He'll grab the other ducks by their beaks and yank them around, especially the females. He's such a jerk. But there's a female duck who will yank him back. It's a wonderful thing."

Lucia picked up a roll that had fallen. "How long have you worked here?"

"Twenty years, give or take. That speckled one there's gimpy. Could be natural causes, but you can't tell. There was a kid here not long ago throwing ice at them—Ice! It could kill them!—and I went to the ice machine and walked up behind him and pegged him right on the back of the neck. The look on his face!

"'How's it feel?' I said to him. And do you know what he says?"

"What?" asked Lucia, caught up entirely.

"He calls me a bitch," Sheila said, her bread-free hands landing on her hips. "Can you imagine? A twelve-year-old. And I can see the little girls at the front desk, smiling. Smiling. They think I'm a bitch, too. But I don't care. The manager comes over, sticking out his chest, telling me to apologize because the boy's parents can sue, just for me throwing ice. I say, fine. I apologize. The girls are still at the desk, covering their mouths with both hands, and they're enjoying the scene. I say to the manager—he quit last year, went into some sort of business with fake fireplace logs—I say, 'Now, Barry, if he'd killed one of those ducks—'"

"'You call me Mr. Price,' he says to me. Mr. Price. Likes he's the principal, and I'm a kindergartner. I wanted to say, all right, Barry, how about I call you whatever I want, and you and those girls at the desk call me whatever they want."

She had to stop for a breath.

"People can be nasty," Lucia said.

"Nasty and fragile," agreed Sheila.

Lucia thought of Earl Conway. *He pulled me aside when he came to pick up the kids,* Sara Conway had said, smiling on the other side of Lucia's desk, *and he asked me why I picked such a bitch of a lawyer.* She said it as if it were the sort of comment that Lucia would chuckle over.

She thought of Garrison Langley. *Amenable.*

She thought of Judge Musgrove. *Just to see your sweet ass walk out the door.*

Judge Simmons, telling her to come see him in his chambers, the walls decorated with one picture of Jesus Christ and one picture of George Wallace in matching frames. *I want to tell you that short skirt makes my blood boil.*

Ben Stallworth, a lawyer. *You'd win more cases with lower-cut blouses.*

Judge Stone, who refused to let her appear in his courtroom because he didn't think feminine ears could handle the coarse details of a paternity case.

Judge Mathison, who slapped her on the butt.

Tim Blankenship, a lawyer, who slapped her on the butt.

Louis Carlson, a lawyer, who slapped her on the butt.

Janet Carlson, Louis's wife, who showed up at Lucia's front door, pushing past Evan, calling Louis's name, as if Lucia would ever touch the man. As if she would have some illicit affair with her own husband standing right in the den. *He has trouble saying no sometimes,* the wife had said, as if Lucia would have coerced him into sex.

That wife whose name she couldn't remember, the one who had called her at the office about yet another husband, saying, *I know you've had drinks with him,* as if half a dozen other lawyers hadn't been at the table, too. If men were fragile, women weren't much better.

"Everyone is just flapping and squawking," Sheila said. "Terrified."

Lucia could only meet the woman's eyes by crooking her head back. The angle showed her a square jaw, a creased neck, and the underside of wide, flattened breasts. She looked like some pagan statue, rough carved.

Sheila tossed another smattering of crumbs. Then another. Eventually her hands were empty, and she slapped them against her pants. A duck ambled up the incline toward her, and she kicked at it, stopping short of making contact.

"No more for tonight," she said.

She told the ducks good-bye. She told Lucia good-bye. Before she had even disappeared behind a wall of broad leaves, the ducks had drifted away. Lucia stuffed her paper napkin into her empty glass. She had spilled crumbs on the chair, and she was brushing them off when she felt someone standing over her.

She saw his shoes first. Black leather, not too shiny. She recognized him immediately, and she thought of bread crumbs. Had she led him to her, somehow? Laid out some invisible path? He nodded to the empty seat next to her. No, not a nod. A tilt of his head. He looked even taller than he had from across the lobby.

"Would you mind?" he asked. "Or were you leaving?"

"No," she said. "I don't mind."

He sat down, his feet extending nearly into the water His jaw was dark with stubble, and he wore no rings on his fingers.

"Jake," he said, holding out his hand.

"Lucia," she answered, offering hers.

He jerked his head toward the turquoise stream. "Was that woman kicking ducks?"

She laughed and leaned toward him.

Rachel

I.

Before our biology quiz on the skeletal system, the boys in the back corner sang a song:

> *Open up her mandible*
> *Or down on her patellas*
> *Doesn't know which way she wants it*
> *So you have to tell her.*

They drummed their hands on the edge of the lab table, keeping the beat, saying the same lines over and over until Mrs. Hughes finally walked into the room, sipping her coffee.

It was a catchy tune. People were laughing. Girls were laughing. Not all but some. I kept both palms on my lab table, fingers spread like when you make turkeys from your handprint. Next to me, Nancy Mann tugged her banana clip loose from her long blond hair.

I wondered, do you really have to tell her which way she wants it?

I felt like I understood sex. We had HBO at home. And yet if I were doing it for the first time, might I appreciate some guy's advice? I might. But that wasn't what Tyler and Kevin and Craig meant, and I knew it. What did they imagine when they sang that song? What girl did they see, or did they see any girl at all?

"Pencil and paper," called out Mrs. Hughes, her slip hanging below her skirt. "Notes and books put away."

Craig Lewis had a belly like a grown man.

Tyler and Kevin had thrown up in the same umbrella stand at Tina's house.

Here is another thing I wondered: how were you supposed to know what you wanted?

II.

Mom and I sat on the couch. We'd picked up baked potatoes and chocolate chip milk shakes at Rax, and the wrappers were strewn across the sofa. We'd gotten into a routine lately, where we brought home fast food most nights and ate on the couch. Or really, I ate, and she used her French fries to draw designs in her ketchup.

I could smell melted cheese and nail polish. I tried to ignore it, but I couldn't.

"I still don't know why you can't just go in the bathroom to paint them," I said for the second time.

"I didn't want to miss the show," she said, forking a bite of cold potato and then setting it down. The bottle of pink polish was balanced on the arm of the sofa.

"You had plenty of time," I said.

"Shhh," she said as the commercial ended, and we watched Jennifer Hart walk into her living room, smiling at the sound of jazz.

I moved my milk shake from between my knees and made myself more comfortable. Jonathan Hart was in a band, and it looked to me like Robert Wagner was actually playing the trumpet. Between songs, Jonathan was chatting with a friend who was a piano player, and since I'd never seen that particular friend before, he was destined to either get murdered or be accused of murder.

"I don't trust him," Mom said.

"You should trust him," I said. "He's Jonathan's friend. He'll be innocent."

The phone rang, and Mom waved a hand at me. It seemed easier to answer the phone than to argue with her. Most likely it was my grandmother or aunt or one of Mom's friends. My own friends knew not to call me during *Hart to Hart.*

"Hello?" I said.

"May I speak to Rachel?"

It was a boy's voice, unfamiliar.

"This is she," I said, winding the coils of the phone cord through my fingers.

"This is John. I asked Tina for your number."

I let the phone cord spring free. I hadn't talked to John since the party, which had been weeks ago. For a couple of nights I'd thought he might call, but I'd stopped waiting.

"Hey," I said.

"Hey."

"What's going on?" I said.

"Do you think that when people say caterpillars are poisonous—"

"Caterpillars can be poisonous?"

"Yeah," he said. "Nobody ever told you that? Everybody keeps telling me. We found this white fuzzy one in our window box, and so we put him in a jar—did you know my mom used to be a biology teacher?—but now guys keep telling me that the white ones are poisonous."

I appreciated that, so far, there had not been any awkward pauses. I wondered if he'd brainstormed before he called.

"What does your mom say?" I asked.

"She says as long as I don't eat him, I should be fine."

I kept an eye on the television. The beautiful heiress had a thin-lipped secretary, and there was something disturbing about her eyes.

"But you still seem worried," I told John. "Exactly what are your plans for this caterpillar?"

He laughed. I wondered why he hadn't called me earlier. Had he wanted to wait so I wouldn't think he was too interested? Had he been unsure whether or not he wanted to call? Did he ask his friends first?

"Do you think if I had, say, licked the caterpillar—just a little—the poison would still kick in?" he asked. It took me a second to be sure he was joking.

Mom had collected our wrappers and balled them up on the coffee table. She tucked her nightgown over her knees. I wished I could tell what the creepy secretary was saying—it was her hair, I realized, that was the warning signal. Usually ladies with long gray hair were psychopaths.

"So is it cocooned yet?" I asked John.

"Yeah. It'll probably be some boring kind of moth, but it's kind of exciting to wait for him to come out. I hope it'll be tomorrow."

I wondered if this was going to be an invitation.

"You'd like it," he said. "It's pretty cool."

"It sounds cool."

I still wondered if this was going to be an invitation.

"Yeah," he said.

All right. Did he want me to invite myself over? Was I supposed to act more enthusiastic about the moth? I hated the phone. It was all words and silence and wondering, and was it any clearer, really, when we were off the phone? This wasn't talking—this was mind reading. It wasn't John's fault. It was the same with everyone. There was no telling what another person was really thinking, and that was one reason I'd taken a break from parties. The wondering sucked up too much energy.

"So what are you doing?" he asked.

"Watching *Hart to Hart*," I said, as Jennifer discovered a dead body in the closet. She called for Jonathan just like she always did when she found a dead body in a closet.

"I've never seen it," he said.

"Really?"

Mom was finally peering at me, her face asking a question. I put my hand over the mouthpiece.

"Homework," I whispered to her.

"You're missing it," she whispered back.

I switched directions, twirling the cord. I pulled my foot loose from a sticky spot on the kitchen floor.

"So next weekend," John said, "I think we're going out to my cousin's farm just for, like, a bonfire with some hotdogs and stuff. They've got four-wheelers. Have you ever ridden one?"

"Once," I said. "I wasn't that good at it. What about you?"

"Yeah. It's pretty fun when I don't nearly kill myself. There are these trails through the woods—"

He kept talking.

It's too dark to tell which way he went, said Jonathan.

What are you going to tell Lieutenant Claire? asked Jennifer.

"My hair actually skimmed the grass," said John. "And it's not like my hair is long."

"Right," I said.

I liked him. I could almost conjure up the giddiness I felt when his knee first landed against mine. I could imagine this bonfire he was talking about, and—assuming he was actually going to invite me—I could see myself being excited about it. I'd tell Tina and Nancy and whoever else, and I'd probably wear my purple boatneck top and my black jeans, and he'd pick me up and maybe it would be really fun—I could picture that—and maybe we would kiss again, and maybe we would fall in love. Maybe we would go out together every weekend, and he would be my date for every dance, and we would sneak snacks into the movies together and his parents would go out of town and I would spend the night with him.

But—come on—chances were that we would sit at that bonfire, and I'd wish for him to hold my hand but he wouldn't or I would reach for his hand and I'd wonder if he was only being polite when he let me hold it, and he'd ask me if I wanted to go to an actual bowling alley and I would wonder if he really wanted to go bowling or if he just thought I did, and, crap, I'd have to introduce him to Mom, and maybe on the second date or maybe on the fiftieth, we would be tired of each other and I would be standing right here in this exact spot, trying to find the words to break up with him or listening to him break up with me, and we would both feel terrible, and all of it seemed so pointless.

I watched Mom stretch across the sofa, taking over my spot, propping her feet on the wooden arm next to her nail polish. On screen, Jonathan wondered about the inscription on a gold cigarette case.

"I think it's the stars," John said, and I had lost him entirely. "Rachel? You there?"

"Sorry," I said.

"The stars are the best, I was saying."

"Right," I said. "Definitely."

"So. What do you think?"

"What do I think—?"

There was a quick wet sound, like either he'd taken a drink of something or licked his lips.

"I get the feeling you're busy," he said.

Too much work. This was too much work, and I wanted things to be easier.

"It's a new episode," I said.

I could hear his footsteps, or at least I assumed they were his. I wondered if he was pacing around his kitchen, too. For the first time, I could hear us breathing, gusts of air from both sides of the phone. I did not fill the silence.

"Well, I can tell you're wanting to watch your show," he said. "I'll let you go."

"Yeah," I said. "Thanks for calling."

I hung up just as tires squealed on the television and Jonathan joined in the car chase.

"He is such a nice-looking man," Mom said, scooting to make room for me. "Did you get the homework thing straightened out? Who was it anyway?"

"Nancy," I said. "It's all fine."

"You comfortable?" she asked, offering me a pillow.

"Yes," I said, and it was true.

III.

If this was ancient Greece, where you had your choice of temples to offer up slaughtered animals to whatever god you wanted, Mom would bow at the Shrine of Kmart.

We needed an ironing board. That's what she told me when she dragged me out of bed at ten on a Saturday morning, and I had no idea why it mattered that our ironing board was ripped around the edges—we did not haul it out and show it to company—but there was no point in arguing. We went to Kmart. We examined all the ironing boards, and she picked one that looked just like all the others. It was on the top shelf, though, so we debated logistics until Mom handed me a couple of dollars to go buy myself an Icee while she found a stock boy to lift down the ironing board.

I didn't always give Mom enough credit: she rarely withheld beverages. When she deposited her paycheck every other Friday, she always let me buy a Slush Puppie at the mall, and I never loved her more than when I watched the pumps of green apple syrup splash against the bottom of the cup.

Coke and cherry were the flavors of the day at Kmart, and I sipped at my swirl as I turned back toward the housewares section. As soon as the ironing board expedition was over, I planned to spend the rest of my day with Edgar

Rice Burroughs. I'd fallen back into my old Pellucidar books, and if I was honest, I'd been spending a lot of time wishing for some sort of tunnel to the center of the Earth, where I would stalk through jungles with mastodons and saber-toothed tigers. What I liked about Burroughs's fantasies was that he told them with confidence. You dug a deep hole. The hole led you to an undiscovered world underneath the earth's crust. Done. Backstory finished by page five. It worked for me because I didn't want to waste time mulling over the science of it: I just wanted to go there. I would be mostly naked, but with good weaponry. Sometimes I thought about how my eyes would be a problem—vision was important when spears were involved, and if I lost a contact—well, the fantasy started to disintegrate once I started thinking about saline solution.

"Rachel?" I heard.

I turned, straw in my mouth. "Mr. Cleary?"

He was angling his cart around a display of buy-one-get-one-free Brawny towels, and he stopped between two aisles. He had stacks of air freshener and Roach Motels in his cart, which made me think the inside of his house was probably not a pleasant place.

"You here with your mom?" he asked, glancing around.

"Yeah," I said. "She's trying to find someone to help her with an ironing board."

"You're wearing more pants than you were the last time I saw you."

I slid a hand down my jeans and stared at my Icee. "Yeah."

"Wait," Mr. Cleary said. "Your mom needs help with an ironing board?"

He was wearing a blue T-shirt shirt and running shorts that showed more thigh than my shortest shorts. His face was tanned like he'd been to the beach. I thought of him as my parents' age, but, under the store lights, it occurred to me that he wasn't that old.

"She thinks we can't reach the shelf," I said, scanning the front of the store to make sure that I hadn't missed her. "But I could. She won't let me because she thinks I'll hurt my back."

"Lifting an ironing board?"

"I know. It's taking awhile. I thought she'd have been at the checkout line by now."

A woman with Crystal Gayle hair and two large-headed children pushed between us, interested in the paper towel sale.

"Well, she probably wasn't looking for just any stock boy," Mr. Cleary said. "She needed a beefy one."

"No," I said. "Just a man. Any size. Any age. Because men lift things and solve your problems and kill your bugs, and women make sandwiches and babies."

He stood there, silent. I assumed he was trying to decide if I was joking, and eventually he decided I was, because he laughed and rolled himself closer.

"So you and your mother aren't peas in a pod?"

"We are not," I said, although I thought of fast-food wrappers on sofa cushions.

"You don't think a man should solve your problems?"

"No."

"Or kill the bugs?"

"I'm okay with that."

He laughed again, and he smoothed a wrinkle in his shorts. Maybe he was a runner. I remembered how I'd disliked the way he puffed out his chest while he was watering his yard, but I didn't see it that way now. He looked like he exercised. He looked solid.

"A women's libber," he said. "Who knew? I haven't had one of those in ages."

That confused me until I realized he was looking at my drink. It was the kind of look that made it seem like I'd be rude if I didn't offer.

"You want a sip?" I asked.

"Thanks," he said.

I hadn't expected him to accept, but I handed the cup over, and he popped off the plastic cover to drink from the side. I appreciated that he didn't use my straw.

"Is this where you hang out on a Saturday?" he said, handing back my Icee. "Not the mall or the Dairy Queen parking lot?"

"No," I said, and now I was the one being slow to recognize a joke. "The Dairy Queen parking lot, Mr. Cleary?"

"That's what we used to do. You can call me Grant, by the way. Which is my actual name. I'm not a thousand years old or your teacher—I'm twenty-nine. So Grant, okay?"

"Okay," I said.

I looked over my shoulder, checking for Mom again. Mr. Cleary—or whoever—lifted his cart onto two wheels and made a sharp turn, heading toward the cash registers.

"Good luck with the ironing board," he said.

"Thanks."

He stopped. "Rachel?"

"Yeah?"

"I liked the shorts better."

I laughed.

He had disappeared through the checkout lines by the time I finally found Mom, who had gone all the way to the Icee counter looking for me. I carried our ironing board back to the sun-soaked car.

"Bend at your knees," Mom said as I lifted it into the backseat, trying to catch the right angle. "Bend your knees, Rachel. You're bending at your back—you know how that can—"

"Mom," I said. "It's in the car."

When I grabbed my copy of Burroughs's *Back to the Stone Age* from the floorboard, it was warm, like a pet who'd been waiting. I opened the book before Mom had even turned on the car, and she made a croupy sound that meant *You read way too much.* I turned the page.

We were stopped at a light, just about to turn left onto the bypass, when Mom's brake light came on.

"Oh no," she said.

I put down my book. "What?"

"The brakes."

She pointed at the dashboard, and I could see the light. There was a line of cars behind us.

"Should we stop at the gas station on the way home?" I asked.

The light turned green, and the car in front of us moved. Mom did not push the gas pedal.

"Mom," I said.

"Something's wrong with the brakes," she said. "That's very serious."

The car behind us honked.

"You have to go," I said.

The car behind us honked again. Somewhere farther down the line, a different car honked.

"Mom! Go!" I said, and I shook her shoulder. Her head jerked back and forth, and when she faced me, her eyes were too wide.

"Step on the gas," I said, not yelling this time. "Go through the light and make your turn."

She did it. She drove too slowly, and the car behind us swerved into the other lane, honking again. It didn't matter, though, because we were on the bypass, and we were moving.

"What if they stop working?" she said. "I'm pumping them a little, and they seem like they're okay, but, Rachel, if the brakes cut out—"

"It's a warning light," I said. "It's only the light. It just means we should have someone look at the brakes. Keep driving."

A couple of tears cut a path through her foundation and powder. Her mascara would run soon. A red pickup veered around us, a bald man frowning at us from the passenger window. I looked at the speedometer. She was going twenty miles under the speed limit.

"Pull over," I said.

"What?"

She stopped panting, at least. She even looked away from the road for a second.

"There," I said. "In that Chevron. Let me drive. I'll take care of it, okay?"

"Okay," she said, and her hand landed on mine. Her skin was cold, but I tightened my fingers around hers. That only lasted a second before she recentered her grip, sharp knuckled, on the steering wheel.

"Turn," I said, pointing. "Turn there. Park in that spot by the dumpster. Now trade places with me."

She nodded and did what I said. I left my book on the seat, and I switched places with her, waiting until she was buckled before I put the car in reverse.

"You okay?" I asked, and I thought of how it might not be the worst thing to have someone who solved your problems.

"Drive to the place on Carter Hill," she said. "I think they're open on Saturday."

I tapped the brakes, which seemed fine.

I waited for a gap in the cars, and I pulled back onto the bypass, too slowly. I checked the brakes again—still fine—and I thought about whether eyeglasses would stay on securely while riding on horseback or attacking a cave bear, and it seemed possible that you could fasten them with some sort of leather cord or vine. They would be a better choice than contacts, surely, although the glass could shatter during hand-to-hand combat.

A bow and arrow?

It was worth considering.

IV.

I leaned back against my antique four-poster bed, which had belonged to my great-grandmother. She died when I was a baby, but I thought plenty about her and this curlicued bed. The wood squeaked and brayed every time I scratched my leg or fluffed my pillow, and I wondered about my great-grandparents trying to get romantic in a farmhouse full of kids. Had they gone ahead and had sex knowing that their kids could hear every bounce? Did they slip off to the outhouse or something?

I centered my lap desk on my legs, and even that small shift made the bed whine underneath me. I chewed my pen and reread what I had written so far:

Dear Ms. Powers:

I share your interest in protecting African wildlife. I read a story about how you liked to help wounded animals when you were a child, and I used to do the same thing. I found a ring-necked dove once that had flown into our window, and I fed it bits of bread and water from a medicine dropper. I would love to help in any way possible on your preserve in Kenya. Do you have an internship program? If so, do you let high school students apply? I am available for the summer of 1982.

I have an A average and have only one B so far in my high school career, which was in Algebra II. (I don't expect you need an Algebra expert with lions and elephants.) I know this might seem like a strange request, so let me sweeten the pot. I will do absolutely anything that would be helpful—I will shovel pens or wash llamas. If you don't need help in Kenya, I'd be happy to do any sort of personal assistant work for you in California. I will answer your fan mail or walk your dogs or make your coffee.

I could see the weak spots. My algebra joke was forced. And "sweeten the pot"? But here was the big question: would these few paragraphs make Stefanie Powers think, ah, this is a girl I would like to meet?

Probably not.

I had already mailed letters to Carol Burnett (who I'd read responded to all her fan mail) and Frank Inn (he trained Benji, and I had made a strong case for how I had once tried to teach Aunt Molly's Scottish terrier to dial a telephone, based on a scene in *Oh! Heavenly Dog*).

"Rachel," Mom called from the other side of the bedroom door.

"Yeah?"

"Have you tidied your room?"

"I will."

"By the time we leave for Molly's," she said. "I mean it. Dirty clothes in the laundry basket. Clean clothes in the drawers."

"All right."

"I want the drawers to actually close, Rachel. No wadded-up clothes sticking out."

"Yes, ma'am."

Or maybe I didn't want to go to Kenya. Maybe I wanted to stay in my bedroom, which I had no interest in tidying. Clothes, dirty and clean, covered the floor. College brochures—Duke and Vanderbilt and UNC and

Amherst and Colgate—covered my vanity. I did need to put those away because Mom huffed when she saw them, and she said it was because of money, but it wasn't. I had a plate with dried ketchup on my bedside table, plus a cup of half-drunk hot chocolate that had been congealing for days. I had stationery and envelopes and books scattered across my sheets. I needed *The Complete Encyclopedia of Celebrity Addresses* for obvious logistical reasons, but I felt a deeper craving for *At the Earth's Core* and *Pellucidar* and *Land of Terror,* where the bare-chested hero barreled from bear attack to ice cliffs to kidnapping, spending more time considering the thickness of ice than the possibility of death or failure. The hero in those books did not seem to consider much of anything, really, and that would not be a bad way to live.

You'll get scholarship money, my English teacher had told me. *Just fill out the applications, and, I promise, you'll have options.*

I kicked at my flowered bedspread until it slid to the floor. I mostly wanted the option of a deep hole that took me to the center of the earth, the kind of place where you could show up and kill a few raging beasts, fall in love, and get yourself declared emperor. I wanted to disappear into a cave and turn myself into someone else.

The best I could do was to keep my door closed.

Lucia

1.

The oven timer would not stop buzzing. Lucia considered the frozen hands on the dial. It was a cheap panel. The whole mechanism was likely only a few wheels and gears underneath the console.

When the phone rang, at first she thought the timer had reached a new level of malfunction. That only lasted through the first ring, though, and then she yanked the receiver from the cradle.

"Hello?" she said, trying to move away from the buzzing.

"Lucia," said a man's voice. "You haven't returned my calls. It's Chris Sanderson."

"Hey, Chris," she said. "Should I be calling you 'lieutenant'?"

"Please don't."

"In fairness, I've only ignored one call, and it was from this morning. I was going to call you back. I assumed you wanted to give me an update."

It occurred to her that she should buy Chris Sanderson lunch. When she'd caught him at his desk on the evening of the shooting, he'd been matter of fact and efficient, no time wasted on shock or horror. Not only had he kept the shooting out of the newspaper, he'd called her every month with an update on the case, which she assumed was far below a police lieutenant's pay grade. It wasn't his fault that he never had any actual news. He'd tell her that sooner or later something would likely turn up. He'd tell her to let him know if she saw any signs of trouble at home or work.

"Yes," he said now. "I have an update. We've found him."

As soon as he said it, Lucia realized she'd stopped expecting this phone call. She'd stopped even hoping for it.

"You found the shooter?" she asked.

The buzzing from the stove continued, a low steady distraction. She pressed her ear against the receiver.

"He was arrested two days ago for firing several shots at a neighbor," Chris said. "Apparently the neighbor crossed into this man's backyard, looking for a cat, and the man pulled out his twenty-two rifle. He clipped the neighbor in the arm. Nothing serious, but it's still assault with a deadly weapon. The gun is the same one fired at your house."

"You're sure?"

"We're sure. His name is Jerry Mackintosh."

Lucia considered. The stove hummed along.

"He hasn't been in town long," Chris continued. "He moved here at the end of last year, right around the time of the shooting at your place. He rents an apartment over by Eastdale Mall. Works at AmSouth as a loan officer."

"The name isn't familiar," she said.

None of it was familiar. It had occurred to Lucia, of course, that the shooter could be someone she hadn't met, someone she'd seen only across a courtroom or as a name on a document. But she had expected the name to mean something. She'd expected that if someone ever gave her that much, she could start making sense of it all.

"Mackintosh," repeated the lieutenant slowly, as if maybe enunciation had been the problem. "Maybe someone in his family?"

"I don't know," she repeated. "I'll check my records. I'll check with my secretary. I'll see if anything comes to me."

She wasn't sure if his next sound was a yawn or a sigh.

"We need to tie him to you, Lucia," he said. "You know the gun isn't enough to get a warrant. No way to prove that it hasn't changed hands a dozen times since the shooting at your house. I'll sit down and talk to him and see what I can get, but if he doesn't offer up anything—you didn't get even a glimpse of the shooter?"

"You know I didn't."

"After I talk to him, I'll check back with you. We could try a photo lineup, too, and see if that sparks anything. In the meantime, you check your records, okay?"

"I will."

"Listen," Chris said, "he'll likely get out on bond tomorrow, unless we magically come up with something. Since he hasn't made any move toward you since December, I can't imagine he'd risk coming near you now. But keep an eye out. His court date for this incident with the neighbor is set for next month. April twentieth."

Her ear hurt from pressing it against the receiver. She switched the phone to her other ear, the cord tangling. She spun, lifting the cord over her head, and, hell, the buzzing was definitely getting louder.

"This one will likely be a felony," Chris said. "He's got a previous arrest for assault in Georgia. Even if we can't make a case for the shooting at your house, he's looking at maybe five years."

When Lucia hung up, she stripped off her pantyhose and settled her briefcase more firmly on the counter. She should feel relief, shouldn't she? She finally knew the gunman's name, and he was in jail, at least for the moment, and whatever legal *i*'s needed to be dotted and *t*'s crossed, this was surely the man. If they couldn't tie him to the crime—well, they would. They would, and even if they didn't, the man would spend time in prison. She should feel something more than the desire to lie down and close her eyes.

She tugged at the zipper of her briefcase, which had snagged on a loose piece of paper. She worked a fingernail into the metal teeth, prying loose a Post-it note, and she scanned the few words taken down in Marissa's neat cursive: Jake from Louisville. No message, but a number where she could reach him.

Lucia slid the note in a circle, enjoying the rasp of paper on the countertop. When she flicked the little square toward the trash can, it missed by a few inches, floating to the tile.

She couldn't think with the buzzing.

She propped her elbows on the stove, avoiding the burners, and considered the logistics. Did they actually need to call a repairman? She couldn't remember which electrician they had used last—Had they called him for the igniter in this same stove? The fluttering in the overhead lights?

"So?" she heard Evan's voice say.

Her husband was standing in the den, not five feet away. She wondered how long he'd been there.

"I thought you were in the bedroom," she said.

"I was," he said. "Who was it on the phone?"

"Chris Sanderson," she said. "I'm guessing you heard at least part of it?"

He lowered himself to the middle of the couch. "They found out something?"

Lucia knelt down and picked up the yellow sheet of paper, wedging it inside the trash can underneath an empty roll of Scotch tape.

"They think they've found the guy who shot at the house," she said. "He shot at someone else, and the gun matched the bullets they found here. I've never heard of the guy. Jerry Mackintosh. He lives over by Eastdale Mall. He moved here in December, apparently. Nothing about him sounds familiar."

"Did he move before or after the shooting?" Evan asked.

"I didn't ask."

"So why did he do it? What has he said?"

"He hasn't said anything," she said. She watched him from across the countertop. "They haven't questioned him yet. They just got the results about the bullets. And the bullets alone aren't enough to—well, they're still working on it. That's all I know."

"Did you ask any questions at all?"

"I asked plenty," she said, exasperated. "God, Evan, it came out of the blue. I'll try to compile a more thorough list of questions and call Chris back."

He rubbed his hands along the couch cushions, back and forth.

"Sorry," he said.

"It's okay. I'll find out more. I'm just now absorbing it all."

"He's in jail, I take it?"

"He is," Lucia said, and it was the truth. The specifics of bond seemed like a complication not worth explaining. She stepped back to the oven, pushing at the timer with her palm, pressing the stem of the clock. She took away her hand. The buzzing was undiminished.

"You should tell Rachel," Evan said.

"What?" she said.

"She'll be thrilled that she can come back over."

"I'm not sure she should."

"What do you mean?"

"I'm not sure her mother would let her. And I'm not sure she'd want to come. Don't you think she might still be shaken up?"

"Did she say that?"

"No. I mean, I don't know. I haven't talked to her."

She turned back to the oven. She was stammering like a teenager, stumbling over her words. She slammed the heel of her palm against the squawking timer, hard enough that her hand absorbed the round imprint of the clock stem. It stung, and she flexed her fist.

"You haven't talked to her since when?" said Evan.

"December."

He pushed off the couch, and then he was right next to her, too close. The smell of Juicy Fruit.

"You knew that," she said. "I told you that I'd promised her mother I would keep my distance."

The fact that he apparently did not know it left her feeling adrift. It was the sort of question that showed he'd been living a life completely separate from hers.

"Yeah," he said. "You said her mother didn't want her over here. I get her mother being nervous. But you cut off all contact with Rachel? You haven't even called her? Bullets fly at her, and then you abandon her?"

"I haven't abandoned her," she said.

She turned so she didn't have to breathe his gum breath. She did not think she could explain it to him, and she was not sure she should have to. Surely it didn't matter, ultimately, if Rachel sat on this particular couch or watched this particular dog gnaw her hind leg. Yes, Lucia missed her. Yes, she'd felt kinship and affection and she'd felt needed in some blurred way, as if she might be the answer to a question Rachel hadn't quite asked. This tipped uncomfortably into the nursery-rhyme rhythm of *make a difference* and *have an impact* and *reach out and touch someone*—and so what if she had felt it? She had also believed that the two of them were safe sitting in her sunroom chatting about the ABC prime-time lineup and true love. She'd believed that if she agreed to sell this house, the tension between her and Evan would ease. She'd believed that if she ever got the name of who had fired that gun, she would understand what had happened. But none of it had lined up as neatly as she'd imagined.

"Margaret is her mother," she said.

"Technically, yes," Evan said. "All right, that was nasty. Yes, she's Rachel's mother. But what are you? You're something."

She shook her head.

"I got some good news," she said.

He stepped back, nearly tripping over Moxie, who had materialized on the kitchen floor. "Other than the man who tried to kill you being caught?"

Lucia absorbed that. They spoke to each other with such sawed-off words. She had thought this was a bad couple of days and then a bad couple of weeks, but increasingly she was afraid that it was a downward slide into the kind of marriage she swore she would never have.

No, she never swore it. She never even considered it a possibility. She never thought she and Evan could be anything other than happy. She thought—secretly, unspoken—that the biggest determinant of a good marriage was choosing well in the first place. She had done that. And although she knew it was possible that they could work through this, she also knew that if you lost some fundamental joy in each other, it was gone. No amount of counseling or good intentions could bring it back.

Sometimes, late at night, she was sure that they had lost it.

"Yes," she said to him. "Other than that. I got a call today that the Montgomery County Women's Alliance has selected me as the Woman of the Year. They said they want to recognize me for, oh, 'advancing the rights of women.'"

Evan nodded. He jerked his head slightly, possibly trying to shake off—literally—his irritation over Rachel. Over all manner of things. She watched him. She expected him to tell her once again that when she did these sorts of events, it only announced her location to the crazies.

"That's wonderful," he said instead. "Congratulations."

"The ceremony is in a couple of weeks," she said. "April second. There's a fancy dinner at the McNally House, and then I give a speech. There might even be a trophy."

"I'll go with you."

She could tell he expected her to object, and she didn't know why. "Great. I was assuming you'd be my date. I thought I'd invite Mom and Dad, too."

"They'd have to drive at night," Evan said. "He'll tell you to bring the gun."

"And she'll tell me to wear a girdle."

"Do you own a girdle?"

"I do not," she said.

"Don't wear a girdle. Or a bra."

She smiled. The joy was not gone between them, not yet. It just faded in and out, the reception spotty.

II.

Katherine Jemison walked through Lucia's doorway, unsmiling, which was surprising. Men, under duress, were comfortable with a nod. Women, though—even if they thought they were going to lose their husband or their house or their children—they smiled. They asked Lucia how she was doing and they told her they liked the shade of red on her walls or the hardwood floors. If they were going to rage or weep, they only did it after they smiled.

"I can't thank you enough for this," Katherine said, offering a press-and-release hug, brisk.

As she stepped back, her chin brushed Lucia's forehead. Her dark hair hung wavy and jaw length; her tanned face was scrubbed. Back in Lucia's Legal Aid days, there'd been a handful of women—a surgeon, a couple of professors, a bank vice president, plus Katherine Jemison and Lucia—who'd kept spotting each other across banquet rooms full of men in suits. They came together and cohered. Lucia had chatted with Katherine over occasional chicken salads and tuna melts for years until the other woman moved to Mobile after her divorce.

"Surely it's unusual to take a client from out of town?" Katherine said, dropping into the leather chair across from Lucia's. Her purse thudded to the floor. "I can't believe you said yes. I don't know—this somehow feels more serious than the actual divorce. Child endangerment? I can't believe Bert is doing this."

Lucia waited: sometimes the insults showed her something important. Sometimes not. Regardless, Katherine did not expand on her ex-husband's faults.

"I'm glad you called me," said Lucia, sitting. "How's Miranda doing?"

They talked a bit about Katherine's twelve-year-old daughter—her good grades and her obsession with *Anne of Green Gables*—and when Katherine's shoulders had relaxed, Lucia skimmed a hand over the papers on her desk and explained how the meeting would work. They would parse each line of the ex-husband's petition to modify the final order of divorce. They would chat. By the end, they'd have laid out all the information so they could get a good clear look at it.

"So you took Miranda to Rio de Janeiro in January?" Lucia asked.

"Yes," said Katherine.

She did not elaborate, which made Lucia nod with approval. "And what did the two of you do on that trip?"

Katherine glanced at the molding of the ceiling then back at Lucia. She might as well have been sitting in front of a class reading some scientific paper on plankton. But when she crossed her legs, Lucia watched her ankle-booted foot twitch wildly, as if it were conducting an unseen orchestra.

"It was a short trip," Katherine said. "Just over a week. I was working with colleagues at the Universidade Federal, gathering samples from Guanabara Bay. You remember the oil spill a few years ago? It was seventy thousand barrels into the bay. The question is whether the mangrove swamps can recover. There's always been a pollution issue there, but domestic sewage and industrial waste is a different animal entirely from—how much detail do you want about my research?"

"That's good. In court, you'd want to give the sort of general answer you'd give at a dinner party."

The ankle boot circled and twitched. It always impressed Lucia in the courtroom when she studied a confident face and steady voice, then looked under the table and saw all the nerves, channeled.

"And the judge?" Katherine asked. "What will he want to see from me?"

It was the most important question, in some ways. It was amazing how few people thought to ask it.

"Competence," Lucia said. "Warmth. No need to mention Cornell or degrees of any kind unless you're asked directly. Your ex-husband's lawyer is likely going to try to show that you're more concerned with specimens under a microscope than your daughter. So minimize how much you talk about work."

"Even when they ask about it?"

"Even then," said Lucia.

"Do you think 'workaholic' is the only thing they'll call me?"

Lucia lifted the corner of one typed sheet and then let it fall. This was, actually, the question that most concerned her.

"Don't forget that your ex-husband has the burden of proof, whatever his claims," she said. "Are you seeing anyone?"

"I am not," said Katherine mildly. "I've gone on a grand total of four dates in the past two years. My options are not extensive. I've never brought anyone home to meet Miranda."

"There's no reason to believe he's taking that angle," Lucia said. "Let's get back to the trip itself. You're gathering samples. What does that mean, day to day?"

"My colleagues and I made several trips out on the bay. There were three of us per small motor boat. We had four sampling stations along the coast, each in a different mangrove forest. In the morning we'd gather sediment and leaf samples. In the afternoon, we'd go back to the lab—"

"Where was Miranda while you worked?" asked Lucia.

"She stayed with Roberta, my colleague's wife. The two of them visited a couple of tourist sites, but mostly they stayed at home. They, oh, cooked Brazilian cheese bread and fudge balls. Miranda practiced her Portuguese. Roberta and her husband live in a nice neighborhood in a lovely sobrado—"

"Sobrado?" said Lucia.

"A loft."

"Say 'loft.' And if you name the university that sponsors the research, call it the Federal University. There's no advantage in speaking Spanish. Or Portuguese."

This had been an issue in a previous custody case where the mother wanted to move back to her parents' house in Arizona, which she kept calling a "casita." Lucia had watched the judge's face screw tighter with every repetition, clearly imagining sticks stuck together with mud. While it was not the entire reason they lost the case, it had not helped.

She waited for Katherine to argue, but the other woman only nodded.

"All right. My point is that while I was working, my daughter spent her days with a competent adult in a safe neighborhood, essentially baking cookies and learning about a foreign culture."

"Good," said Lucia. She had nearly forgotten how much she liked this woman. "That's good. So Miranda was never alone in Rio?"

"Never."

"The petition mentions the murder rate in the city. The statistic alone isn't a problem. Your husband would have to prove she was actually in danger. Was Miranda threatened at all? Did she see any violence?"

"None," said Katherine. "No blood, no guns, no criminal activity."

"What does he mean by the phrase, 'allowing inappropriate contact with prostitutes'?"

Katherine smiled for the first time. "We walked to a food market one morning, and we passed a couple of hookers. It was obvious—one of them wore a see-through blouse. The other one reached out to Miranda and caught a piece of her hair. Very gently. It's curly blond, do you remember? The woman said it was pretty. Miranda said thank you, and she told the woman that she liked her hair, too. She was taken with the prostitute, that's true enough."

She was still smiling.

"You don't want to do that in court," Lucia said. "Don't act amused."

"Well, of course not." Katherine smoothed her hands over her knees.

"I was thinking how I once read an interview with Dolly Parton talking about the first time she saw a 'fallen woman' with bleached hair and too much makeup and tight dresses, and she thought, 'Yes. I want to be that.'"

"Miss Kitty on *Gunsmoke,*" Lucia said, and she thought of Saturday nights sitting on her parents' couch, her cold toes tucked under her father's thigh. "There is an appeal."

"I was proud, actually, of how kind Miranda was," Katherine said. "The woman just came lurching across the sidewalk. But Miranda was gracious. They really like blond hair there. You'd be popular."

"I get touched enough in this country, thank you," said Lucia.

Katherine tilted her head, and the polite confusion in her expression struck Lucia. She wondered how often men groped a botanist. Even sitting, Katherine looked formidable. Broad across the shoulders, taller than some men. She was compelling but not pretty, and how much did prettiness have to do with the frequency of groping? Might height be a factor—sheer physical space occupied? Lucia considered that there might be some equation—if you were blonde and five foot three, you might be, say, three times more likely to have your ass remarked on as you left a courtroom than a solid five foot ten brunette. And if you avoided the ogling, did you pay a price for that lack of attention? There had been plenty of moments when Lucia had wished for more wrinkles or gray hair, and yet she knew that she would not make that trade, and was that because of vanity or because of power? If they were in a bar instead of in her office, she would ask Katherine's opinion.

"Miranda told her dad about the prostitute," Katherine said. "She thought it was a funny story. Bert would have laughed at it. Before."

Lucia did wonder about Bert Jemison. She hadn't spoken to Katherine at all during the divorce. In the event of a floundering marriage, friends either grilled her for free legal advice or they vanished entirely, self-conscious about trading on friendship. Katherine had been in the latter group. Lucia found out about the divorce over lunch with a mutual friend: it was not every day that someone they knew told her husband she was leaving him because she preferred women. But instead of making Katherine's sexual preference an issue in the divorce, Bert had named only "irreconcilable differences." That did not seem like the action of a mean-spirited man.

Had his sense of aggrievement intensified? Would he belatedly bring sex into this? Lucia did not relish that scenario. If he chose to go that route—and if he got the right judge—Katherine would likely lose her daughter.

"He mentions Mexico," Lucia said. "When did you take Miranda there?"

"I'm not sure what he means," Katherine said. "I took her to New Mexico last year. Las Cruces. It was a conference."

Lucia felt a swell of anticipation, like when her younger self was bodysurfing chest deep in the Gulf and she spotted a ripe, easy wave she knew she would catch just right.

"You took her to New Mexico—never Mexico?" she said.

"Correct."

"And your ex-husband—"

Katherine smiled for the second time. "Does not seem to recognize the difference."

Lucia looked down at her desk drawer, which was slightly open, showing paper clips and two pens, both from Rachel. A hot-air balloon floated in one of them, and the other was topped with a woodpecker on a spring.

"If you have any contact with him," she said, "don't correct him. Was there anything else about the Rio trip that he might possibly bring up?"

"It was no more dangerous than going to Atlanta. Lord, Lucia, Bert's never been out of the country. Once I thought he would—well, I don't know: I suppose I gave him enough surprises."

Katherine leaned forward, feet flat on the floor. She no longer looked like she was reading a scientific paper.

"The trip wasn't dangerous," she repeated. "It was—lovely. On our third day, Miranda and I hiked to an abandoned sixteen-story hotel in the middle of the jungle—Esqueleto Hotel, which means Skeleton Hotel." She flapped a hand. "I know. I'll only say it in English. But the two of us and a few other tourists wandered through this beautiful ruin of a place, vines wrapping around the walls. Miranda ate cod balls. She tried coconut juice. She surfed, sort of. I didn't visit a foreign country until I was thirty years old—two weeks in Costa Rica looking at high-altitude vegetation."

Something had loosened in Katherine. Her face was wide-eyed and open, and the words came fast. Lucia was not sorry to see it. She preferred to know—before the court date—what it looked like when the dam burst.

"Bert wants her safe and tucked in," Katherine said, "but so what if she meets a prostitute? So what if she sees breasts? She has them, for God's sake. So what if she sees some ugliness and it makes her uncomfortable? Why should you want to feel comfortable and safe—where does that get you? She's not safe. That's a fairy tale. She's going to suffer at some point. Bert can't stop that, but he can stop her from falling off a surfboard or climbing on a plane, and maybe he can even stop her from wanting anything at all. And you know what? She still won't be safe. He's keeping himself comfortable, not her, the prick. I want her to know there's a world out there. A whole world, waiting. And, yes, I know I sound like a bitch."

Lucia glanced at the pens again. "If you were a man, they'd say you were a prophet."

What difference would it have made, she wondered, if Rachel had this woman for a mother? The girl was dying to ride a train—any train, preferably the kind where murders happened—but other than that, the most exotic dream trip Lucia had ever heard her mention was the glass-bottom boat in Pensacola. What might she make of a trip to Brazil?

"I won't be a prophet or a bitch," said Katherine, giving something close to a laugh. "I will be warm and loving, and I will be completely uninterested in sex with either gender, and I will talk about cooking and knitting and Wednesday night church services. I will be whoever I need to be."

She was not quite finished. Her hands flexed and unflexed.

"Bert loves her. I know he loves her. But I wonder if he knows her at all or if he just sees some Miranda-shaped space and fills it in however he wants. How is she supposed to know what *she* wants? You have to see it first, don't you, to know you want it? She begged to go on this trip. Do you think he's even asked her for her opinion?"

There, thought Lucia. This was the other thing that sometimes happened when the dam burst. She was back in the Gulf again, shell shards under her feet, and she looked out at the waves, too many to count. When a client overflowed, she watched the waves roll in. Sometimes the peaks were unmanageable. But often she could pick one that was coming at just the right angle. The perfect arc. She saw what was there, ebbing and flowing, but what she did in this moment also had a hint of Poseidon. She could sometimes control the waves. She could take a thought and shape it into something you could ride all the way to shore.

"That's the ideal tone," she said. "It's important that she asked to go. And that he never asked her what she thought. You had an opportunity to add to her education, and you took it."

"Got it," said Katherine. It was a bonus for Lucia that this woman understood that you could be real and engineered at the same time.

III.

When she was the only one in the house, the buzzing oven timer sounded louder. Lucia added a scoop of food to Moxie's bowl, then pulled out the Conway folder, since the trial would start in two days. She nested on her usual corner of the couch, and she stared at the first page of the deposition summary, but there was no concentrating.

She'd gone by the police station and looked at photos of middle-aged white men today, and she had recognized no one. Not the slightest spark of familiarity, although that failure was not what was distracting her, surely. The humming. She could not unhear the humming. The more she tried to block it out, the louder it got. She'd gone to the store to buy more foundation—Lancôme, porcelain—and she'd walked out with a multicolored bangle bracelet that had made her think of Rachel. It was the third gift she had bought the girl in the past months, all undelivered.

The house was so empty. It was louder without Evan in it.

He had been gone for the last two days to a conference in Chicago. She'd had another call at the office from Jake. Another yellow square left on her desk. Could the man not take a hint? Now that she was back in her home, she was mystified by the woman who had sipped a martini with a stranger in the middle of an indoor forest. She had spent a pleasant half hour with him and then she'd headed to her room, and who knew if he would have asked her for more than a drink? She hadn't given him the chance. It must have taken some work on his part to find her work number—she didn't recall giving him her last name—and she distrusted any man who made that sort of effort for a woman who had shown no interest.

She could not fathom why she had constructed shallow hotel scenarios. Everything she had ever wanted was in this house, or rather, it was most nights. Now the stove was the only thing talking to her, and the room was crowded with empty spaces. She should not have pushed Rachel away. She had made a mistake there, and she must have made a mistake with Evan, too, although she was not sure what it was. She thought, still, soul mates. She did not want them to drift any further away from each other, and yet she did not know how to change their trajectory. He would be home tonight, and she was euphoric at the thought of him, but she wondered if she would love him as clearly and sharply when he was sitting next to her.

The stove. Dear God, it was driving her crazy. She stalked to the kitchen and stared at the timer, at the fragile panel framing the clock mechanism.

She would fix this.

She would fix it right now. Things did not just fix themselves, did they?

The hammer, for once, was exactly where it was supposed to be. She yanked it loose from the junk drawer—the handle was wrapped in string and jammed inside a roll of duct tape. She did not recall ever buying a rubber band, and yet the drawer was clogged with them. A gentle tap, she thought. All she needed to do was to lightly tap the center of the clock face. It might knock the moving parts off track and stop the noise.

She lifted her grandmother's ancient cast-iron skillet off the front burner, setting it aside. She could still see the old woman wielding it—cornbread batter sizzling in hot Crisco oil—her pale forearms roped with muscle and striped with oven burns. Even when her leg was gone, she'd stalked through the kitchen, never holding on to a counter, not an ounce of caution in her. (How had that woman produced Lucia's mother?) She rejected electric mixers, beating by hand until her arms gave out, and Lucia imagined that she found the ache necessary. It was proof of the work, and work was the lasso her grandmother laid down to keep the snakes away. If you worked hard enough— if you felt the effort in your joints and your muscles and behind your scratchy eyelids, if you worked well enough and long enough and you could manage to be good enough—well, then, everything would turn out fine.

Lucia had never owned an electric mixer.

She considered her angle, hammer in hand. She centered herself, her belly against the edge of the oven, the incessant whir sounding like a taunt. She tapped twice, directly on the knob in the center of the clock. The oven continued to whine. She tapped several more times, increasing the force, feeling each hit more deeply in her wrist. She imagined what lay behind the dull silver panel, back behind the knobs and numbers. She thought it must look something like a travel alarm clock.

Moxie bumped against her knee, curious. Lucia stroked her head.

She could destroy the clock. Easily. It made so much more sense than calling an electrician, which would take days, potentially, and likely cost hundreds of dollars, and all she needed to do was break the clock. She could break a clock. What kind of idiot couldn't break a clock?

She thought it as she continued hammering away, never missing her tiny target, each hit well calibrated. She could stop calibrating. That was an idea. She could stop being careful.

She hit the knob harder. Five times. Each hit was more satisfying. On the sixth stroke, the glass shattered around the timer, the jagged pieces spraying across the burners and onto the countertop. The glass was thicker than she'd expected. The panel was naked now, hardly a remaining shard, and the whole contraption looked cheaper. The metal backing seemed no more solid than a sheet of notebook paper, so she went back to the tool drawer and traded her hammer for a pair of pliers. The metal peeled back like the top of a sardine can. This work was precise, gratifying in a different way. Her index finger was bleeding, but not enough to make a fuss over. Two drops of blood splatted next to the glass bits, and Lucia stopped to wrap a bit of paper towel around her knuckle and got back to work.

The alarm was no longer just whirring. The sound now was louder and sharper. More like a leaf blower. The oven sounded threatened. Lucia poked and pulled the metal panel, peeling it farther back. She sliced her thumb, but she didn't stop to wrap it, only wiped the blood against her thigh.

Finally she managed to bend the metal on three sides, every edge turned petallike. Using her needle-nose pliers, she lifted the panel free, only it was not free. She found the gears of a clock, yes, but also a mass of electrical wiring, blue, yellow, and white. The wires were attached in at least four places to the clock mechanism.

Whaaaaaaaaa, went the stove.

She wiped her thumb again, another red streak across her thigh, and she was proud of the blood. The mechanism did not look anything like a travel alarm clock. It looked like a bomb.

She should stop, she thought.

She tugged at one of the wires, testing, and a jolt of electricity shot from her fingers up to her elbow. She dropped the mechanism, her arm slightly numb. *Foolish*, she thought. *Dangerous.* And yet she stared at the stove, metal ripped and torn, wires dangling, and she had come this far.

She went back to the drawer for the hammer. She aimed carefully, and she hit the mass of wires where it connected to the timer. Sparks flew, arcing like actual fireworks, and there was a popping sound and a brief rush of terror, but then the buzzing stopped. She stood there in the silence—silence!—with the hammer in her hand, and she felt an overwhelming satisfaction.

Soon, though, she felt other things.

Shame. Dread.

She had utterly lost control.

She could still hear the echo of the popping sound. The air smelled of burning. She reached for the oven and turned the cook setting from "Off" to "Bake," watching for the power light to flash red. There was no light, though.

Not when she tried to bake or broil, not on any temperature setting. The burners, too, were cold and dead.

She had overdone herself.

She wanted a vodka tonic, but she also wanted to tell Evan when he came home that she had not been drinking, so she made a cup of tea and sat down with the Conway file, and eventually Evan opened the door. Before he even set down his suitcase, she was standing.

She wrapped her arms around him and kissed his neck, and he was saying hello and something else, but she cut him off.

"I broke the oven," she said.

He shook his head once, frowning.

"Oh," he said. "You stopped the buzzing?"

"Yes," she said. "That's the good news."

He stepped around her into the kitchen. She watched him take in the sight: the metal panel, peeled back. The wires, bursting out like tentacles. The few glass fragments still attached to the control panel.

"What did you do?" he asked.

"I broke the oven," she repeated.

"How?"

She could not read his expression. She explained. He did not look away from the oven the entire time she talked.

"A hammer?" he said finally.

"Yeah."

"A hammer." He glanced at her and then looked away. "Well, it was ancient anyway. We needed a new one."

She told herself that she should be relieved. He had not yelled or looked at her as if she had lost her mind. He had seemed surprised, but that was all. And yet she thought, *Really? Is he so far away that I can rip apart our appliances and it doesn't even phase him?*

An hour later, she hefted the iron skillet from the counter and considered whether she could use a crème brûlée torch to cook a frittata or whether cheese and crackers might make an acceptable dinner. She turned as Evan stepped into the kitchen, his Nikon camera in his hands. He loved that camera. He held it like a newborn, two handed and well supported.

"What are you doing?" she asked.

He hip-checked her gently, taking her place in front of the stove. He twisted the lens of the camera, barely glancing at her.

"I wanted a picture of this," he said.

He leaned closer to the ruined panel, and she'd always been confused about why you needed to be physically closer to a thing when you had a zoom lens. She watched him twist and sidestep, and she wondered if he was trying to document her descent into madness.

"Why do you want a picture?" she asked.

"Because it sums up what I love about you."

She absorbed that for a moment.

"That I'm crazy?" she said.

"That you don't just sit there," he said, and she was surprised to see that he was smiling at her. "This thing starts buzzing, and it won't stop, and you don't think, oh, well, I'll just live with it. You don't call someone and wait for them to come and fix it. You're the Little Red Hen. I mean, I would have eventually called someone, but—let's face it—it would have been next week. You went looking for a hammer."

He started to laugh and kept going until he had to brace himself against the edge of the stove. He slanted his face toward her, and it had been a long time since she had seen his face light up when he looked at her.

"It was stupid," she said.

He poked at the exposed wires of the stove with one finger. "It wasn't *only* stupid."

"You like that I'm the Little Red Hen?" she said. "Because it sometimes feels like—"

"It feels like what?"

"You don't like how I do it myself."

He faced her, the whole mess of the stove behind him. Her wrist was feeling the weight of the iron skillet, and she eased it onto the counter.

"Lucia," her husband said, his face still alight. "It drives me crazy how you do it yourself. And I love how you do it yourself. It's not an exact science."

He picked up the hammer, tossing it and catching it. She thought of him reaching onto a top shelf, handing down a bowl into her grandmother's butter-slick hands. He had known almost everyone she had ever loved.

"It feels satisfying, doesn't it?" she said, as he flipped the hammer once more.

"It does."

"I don't want to leave this house."

"I know," he said. "I don't really want to move, either, but I think we should. We haven't even had a solid offer for it yet, so who knows? But I imagine we'll get an offer eventually and we'll go back and forth a few hundred times and eventually we'll figure it out."

He stepped behind her, and she assumed he was headed for the tool drawer until she saw his tie flick through the air. His arms came around her, and he looped the tie around her hips, pulling her against him, chest to thighs. She felt his stubble against her cheek, and she leaned against him as he held her there, lassoed.

Rachel

I.

The mailman came by a little after 4:00 p.m., just like he always did. I walked barefoot down the driveway not long after that, just like I always did. I pulled a handful of mail out of the mailbox. The first two pieces were letters for Mom—bills, probably—but the third was a small box wrapped in brown paper with my name written on it.

I had thoughts of Stefanie Powers until I recognized Lucia's writing.

I stood in the shade of Mr. Cleary's pecan tree and I spun the box in my hands. The brown paper was folded, perfectly symmetrical, and the ends were slick with tape. I ripped open the wrapping, letting the paper fall to the concrete. The spider lilies lining the driveway tickled my legs.

I was holding a white box—a jewelry box—and when I lifted the lid I saw a square note on a kind of stationery I'd never seen. It had a swirling texture, like fingerprints, and it was the almost the color of my skin. Lucia had written in a purple pen: *I was thinking of you on St. Patrick's Day*, it read. *I missed that window, but I'm early with these. I know how much you like holidays. I hope they don't weigh down your ears.*

When I lifted the note, I found a pair of earrings, egg shaped. Almost actual egg sized. They were tacky and glitter covered, and I loved them, but I went back to the note and I soaked up Lucia's writing.

The last time I cried in public was at *Charlotte's Web* when I was seven, but I started weeping over earrings, not able to do more than turn my face away from the road. I had almost forgotten what it felt like to have Lucia choose me. I had chosen her first, of course, but every time she poured me a ginger ale, she chose me back. When she took me to the Crab Shack for my birthday and snuck over ahead of time to arrange for cupcakes—she chose me. When she maneuvered this box exactly in the middle of the wrapping paper, making sure the tape was evenly spaced—she chose me. It was my name she had spelled out letter by letter. My mother didn't get to pick me, but Lucia did, and that meant I was someone other than the girl who lived in this house.

I was still standing next to the spider lilies when Mr. Cleary called my name. When I turned, I saw him standing on his front porch, his hands full of wires and cords. I pretended to cough, an excuse to swipe at my eyes.

"I had an idea," he said to me.

He clearly hadn't noticed the crying.

"What is it?" I said, and my voice sounded weird, but he didn't notice that, either.

He stepped into the grass, and I realized the cords he was holding were Christmas lights, long knotted strands of them.

"I'm going to light the pool," he said. "These things sit around in the basement all year long, and I'm going to make use of them."

I stepped into his yard, bits of shell and nut and root cutting into my feet. The shade was denser close to the trunk of the pecan tree.

"You're going to put lights in the pool?" I said.

"Not in it," he said. "Around it. Now I'm wondering about your science curriculum. You know the earth isn't flat, right? And women weren't created from a rib bone?"

"My curriculum is fine," I said. "I know you can't put lights in a pool. I just wasn't sure that you did."

He tilted his head. Now, of course, he chose to be observant.

"You got a look on your face there," he said. "I'm confident you don't believe the earth is flat. Do you believe in Adam and Eve? The whole earth-in-seven-days notion?"

"I—I believe in the Bible, if that's what you mean."

"I apologize," he said, and his voice had turned gentle. It didn't suit him. "I shouldn't have said that. There are multiple ways to read the Bible, and you seemed like you were—well, it just didn't occur to me that you believed it was literal. Which is absolutely fine."

Standing there facing him, I couldn't sort through my thoughts. I understood, of course, that plenty of people did not believe in the Bible, but he was implying something other than lack of belief.

"You don't believe it's literal?" I said.

"No."

"You don't believe it's true?"

"That's not quite the same thing. I don't read it as a collection of facts."

"How do you read it?"

He rolled his shoulders. He played with a loose loop of cord.

"As a collection of stories," he said after a few seconds, leaving a pause between each word. "Powerful stories that might be based on real people and real events. Stories you can interpret as you like. You can find wisdom in them, but I don't believe they actually happened."

I had no frame of reference for what he was saying. This was not a debate about wine versus grape juice. This was unfathomable. "You don't believe it happened like it's written?"

His voice stayed obnoxiously gentle. "I don't."

It was an absurd conversation to be having standing in the front yard, cars rumbling past. My hands were stuffed with mail and his hands were stuffed with lights, and we both had things to do.

"I've never once seen you in your pool," I said. "Can you even swim?"

His eyebrows jerked. "Can I swim?"

"Yeah."

"Yes, I can swim. Of course I can swim. I'm a grown man."

"I'm not sure I believe you."

"I'm definitely grown. And a man."

"My mother is grown, and she can't swim," I said. "Adults do not all know how to swim."

"Well, this one does."

"I still don't believe you," I said, picking up steam. "No one is ever in that pool."

He looked at me and I could see his gears turning. He was in a patch of sun, and I'd never noticed that his eyes were blue.

"Fine," he said. "Let's fix that. The weather's getting warm enough—come over and swim tonight. Bring your mom."

"My mom doesn't like the water," I said.

He snaked his wrist through the tangle of lights until they were looped over his elbow. With his free hand he picked at one strand, loosening the knots slightly.

"Then come over by yourself," he said.

"Tonight?"

He nodded. "I'll prove that I know how to swim."

Eventually—very soon, actually—I would look back at this moment and try to decipher myself. While I wasn't deaf to the voice that whispered *Be careful,* I thought it was my mother's voice. I was still flush with the confidence of earrings, and that voice did not make the idea less appealing.

He was my neighbor. I had once spent three consecutive Thursdays—at Mom's insistence—trying to learn knitting from Mrs. Hightower down the street, and I had carried casseroles to plenty of other neighbors and navigated the hallways of their houses by myself. I would be swimming right next to my own backyard, even though this was technically a man inviting me to spend time with him alone. No, it was not even that. He had invited my mother, too.

He was my neighbor.

"Okay," I said.

"Okay," he said, jarring loose one loop of lights so that it fell to his knees. "Come over after dinner. I'll be here. And now I have some lights to hang."

He nodded at me, squinting in the sun so that the blue of his eyes completely vanished. In two fast steps, he'd disappeared back inside his house, and I wondered why he'd come outside in the first place when the pool was in the backyard.

I made my way back up the driveway, picking a handful of spider lilies on my way. By the time Mom came home, I'd put them in a plastic Hamburglar cup in the middle of the kitchen table, and I was labeling a map of World War II battle sites for U.S. History class.

"I like the lilies," Mom said, shrugging out of her sweater and untucking her tank top. "We have a vase somewhere."

"We do? Where?"

"Well, that's a good question. Maybe in the garage."

She reached for my ice water and took a long swallow. The neck of her blouse was damp.

"I think I'll just leave them in the cup," I said. "I ran into Mr. Cleary when I was getting the mail—it's in the rocking chair—and he told me we could use his pool. Which would be cool."

"Really? When?"

"Tonight," I said. "He's got his son for the night, and they're going out to ShowBiz or somewhere for dinner, and they won't be back until later. He said you and I could come enjoy the pool—weird, huh, that it finally occurred to him to offer after all this time?"

Once I had been surprised by how easy it was to lie. Now I knew it was nothing but acting. You caught hold of the rhythm, and after a sentence or two it didn't even feel untrue.

Mom opened the refrigerator, stared inside, and then closed it again. I got a glimpse of a dish of baked beans, uncovered, rippled like old asphalt.

"You know I'm not going in that pool," she said.

"I figured."

"You're sure he won't be home? He definitely doesn't mind?"

"Yep."

She opened the freezer now, contemplating its innards. She hadn't even looked at me since I'd mentioned the pool, and it occurred to me that all these recent nights with me tucked away safely in my bedroom had probably left her feeling very secure.

"You should stay out of the deep end," she said, lifting a box of broccoli. "You could get a cramp, and no one would be around. But if you're sure you're all right by yourself, then I suppose for just an hour or so—"

"Thanks," I said.

II.

That night I left Mom napping on the sofa, and I hopped across the cobblestones and let myself through our gate. I looked into Mr. Cleary's yard, and he'd done what he said. The Christmas lights were hung along the brick wall of his house—duct tape?—right above the row of flower pots that had nothing but dirt in them. The lights looped from his back door to the last set of shutters, and they flashed blue, red, and green across the surface of the pool.

The two deck chairs on the patio were empty. The door by the patio was dark. I stood there in my spaghetti-strap sundress, which completely covered me from my chest to my ankles, and it wasn't the right outfit for climbing over a fence. Aside from that, it seemed rude to start swimming without saying hello, so I didn't have much choice other than to go around to the front door.

The driveway was dark enough that I couldn't see where my flip-flops were landing. I passed through a square of light under our kitchen window, and a moth brushed against my face. When I reached Mr. Cleary's door, I took a breath and knocked.

"It's unlocked," he called.

I barely gave the door a push, and it swung open. I caught it before it slammed against the wall, and then I was standing in a room that might have been a dining room or a living room. It had a sofa, a long table with chairs, and a bookshelf. Next to me, a floor lamp cast a weak kind of glow.

"I'm in the den," Mr. Cleary called.

I followed his voice, passing down a hallway and through a kitchen, and all of it was dark, too. A half wall separated the kitchen from the den, where the only light was one lamp, pleated like a fan, that spotlighted Mr. Cleary. He sat at one end of a plaid couch, and he had stacks of paper around him and a notepad in his lap. He held a pen in one hand and a juice glass in the other hand. His feet were propped on a coffee table that was empty except for an ashtray with two ceramic alligators biting each other's tails.

The house smelled like smoke, but only a little.

"Hey," he said.

"Hey."

It seemed strange to call him Grant, and yet he'd told me not to call him Mr. Cleary. So I didn't call him anything. I only stood there as he sipped his drink. It was gold when it caught the light, pretty and alcoholic.

"You want something to drink?" he asked, and he crossed one leg over the other. He was in shorts, and his shirt was unbuttoned—only two buttons, nothing immodest, but the bit of chest hair bothered me. The darkness bothered me and the way his thighs were stretched apart bothered me, and the offer of a drink bothered me more. I took a step backward, my foot nearly catching in my long dress.

"I have some iced tea," he said. "It might be kind of old. I have orange juice. My son loves orange juice, but no pulp. He hates pulp. Do you have any strong feelings about pulp, pro or con?"

He set his drink on the rounded arm of the couch, then he grabbed for it as it nearly toppled. He grinned, sheepish, and he looked again like a man who didn't know how to work a garden hose. I almost laughed. I was an idiot, imagining I was in the middle of some HBO show.

"I'm fine," I said. "I just wanted to let you know I was here. I thought maybe I'd try the pool now?"

"Your mom was a definite no?"

"She's asleep on the couch already," I said.

"Then go ahead," he said, giving his pen a twirl. "I'm going to finish up a few notes first. The water's a little chilly, but you'll get used to it."

"How chilly?" I asked, half turning, scoping out the pool through the glass of the kitchen door.

"Bracing," he said.

The water looked tropical with the sparkle of lights and the shadows of the trees. When I tugged at the door, it didn't open.

"Pull harder," Mr. Cleary said.

I did. The door scraped my toes when I jerked it open. As I closed it behind me, Mr. Cleary was drawing lines on his notepad, either underlining or crossing something out.

I kicked off my sandals and set them in one of the patio chairs. The concrete was rough against my feet, and I thought I smelled magnolia. It only lasted as long as one stroke of the breeze. I glanced back through the windows, where I could see Mr. Cleary still on the couch, and it was not a bad thing to be alone. There was something about the light and the darkness. The sky was star speckled, and the moon was thin and sharp, like a Russian weapon. The Christmas bulbs and the reflections on the pool lit up the space around me, but beyond that everything was dark shapes and flutterings. I could see the outline of my house, the kitchen window still lit up—but it was only another shadow.

I could be anywhere.

I walked around the edge of the pool, prolonging. I dipped one foot in and, yes, bracing was one word for it. It was like ice. I looked up at the stars again, and I liked the image of me swimming under them, kicking from one end of the pool to the other, Christmas blinking on my skin.

The temperature didn't matter. I'd get used to it.

I reached for the bottom of my sundress, hiking it up, and as my elbows caught in fabric, the porch light came on. I pulled free of my dress just as Mr. Cleary stepped through the door.

He stood there under the eave of the house, the glow of the porch light brightening his feet and legs but not his face. I folded my dress, and I could tell he was watching. We were separated by the pool, and my bathing suit was a one-piece—all my bathing suits were one-pieces—but still here I was half naked with a grown man who was clothed, even though he'd said he was going to swim, and I wasn't sure whether that was better or worse than having him in his bathing suit.

He kept watching, only watching, and I still couldn't see his face. I didn't want to walk over to the patio chairs, which would take me close to him, so I dropped my dress onto the concrete. I dropped myself to the concrete, too, scooting to the edge of the deep end and folding my legs up to my chest.

"Did you finish your work?" I asked.

"I did."

"Are you going to swim?"

"I need to get my suit," he said, but he didn't move.

You knew I was coming, I thought. *You had plenty of time to put on your suit.*

"It's nice to have someone use the pool," he said, standing there, faceless and unmoving.

"Yeah. Thanks."

"I should have invited you over before now."

I'd only have to scream, I told myself. My mother is about fifty steps away, and she could at least call the police.

Mr. Cleary took a step toward the pool, and he looked more human in motion. He lowered himself into one of the patio chairs, legs stretched out in front of him. I could see him better.

"Is it too cold for you?" he asked.

"No," I said, as I eased my legs into the pool. My feet went slightly numb. My arms broke out in chill bumps.

"I wanted to finish up work before you got here," he said, flexing his feet.

"And swim trunks are not comfortable in terms of sitting for long periods of time. Now, honestly, I'm so damn tired that the thought of changing into my suit is exhausting. Maybe I'll just jump in like this, huh? That would wake me up."

"Yeah," I said.

"Are you sure it's not too cold?" he asked. "You don't have to swim, you know. It's fine if you want to go home and come back some other time."

He yawned, stretched, and let his arms drop, hands skimming the concrete.

I felt tired, too, from ricocheting back and forth between fear and comfort. Or, no, between fear and embarrassment. Because just as I decided that I shouldn't trust this man—just as I decided that I shouldn't jump in the pool because he could trap me there more easily than if I had space to run—just as I was planning escape routes, I'd look at his face and feel sure that I was imagining things.

"I'm fine," I said. "But if you want to go to sleep, I can leave you—"

"No," he said. "Although I'll admit that I'm not sure I'll join you. Even though you'll accuse me of not knowing how to swim. You may have to take my word for it."

"That sounds like what someone would say who doesn't know how to swim," I said.

"Hasn't your mother ever taught you that you should flatter men's egos?"

"Yes," I said.

He did not want me to flatter his ego. I knew that much. If I hadn't been rude to him that first time in the driveway, he would never have invited me to swim in his pool.

The water was feeling warmer. My chill bumps had settled down, and I slid a little farther until the water came to the middle of my thighs. He stood up and moved to the opposite side of the deep end, sitting on the concrete and dangling his feet in the water.

"Shit," he said. "Why didn't you tell me it was too cold?"

He didn't apologize for cursing. He didn't move his feet, either. We sat across from each other, twenty feet of water and chlorine between us, and the stars stretched everywhere.

"It's tricky going against your parents," he said. "I wanted a pool, and when I told my dad I was thinking about putting one in, he said, 'You'll regret it. You won't use it. It's a lot of trouble.' And, of course, that made me get the pool. Even though I was going in the opposite direction, he was still the point of departure."

"The point of departure," I said.

Grant shrugged. "My parents took us all to Mexico when I was ten—Acapulco—and we stayed in this place with a pool shaped like a big bean. It had all these huge flowers around it, maybe canna lilies, and it was the most beautiful thing I'd ever seen. So maybe that's why I wanted a pool."

"You traveled to other countries when you were a kid?" I asked.

"Just that once."

"Have you ever gone to the airport and just bought a ticket somewhere? Like, spur of the moment?"

He leaned back, resting on his hands. His shirt pulled up, showing a strip of his stomach. It didn't bulge over his waistband.

"Never done it," he said. "I like the idea, though."

"Me too," I said.

I leaned back on my hands, matching his pose. I made circles in the water with my feet. I could hear the bass rumble of a car as it drove past, and I thought of my mother sleeping on the couch. She might wake up and decide to check on me, and she'd find me sitting here in the dark, dress discarded, with this divorced man who was not so much older than I was, and I thought of the excuses I could make. He got home earlier than expected, I'd say. He was checking to make sure the filters were working, I'd say.

"You know what you said about the Bible?" I said.

"Yeah."

"Since God wrote it," I said, "doesn't it all have to be true? He would get it right."

"Men wrote it."

"Right. But God told them what to write."

He kicked back and forth, splashing. "I see. All right, I believe men wrote it, and maybe there was inspiration at work, but they were only men. They did the best they could. The finished product is—messy."

I let the words eddy, and I watched the blues and blacks of the water.

"You were writing something when I got here," I said.

"Not really. More like thinking on paper. Just work."

"What do you do?"

"I'm a lawyer, I think."

"You think?"

"Let's just say that it's not all that I hoped it would be."

"I have friend who's a lawyer," I said, because I wanted to say her name. "Lucia Gilbert."

He leaned forward, and the colored lights freckled his face. "Lucia Gilbert?"

"You know her?"

"Well, yeah," he said. "In passing. I could be listening to her right now."

"What?"

"You know that award she was getting tonight?"

"No."

The breeze blew, barely, but it was enough to make me shiver. The leaves rustled behind me, and I crossed my arms.

"It's a banquet downtown," Grant said. "A Woman-of-the-Year thing. My firm bought a table at it, and I thought about going. What time is it now? I bet she's right in the middle of her thank-you speech. How do you know her?"

I watched a small frog, belly up, float past my feet. It was as small as a toenail.

"My mom talked to her about the divorce," I said. "Mom didn't hire her, but I just, sort of, showed up at her house and she let me in."

"Huh," he said. "Okay then."

"I haven't seen her in a while," I said. "Mom is not a big fan."

"No," he said. "I'd imagine she's not. Who is your mother a fan of, by the way?"

The current in the pool shifted, and the frog drifted back in my direction.

"Princess Diana?" I said. "Anyway, Mom told me not to go over to Lucia's house anymore, and she also told Lucia to stay away from me."

These were not sentences I had said to anyone else.

"Why?" he asked.

"There was a shooting," I said.

"You were there when it happened?" he said. "At her house?"

"You know about it?"

"Yeah. Everybody knows about it. Somebody shoots up a lawyer's house and drives away? It's the sort of thing other lawyers find worth talking about."

"She sent me some Easter earrings today."

Grant let his head fall back, and he stared at the sky for long enough that I thought my earrings comment must have been either incredibly boring or somehow offensive. After a few breaths, though, he slapped his hands against the concrete and jumped to his feet, water sloshing over the side of the pool.

"Let's go," he said.

"What?"

"Let's go hear your friend. You get your dress back on, and we'll drive downtown and check it out. Maybe we can catch the end of it. You can surprise her. Come on. Spur of the moment."

It took me several long seconds to move. When I did, I only lifted my legs from the water and curled them under me. I looked over at my house again, so close, and Mom had told me countless times that if someone tried to grab you and pull you into a car, fight with everything you had because once you were in the car your chances of surviving dropped by half.

I looked up at him, and the lights were blinking faster against the wall, like maybe there was a short in the strand.

"Are you serious?" I asked.

"Completely," he said. "You've got a dress. You're barely damp. I'll throw on something decent. Your mom never has to know. Unless, I don't know—you'd rather go back home and curl up on the couch next to her? Have a little nap and watch some Lawrence Welk?"

I thought of my mother making her way over the cobblestones, opening the gate, and looking across our driveway at the empty pool. She would panic, surely. I felt the pull of her, but I didn't want to feel it.

I thought of Lucia.

Watch this.

"In your car?" I asked, standing.

"Are you saying you want to drive?" he asked. "Here I was thinking I was being gentlemanly. Come on. You got me thinking with your talk about plane tickets. It's been ages since I've done something fun and stupid and unplanned."

I picked up my dress and pulled it over my head. I ran my fingers through my hair.

"This sounds fun to you?" I asked. "An awards dinner for someone you hardly know?"

"You'd be surprised at what I think is fun," he said. "Here's your shoes."

I jogged toward him, ignoring the voice in my head telling me not to run at the pool. As I slid on my flip-flops, Grant opened the kitchen door. A moth jounced off the glass and slipped inside.

"So are we doing this?" he asked. "Or are you escaping back to your couch?"

"We're doing it," I said.

He took off through his kitchen, not quite running but close to it. I'd caught some of his excitement. I liked this pace. No thinking, only gliding from one step to the next. I locked the door behind me as I stepped into the kitchen, which was still dark, lit only by the lamp next to the sofa.

Lucia, I thought. She would be surprised—pleased?—to have me appear at a lawyerly banquet, out of nowhere, and she'd surely recognize Grant, so maybe she would say hello to him, and then she'd see me standing there, too, and she would smile. I'd tell her the story of how Grant and I headed off in the middle of the night, and Lucia would laugh up at the ceiling, and I had not seen her do that for so long.

"Come on," Grant said, coming back to the kitchen, a suit jacket and a tie draped over his arm. He was buttoning up a white shirt, and I didn't mind the chest hair so much this time.

I couldn't quite keep up with him as we cut through his front yard. He climbed in the driver's side of his red VW Bug and stretched across to unlock my side. It was only once I was inside that I felt the discomfort inching back. The car was small, his knee was maybe three inches from mine, and if he took a corner too sharp, my shoulder would bump against his. I could smell chlorine, which was probably some combination of both of us. It made the space feel more claustrophobic, like indoor pools and locker rooms. As Grant backed out of the driveway, I lifted the lock of my door up and down, making sure I could unlock it.

It didn't take long to reach downtown at that time of night. We were out of our neighborhood in a couple of minutes, and soon we were in Old Cloverdale, which you could recognize by the size of the mansions and the tree branches that stretched over the road and met in the middle, blocking out the sky in places.

"The McNally House," Grant said. "It's at the McNally House. I always forget whether that's on Court or Perry or Hull. Or even on Gilmer? I still confuse them after all these years. They all look the same."

"My school is on South Court," I said.

He pulled up to a stop sign. "That doesn't help me a whole lot. Unless the McNally House happens to be next to your school?"

"Sorry," I said.

"Let's try Perry," he said, making the turn. "We're looking for a three-story colonial. White with columns. Very *Gone with the Wind*."

"All of these look like *Gone with the Wind*," I said and kept my face to the window, enjoying, as always, the gas lanterns and the stone fountains, the never-ending porches and the gazebos and the Julietish balconies. The Governor's Mansion. And then we were deep into the part of downtown that felt like a foreign country, the one-way streets turning into a maze. The mansions had evaporated by the time we crossed under I-85, replaced by apartments and tiny brick churches and stores with bars on the windows. We stopped at a red light, and I watched a black man walk down the street, unsteady. The light changed to green. In another block we passed a couple of skinny white men, baseball caps pulled down, laughing so loud I could hear them as we passed. A hardware store had the glass knocked out of a window.

Next to me, Grant had gone quiet. He was frowning at the road as he slowed at yet another light.

"Is this right?" I asked.

"No," he said, as the light turned green. "I've gone too far. And the one-way streets make this such a pain in the ass. Which way, now, let's see— Adams won't go through. Oh, damn it, Adams did go. It's Washington that's only headed west. Okay, let's see. We'll turn here on Dexter and then we'll head back up on McDonough—or maybe Hull?"

It seemed like his sense of direction must be even worse than mine—we'd wound up in the worst part of downtown, nowhere near anything that looked like Tara. We passed a building that had clearly burned and never been repaired, a world away from marble columns. Surely Grant had known that he'd made a mistake long before I said anything. He was nervous, I thought.

"Do you mind driving at night?" I asked.

He'd managed the turn onto Hull, so we were at least headed back into the right neighborhood. He aimed a quick look at me.

"No," he said. "Not at all."

"Some people have trouble seeing in the dark," I said. "Because of the reflections and everything. Mom won't drive at night."

"I'm not your mother, Rachel."

He made a right turn and then, a few seconds later, a left turn. I didn't see a street sign at either turn, and nothing looked familiar. Aunt Molly's house couldn't have been too far away—maybe even walkable—although she didn't live around the mansions. I knew I had to be close to my high school, but I had no idea how I would get there. We hadn't passed another car in several minutes.

"Do you know where we are?" I asked.

"I have a general idea," he said. "But I'm still working on how we get to the McNally House from here."

With a jab of his foot and a swirl of the stick shift, he slowed down and pulled over to the curb on the one-way street. It was even darker here—we were in a gap between streetlights, and the branches overhead blocked the slice of moon. I pressed my face against the window, looking for a street name. My foot kicked an empty Coke bottle on the floorboard.

"What street are we on?" I asked.

"Not sure," he said. "Just give me a minute. I'm trying to orient myself."

He leaned to the right, peering up through the windshield, although there was nothing to see. His hand landed on the edge of my seat, and if he stretched his fingers out, he would touch my thigh.

"Maybe I am a little jittery," he said. "The truth is that I haven't driven a whole lot around this part of town at night. Let me think—how would I get to Gilmer from here?"

"The McNally House is on Gilmer?" I said.

"Yeah. At about Gilmer and Felder, I think. We just have to figure out where we are now."

He turned to me, one hand still on my seat and the other hand on the steering wheel. The chlorine smell was stronger than it had been. I could only see the outline of his face, and I thought of old games of hide-and-seek in closets, the breath of a friend on my face, the smell of root beer Dum-Dums.

I could hear his slacks as he shifted on his seat.

"You remembered?" I asked.

"What?" he said.

"You said you didn't know which street the McNally House was on."

"Did I?" he said. "Maybe I'm more tired than I realized. Maybe I shouldn't be driving. Lord, I am sick of work. Work and sleep, work and sleep. That's all there is. But, yeah, it's definitely on Gilmer near Felder."

Although my back was against the door—the handle jamming into my spine—he was still only inches away. We sat. I faced the windshield, but I could feel him watching me. Felder Avenue. I knew Felder. I turned off Felder on the way to school.

"You don't like being a lawyer?" I said.

"Oh, Rachel," he said, and he wasn't touching the steering wheel or the gear shift or any reasonable part of the car. His hands were free.

"Should we go home?" I said.

I spotted a flash of yellow ahead, a light hanging above the street. It could be the left turn I usually made going to school. If I was right, this street was South Court. My school would be a few blocks ahead on the right.

Mr. Cleary hadn't answered me. He put his hand on the back of my seat, and I could feel his fingers brush my hair. It could have been an accident. A car drove past, and I caught a quick glimpse of his face, familiar in the headlights. Eyes still blue and tired. No fangs or claws.

I didn't know him at all.

Maybe he was just an exhausted guy who was lost and confused and lonely, and if I asked, he would move his hands away from my hair and turn around and take me home. Or maybe he was a different kind of guy entirely.

His hand in my hair again, stroking this time.

Be careful, said my mother's voice.

Watch this, said Lucia's.

I listened to both of them. I grabbed at the handle and opened my door just as the red taillights from the passing car vanished.

"I'm going to walk," I said.

"What?" said Mr. Cleary, his hand landing in the empty space where I'd been sitting. "What are you talking about? Get back in the car, Rachel. We're in the middle of downtown. It's not safe."

I slammed the door behind me and darted to the sidewalk, a chunk of worn concrete moving under my foot. I started running, and I wished I was wearing something other than flip-flops. It couldn't be rocket science to find a street sign. I'd know soon enough if this was South Court, and if it was,

Felder Avenue would be just ahead at the flashing light, and that should take me to Gilmer, and even if it didn't, I could get to Molly's from my high school, and the thing that mattered more than any of that was to get away from Grant Cleary.

I looked behind me and saw that he'd turned off the headlights. He opened his door, jumping onto the curb at the same time.

"I can't just leave you wandering around down here," he called. "You know that!"

When I realized that he was running, too, I picked up speed. My toe caught on an edge of raised sidewalk, and I stumbled, landing hard on one knee. My palms burned against the concrete as I shoved myself up.

"Rachel!" he called. "I'll take you home. Get back in the car!"

I could hear his feet hitting the pavement. It would be embarrassing, wouldn't it, if I was wrong about him? I did not think of embarrassment. I looked ahead. I could feel wetness on my hurt knee, but it was easy to ignore. I let my feet slam the concrete, and soon I couldn't hear him anymore. I took my first left turn, under a massive tree that was splitting the sidewalk, and I thought he might not see me change directions. The moon was hanging over the houses, and roaches zagged across the concrete, blacker than black. Soon it didn't feel like running: I was diving into the dark with both feet, and the shadows flew up around me.

Lucia

I.

The waiters and waitresses were clearing the round tables by the time Lucia, Evan, and her parents were able to step through the side door of the McNally House after her speech. A line of cars wound through the parking lot, bottlenecked at the single exit. Her mother carried a centerpiece—daisies and nasturtiums—which the emcee had encouraged guests to take home.

"You just did so well," Caroline said. "You never seemed the least bit nervous in front of all those people."

"Thanks," said Lucia.

It had barely been a speech at all. She'd thanked everyone, and she'd quoted Proverbs—*To do righteousness and justice is more acceptable to the Lord than sacrifice*—because it never hurt to lead with the Bible. She'd made some well-polished comments about how not only had women been robbed over the years—robbed of property, of education, of possibilities—but the state and the country had been robbed, too, of all that women could have taught and created and discovered. She talked of mothers and daughters and of what came next.

"Those green beans with almonds," said Caroline. "So delicious. The chocolate cake was a little dry, but the icing was good."

"I liked the cake," Evan said, his hand on Lucia's back.

"They had someone introduce the woman who introduced you," her father said. "Is that usually how they do it? If they'd have cut all those introducers, we'd have gotten out of here an hour earlier."

Lucia tugged at her silk skirt, which was long enough that it kept snagging in the straps of her high heels. Her father had tilted his forehead against hers as she hugged him hello tonight, asking her if she had the gun in her purse. *I hate to think of you defenseless,* he'd said, and he'd run a hand over her hair like he used to do to their Lhasa Apso. She liked being with her parents after a public event, when she was still, at least partially, the stage version of herself. That Lucia had endless patience and humor.

"I think they wanted to let as many people as possible participate," she told him.

"Mission accomplished," her father said. "Y'all up here on the left?"

"Yeah, we're right there," Evan said. "Where are you?"

"On the street," Oliver said, pointing. "We thought they might charge in the lot."

Lucia hoped her father would be safe driving back this late. He didn't drive much at night anymore. Behind them a line of men and women in white shirts and black pants carried trays covered with foil and boxes loaded full of wine bottles. The caterers followed one another, antlike, emptying their arms into the back of a white van and then heading back inside for more.

"I thought the black woman who introduced you was very attractive," said her mother, jingling her topaz tennis bracelet. "Don't you think? And you looked so pretty up there, too. You know, I remember that there's a rush to it. Being on stage."

"When have you ever been on stage?" asked Lucia.

Her mother laughed her saloon girl's laugh. Her lipstick had worn off, and she looked younger in the moonlight. "Fifth-grade spelling bee. I thought I'd wet my pants I was so scared. I made it to the final three, and when I walked off the stage, I tripped and landed with my face in Gabriel Anthony's neck and he smelled like cheese. But after it was done, it was like all that nervousness came to a boil and turned kind of good. Is that what you feel like?"

"I feel the good part onstage, too," Lucia said. "Not just after. You never told me you were in a spelling bee."

"I liked spelling. And Gabriel Anthony, until I smelled him." Her mother stopped in the middle of the sidewalk, reaching over to touch Lucia's thumb. "You've got a burn there. Did you use aloe?"

"Did you?" Lucia asked, halting next to her.

Even in the dim light, she could see the fresh mark on her mother's wrist. Likely another brush against the oven rack.

They were a family of reckless cooks.

Her grandmother would have enjoyed tonight. She'd have worried over her wardrobe, flat refused to go shopping, and ultimately would have felt deeply satisfied to get more wear out of one of her two party dresses: the ancient navy polka dot or the beaded lavender. They'd buried her in the lavender, and Lucia had worked equations as she gripped the metal casket. Her grandmother was born in 1892. Lucia's own children, when she had them, should live past 2050; her grandchildren might live until 2100, and if she told them of tractors and milk cows and burned-off eyebrows and the flirting soldier who crushed a favorite hat on the train to Birmingham—if she got the stories right—then Ingrid Alma Bledsoe, a woman who never left the state of Alabama and never wore a pair of pants, would stay alive for more than two centuries.

Her mother was holding her burned wrist toward the light, trying to see it around the nasturtiums.

"I always kill the aloe," she said.

"You don't need to water it every day, Mother," Lucia said. "You overwater."

"Traffic's cleared up some, don't you think?" said Oliver behind them, shifting from loafer to loafer. "We'd better head on."

"Let me take those, Caroline," Evan said, reaching for the flower arrangement. "I'll carry them to the car for you, and Oliver can get the door."

Lucia watched as her mother handed over the arrangement. Even in the kind light, the illusion of youth didn't hold. Caroline moved more slowly than she used to, and she was thicker around the waist. Underneath her topaz necklace, freckles covered her clavicles. Lucia remembered lying in her mother's lap during a thousand sermons, her hair ribbon hanging against her mother's stockings. She would pinch the ribbon between her fingers, a magnifying glass, and every peek through the loop captured some piece of her mother. Smooth, filed nails. Vaccination scar on her arm. The freckles across her throat, which Lucia had once been able to count. They were uncountable now. She had watched the dusting across her own throat darken and spread, and she knew they would cover her, too, one day.

"Essie and Matthew are headed this way," said Evan, vase tucked in the crease of his elbow.

"I barely got to speak to them tonight," Lucia said.

"I'll go with your parents," Evan said, shifting his grip on the arrangement. "You stay here and chat. I'll meet you at the car."

They exchanged a quick round of hugs, and Evan shepherded her parents away. Lucia watched the three of them head off at an angle—"up by the fire hydrant," her father was saying, and she admired the width of her husband's shoulders. Matthew and Essie Green stopped and congratulated her, and they had news of their son, who'd been accepted at Florida A&M. She saw how close the Greens stood to each other, no space between their arms, and she watched Essie straighten Matthew's collar. Over their shoulders, she could still see Evan between her parents, his hand under her mother's elbow as they stepped around a buckled bit of sidewalk.

In the beginning, she had kept track of how often he touched her like that. She'd noticed every single brush of his hand against her back, every linking of his fingers through hers.

After a while, the touches became uncountable. She felt him all the time.

She had talked to clients before about the ebb and flow of marriage, but she had never really believed in it. She had seen clients inching toward a court date, claws extended, and then both of them would magically realize that they were still deeply in love with this person who they'd just claimed shouldn't be allowed to see their own child unsupervised or ought to have mandatory drug testing, and every time she had secretly thought that those people were unbalanced. Still, she'd constructed a speech about how every marriage had low points and high points, and she'd warned plenty of clients that a low point wasn't the same as an ending.

She still thought people were crazy who reconciled after hiring lawyers and drawing up custody schedules and screaming threats over the phone at each other. There was a point at which you could not go backward.

But maybe at times you could. And maybe it wasn't even backward. Maybe it was an ebb and flow, and it all came together—not an exact science—and you had to trust that it would. It didn't fully cohere, but there was her husband, disappearing into the darkness with her parents, likely still talking of traffic and green beans, and she kept watching the spot where she had last seen him.

Matthew and Essie said good-bye, and Lucia turned toward Evan's Datsun, which was at the far end of the lot, separated from the street only by the sidewalk and a narrow patch of grass and dandelions. Her shoes were cutting into her feet, so she paused, lifting one foot to run a finger under the edge of the strap.

A car on the street pulled alongside her, and at first she thought it was parking in one of the parallel spots. She finished adjusting her shoe and headed down the sidewalk, and the car did not stop. It followed behind her, keeping pace. She could see the headlights and front fender from the corner of her eye, and she thought of bail hearings and rifles, and she thought that maybe her father was wiser than she had given him credit for. She thought, too, that if the shooter was in the car, she would very much like to see his face.

The line of cars exiting had finally cleared out, and Evan hadn't returned. The catering staff seemed to have vanished en masse. The car crept along next to her, still barely in her peripheral vision. There was no one else in sight. She stepped into the broad bright circle of a streetlight, and she slowed her pace, because surely the light was preferable to the shadows. Some small degree of protection. She skimmed her hand along her purse strap, acting as if she were adjusting the weight. She dipped her fingers past the open zipper, feeling the edge of her wallet. The cap of a pen. Her checkbook. She felt the curve of metal as a woman called out her name.

"Lucia Gilbert," the voice said. "I thought that was you."

Lucia turned, her hand still in her purse. She didn't recognize the driver. The two-door car was in shadows, and the woman had leaned across the passenger seat to roll down the window. She was sprawled across the front seat awkwardly, and Lucia could only see long dark hair. Then the woman turned her head, and her perfect face caught the streetlights.

Bo Derek cheeks.

"Donna?" Lucia said, dropping her hand to her side.

She hadn't seen Donna Lambert since she'd told her to find a new lawyer. It was strange that her former client would stop to say hello on a downtown street after dark. They hadn't parted on friendly terms. But no, that was not what was happening. The look on Donna's face was not friendly.

"Are you going to do it?" Donna asked, faint lines creased between her symmetrical eyebrows. She had one hand on the window frame. The angle of her neck looked uncomfortable.

Lucia walked to the passenger side of the car, a pointy-nosed Mazda, and, of course, this woman had a red sports car. Lucia leaned down, nearly at eye level.

"What are you talking about?" she asked.

"Jerry wasn't trying to hit anyone," Donna said. "He lost his temper—I know that, and it's a problem, honestly. But no one got hurt, and he never came near you again. He told me that. Afterward. Not that I knew anything beforehand."

By the time she finished speaking, Lucia had pieced it together.

"Jerry was the man you were seeing in Atlanta," she said.

"I thought you must know."

"No," said Lucia. "No. I didn't know."

Another car drove past, the headlights blinding for a moment. Somewhere in the darkness, a woman laughed. Lucia thought of glass breaking and the taste of carpet, of Rachel's thick hair against her palm and the empty space where Evan had been standing.

She thought of the gun in her purse.

"I don't understand the purpose of it," she said. "I no longer represented you. I didn't have anything to do with you. Was that the issue? You were mad at me for refusing to keep your case? He was mad at me for saying you shouldn't see him? Is that really what was behind him nearly killing me—nearly killing my husband and a child?"

"I had nothing to do with it," Donna said.

Lucia bent closer, ducking her head into the car. Donna pulled back, latching on to the steering wheel.

"He wouldn't have known my name unless you told him," Lucia said.

"Well, yes, I mentioned you. He obviously knew the name of my lawyer."

Lucia breathed in and out.

"Why?" she managed.

"He didn't mean to hurt anyone."

"I asked you why." She backed up and grabbed hold of the side mirror as she saw Donna glance at the gear shift. "Oh, don't think about leaving now. Why did you stop if you didn't want to talk to me? He shot six bullets into my house, Donna, and I never even met the man. I never even knew his last name. I think you can suffer through explaining why."

The shadows played over the woman's face, and she looked like some Pre-Raphaelite painting, all hair and lips. She gave every appearance of being desperate to escape, and yet she was the one who had stopped the car. Lucia wondered what she had planned. A tearful monologue? A screaming and gnashing of teeth? Had she lost her nerve?

"I ended things," Donna said.

"Your boyfriend tried to kill me and my family because you broke up with him?"

"I told him what you said about how I couldn't see anyone until the divorce was final. I said we should stay away from each other, and he didn't like that."

"You didn't like it, either," Lucia said. "Which is why you ignored my advice."

She shifted her sore feet, suspecting her shoes had broken the skin. She did not let go of the car.

"That was stupid of me," Donna said. "I told him that. I told him that you were right and that I should wait. He just—I don't know. Maybe he'd been drinking? He had a bad spell. He's not normally like that. I mean, I feel bad for him. I think he has some problems."

"Yes, I'd say he does," Lucia said.

"He's not my boyfriend," said Donna, straightening so that Lucia could only see the lower half of her face. "That's done. But I wish you wouldn't press charges. It won't help any. He regrets everything."

Lucia was about to ask why, if the man so regretted it, he had tried to shoot holes in his neighbor, but the sound of footsteps on the asphalt made her look up. She saw Marlon jaywalking across Gilmer, veering around a puddle, and he was in a suit. The jacket and tie made it clear that he had come to the banquet to see her tonight, and she hadn't even noticed him. He fumbled in his pocket and pulled out his keys, and she recognized his car parked at the curb because of the beagles scrabbling against the backseat window. Why in the world had he brought the beagles?

Overhead, something fluttered past the streetlight bulb, and Lucia felt a rush of affection and disbelief. This man had held her dog captive and yet these days he chatted with her in her driveway and rolled her emptied trash can back to the carport, and all of it was possible because she had forgiven him for taking the dog—an act of complete lunacy—and of course she had forgiven him because what other choice did she have? You could not accumulate all these resentments. The weight of them would crush you. Meanwhile Donna stared up at her, lavender eyeshadow glittering, compelled for some reason to defend a no-good, violent ex-boyfriend, a man who must have frustrated and disappointed her, and forgiveness did not seem like the right word for whatever this was.

Across the street, Marlon walked around to the driver's side of his car.

Lucia caught a glimpse of hind legs and tail as at least one dog sailed over the front seat.

"Just a minute," she told Donna. "Marlon!"

"I knew this was pointless," said Donna, reaching for the gearshift. "I knew it wouldn't help anything."

Lucia looked from Marlon to Donna, noticing how the woman's hand shook slightly. Her voice, too, hadn't seemed quite steady, and Lucia wondered if she should be driving. Marlon had spotted her, though, and she could see his grin from across the street. He waved wildly, and she lifted a hand. He was still waving as he opened his car door, only partially, but enough.

The beagles pushed past him.

The dogs raced across the street, which was miraculously empty, and Lucia stepped away from the car, ready to corral them. As soon as she stepped back, Donna shifted into drive, shaking her head at Lucia, not looking toward the street at all. The dogs kept coming, and Lucia didn't have a chance to voice a warning before Donna jerked the wheel and a tire slammed into the faster dog.

It was possible that the beagle hit the car, not the other way around. But the thud was sickening, and Lucia screamed, the sound breaking out of her without thought.

Brakes, squealing. Donna, screaming, the passenger window still open. Marlon, crossing the street as heedlessly as his dogs, and his screams took the shape of one word.

"No," he called. "No! No!"

He said it again and again, and by the time he reached the car, he was barely whispering. Lucia ran around the front of the car to meet him, holding a hand up against the glare of the headlights.

One dog was on its feet, unharmed, nosing along the spine of the second beagle. That one—why had she never asked Marlon their names?—was lying on its side, unmoving, legs bent, front paws crossed.

Marlon dropped to his knees, running a hand over the dog, his hand slowing along the curve of its skull, stroking its ears.

Lucia leaned down, then straightened, realizing she was blocking the light. "Marlon," she said.

"He's breathing." Marlon was kneeling in a traffic lane, and it seemed possible that the next passing car might sever his feet. Lucia grabbed at his hand to tug him closer to the curb.

Marlon didn't understand at first, resisting, and his weight threw her off balance. She put a hand down on Donna's sporty two-door to steady herself and she felt the engine thrumming, the metal warm against her palm. She realized that Donna was still sitting at the wheel with the car running. She wondered if Marlon had the same thought, because he stood, giving the injured dog one more stroke and scooping up the other dog under one arm.

"You hit my dog," he said.

Lucia shook her head, tugging at his hand. They were in the glow of headlights and streetlight, well lit.

"Calm down," she said, because she could see Marlon as Donna must see him, and he was not a big man, but he was thick and his face was red with possibly fear but maybe anger.

Lucia couldn't make out Donna's expression against the headlights, but over the angled hood of the car, she could see hands gripping the steering wheel.

"You hit my dog," Marlon said again, and his voice was shaking. "You need to get out of the car so we can call the police."

Lucia stepped closer to Marlon, still unable to see Donna's beautiful face, but well able to see the Mazda jump forward slightly. She was sure that the woman had shifted the car back into drive.

"No," she said firmly, not shouting. She held out a hand. "Stop, Donna."

She had no idea, it occurred to her. She had no idea if a single word that Donna said was true. Who knew, maybe Donna had taken the gun from her boyfriend and fired those shots herself? Maybe she had told the boyfriend to do it or maybe she really was blameless. Maybe at this moment she was terrified that this red-faced man would attack her, or maybe she liked the idea of making Lucia bleed.

Regardless, Lucia planted herself in front of the car. The prone beagle was slightly off to the side, out of the path of the tire, but Marlon was directly in front of the hood. She angled herself in front of him, her skirt brushing against the bumper, and she backed up so that he had no choice but to back away as well. Keeping him behind her, she felt the pistol in her purse slap against her hipbone. She knew what would happen if she reached into her bag: this seemed to be one of those scenarios that Evan warned about. By the time she got the gun, the front fender of the car would have broken her knees, leaving her bloody like a dog on the pavement.

She would have to tell Evan that: he had been right. The gun had not made her safe. Although it had made her feel safe, whether that was a false sense of security or a legitimate comfort—she and Evan could argue about it, she would love to argue it, him stealing a sip of her drink, his hand warm against her hip. He would shake his head at the fact that after all the boys' club stonewalling and sexist slurs and ass grabbing, it was a woman who decided to run her down.

Marlon threw an arm in front of her, shouting. She could see them both, from a distance, like a movie, going through the motions of an absurd dance, and the car seemed to be moving in slow motion, too, but it would not be slow enough.

Lucia braced herself, even as she stumbled.

Rachel

1.

I'd been running for a few blocks when I realized that I couldn't hear or see Mr. Cleary behind me. I suspected he'd gone back to his car, and I could see how it made more sense to come after me that way. I didn't feel afraid, though. Adrenaline had sapped away the burn in my lungs and the ache in my legs, but I was eating up sidewalk, weightless, passing house after house with blurs of lighted walkways and porch swings and gingerbread curlicues around the roofs.

I was almost sure that I would make it to Lucia's banquet before Mr. Cleary found me, and if not, I would run up to one of these houses, and I would scream my head off. I might enjoy screaming.

I wondered if Mr. Cleary had been right about Gilmer. It was possible that the McNally House was a separate street entirely, and I might be blocks off course. It didn't worry me: I would find my way. The street was silent enough that I could hear the leaves on the trees, and I'd have thought that downtown would be all horns and sirens.

It was a night full of surprises.

It was possible Mr. Cleary had given up and gone home, and he might even head next door and tell my mother what had happened. Maybe he would stand there in his jacket and tie and explain how he'd done nothing but offer me a ride, and then I'd burst out of the car and disappeared into the night. Maybe my mother would even believe that version, but I doubted it. My horror story would suit her better.

A collection of stories, Mr. Cleary had said. *Interpret as you like.*

I clenched my toes tighter around my flip-flops, and I thought of Grant Cleary: he struggled with garden hoses and analyzed the Bible like he was sitting in English class and touched me too often for it to be accidental. Then there was Margaret Morris: she bought me Icees and hurled razors and would give her life for me even though she hardly knew me. And Lucia Gilbert: she threw her body on top of mine when the bullets came and she shut the door in my face. It was all a mess, everything overflowing out of drawers that were never going to close, and I did not mind because I was overflowing, too.

I was open to interpretation.

I saw a stream of headlights a block or two ahead of me. A line of cars, all turning right from the same parking lot. I saw windows, lit, and a gas streetlamp by a stone fountain.

I didn't slow down until I reached the curb. I noticed the street sign that said Gilmer, and I waited for a gap in the line of cars. When I was midway across the street, I spotted Evan's car in the parking lot, and then I saw Lucia near a car I didn't recognize.

Lucia.

It felt like years since I had seen her.

I stopped next to a white van that was pulled up close to the house, which wasn't quite as big as I'd expected, although it was like Mr. Cleary described, Tara-ish. The black shutters were glossy, and through the front windows I could see chandeliers and fireplaces and pictures on the walls so vivid that they looked like the paint was still wet. The side door of the house was propped open with a broom. The back doors of the van next to me were wide open, too, with stacks of aluminum trays and cardboard boxes crammed across the entire floor. The inside of the van was unlit, but all the aluminum reflected the streetlights, and I could see my face looking back at me in one of the lids. The boxes mostly held wine, dozens of bottles, only their necks sticking out. I could hear the water in the fountain splashing, and, from inside the McNally House, I could hear voices that I imagined belonged to whoever owned all the stuff in the van.

I stepped behind one of the open doors, thinking it would make me less obvious. I didn't want to interrupt Lucia, but I also didn't want her driving off without seeing me. I'd need a ride home, wouldn't I?

I glanced into the street again. No sign of Mr. Cleary. I glanced down at my skinned knee, and the blood had started to gel.

Lucia was wearing a gown that caught the headlights, and her hair was piled up in the way I loved. She was fidgeting, lifting one foot and then the other as she leaned into the passenger side of a red sports car. I heard footsteps behind me, and when I turned, I saw a man in a dark suit stepping off the curb, head swiveling. *Left, right, left, right,* he looked, all the way across the pavement.

I didn't recognize him until I saw the dogs smack against the car window. The Moxie kidnapper had come to the banquet? I looked back at Lucia, who was pushing away from the car, seeing him, too. She called his name, and he opened his car door. The dogs slipped out and ran.

No one has any reason to be out after 9:00 p.m., I thought of Mom saying. *Nothing good happens.*

The headlights were too bright, and I had to put a hand over my eyes. Someone screamed—maybe Lucia. The sports car jerked, cutting sharply into the street, and the dog just kept coming, and then it lay there in the road. I looked around the parking lot. The door to the house was still open, and the white light came through it, comforting and safe, and I willed someone to step into the doorway. Someone would come.

Only they didn't.

Lucia leaned over the dog, and so did the man—Marlon—and he looped an arm around his other dog, pulling him close. Then Lucia and Marlon were standing, and Lucia held a hand out, like Diana Ross.

The car, I realized. The car was still running. I saw it jolt forward as Lucia and Marlon backed away, too slowly. I couldn't see anything of the driver— there was only a dark rectangle of windshield—but I could tell the driver was aiming for them. I felt the anger wash over me, and it simplified everything. My hands were empty, but I was capable of slaying all sorts of creatures.

Watch this.

Maybe terrible things happen. Maybe riptides and car wrecks and divorce and gunshots fall out of the sky, and maybe you are powerless against it. But maybe not.

I reached into the dark cave of the van and grabbed two bottles of wine, heavy and solid, and they fit perfectly in my hands. The car jerked toward Lucia, and as it did, I swung the bottles and let them go. One crashed against the road but another sailed over Lucia's head and smashed against the hood of the car, and it was as if I had some hidden talent for freezing time. The car screeched and stopped. For a moment, so did Lucia and Marlon and even the beagle in his arms. The bottle wasn't a bottle anymore—the glass had turned into confetti. Wine ran down the fenders and bumper, pooling on the asphalt, and any fear or anger inside me all at once tilted toward something like joy.

A woman inside the car shrieked, high pitched and helpless. Marlon leaped back, his hands wet and shining, barely keeping hold of his dog. Lucia turned, too, stepping to the curb and dragging him with her. Wine spilled everywhere.

I picked up another bottle, swinging it, and I was denser and lighter and more. I had no idea there would be such bliss in breaking things. A woman leaned out of the driver's window and then pulled her head back into the car like a scared turtle, and I wanted her scared.

I could see when Lucia spotted me. Her hand stretched toward me, nails shining, so familiar that they were almost my own hands.

"Rachel," she called, and I had missed hearing her say my name.

Lucia

1.

There was red wine everywhere. It looked as if the car had slaughtered her and Marlon then rewound back to where it started.

Donna was still screaming. The woman could do nothing but scream.

"What the hell?" said Marlon.

Lucia didn't bother answering. Her skirt was soaked. Marlon, on one knee next to her, had wine running down his beard and his arms. He looked almost biblical. A shard of bottle had jammed under a windshield wiper, so when Donna turned them on, only one blade cut a swathe through the red. The other jerked and jolted, paralyzed.

The neck of the bottle was on the hood of the car, still corked.

Lucia looked at Rachel, who looked unhinged but ecstatic, smiling, another wine bottle in her hand. Claws scrabbled against asphalt: a few feet away, the injured dog was easing to its feet. Marlon still held the other beagle in his arms, its tongue curling at the air.

Lucia sank to the curb, something shellacked and leggy moving against her fingers. The glow of the streetlamp circled her, and she welcomed the light, even though the last few minutes had proven that it offered no protection at all.

Donna, head down in her burgundy-spattered car. Evan running down the sidewalk, his jacket flapping open like a cape.

Dark shapes fluttering around the streetlamp.

The moon, pearled and pointed.

All a jumble, spilling around her, and Lucia tried to follow each curl of sound and movement. The bright light seemed to be, in fact, the opposite of a barrier—it was drawing everything closer, and that was a good thing. She was surrounded. Evan's hands on her shoulders. The quick slap of his dress shoes—a car door opening and the jangle of keys ripped from the ignition. Headlights gone dark. Marlon threading his fingers through hers. Rachel, wine bottle in hand, edging into the bright circle. Lucia had missed all the pieces of her: falling-down hair and flip-flops and sharp jaw. Her head thrown back as if she found something funny in the tree above. A skinned knee—from broken glass or something else? Blood oozing slick and dark, and there was no telling what had marked her, but Lucia would ask. She would ask and Rachel would tell and Lucia would have all the time in the world to listen.

The burn on her thumb pulsed.

Rachel took another step, swinging the bottle in a slow rhythm. A metronome. Lucia could almost feel the sloshing weight of the wine. When the bottle hit the asphalt, she felt the shattering, and it occurred to her that maybe this was not her story.

ACKNOWLEDGMENTS

This book draws from my own childhood in Alabama, as well as from plenty of other women's experiences. I'm forever grateful to Lisa and Jeff Woodard, who were always willing to open the door. You showed me many things, including what a great marriage looks like.

I couldn't have written this book without Judy Crittenden, who made Lucia's world come to life with incredible intelligence, charm, and wit. I deeply appreciate all the hours, all the stories, and all the notes in the margins!

Thank you to the smart, funny, kind, all-powerful women who had a hand in shaping my younger self (and who had no obligation to do so since they weren't even related to me). Mary George Jester, you showed me—you showed all of us—what wonderful things happen when a woman is in charge. Diann Frucci, you made me love John Donne, and I can never hear the words "Truman Capote" or "The Three Witches" without hearing your voice. I'd give a great deal to sit in your classroom one more time and listen to you work your magic. Karen Etheridge, you taught me to love Shakespeare and Dickens, and you showed me that there's such a thing as a healthy level of intimidation.

I appreciate Phillip Harris for sharing his time and expertise and for repeatedly steering me away from stupid mistakes about police procedure in the 1980s. Thanks to Rev. Sarah Shelton, one of my favorite prophets, for talks about rocks

Acknowledgments

through windows and feminism. Any and all uses of "murmuring" are for you. Thanks to Audreyalice Kubesch Warner for the epigraph, as well as to Polly Dobbs, Alistaire Tallent, and Tina Noyes for lines that stuck in my head enough for me to write them down. Lucia Watson, I've always loved your name!

Thanks to Anne Collins for her elegant edits and for, in general, sharpening and deepening every page of this book. Thanks to Kim Witherspoon for perpetual competence and force of nature-ness—you were on my mind in the early stages of imagining Lucia. Jane Cavolina, you did a beautiful job with the copyedits. And, Laura Tisdel, work never feels like work when I'm doing it with you. Every conversation is a joy.

Thanks, as always, to Fred. You leave no part of me floating.

Gin Phillips is the award-winning author of *Fierce Kingdom* and *The Well and the Mine*. She lives in Birmingham, Alabama, with her family.